THE GETTING PLACE

THE GETTING PLACE

nine stories

■ ■ ■

FRANK SOOS

borealbooks

Book design by Mark E. Cull

Cover artwork *Winter Birch* by Margo Klass
Cover photograph by Chris Arend

ISBN: 978-1-59709-921-9 (tradepaper)
Library of Congress Control Number: 2021946185

The National Endowment for the Arts, the Los Angeles County Arts Commission,
the Ahmanson Foundation, the Dwight Stuart Youth Fund, the Max Factor
Family Foundation, the Pasadena Tournament of Roses Foundation, the Pasadena
Arts & Culture Commission and the City of Pasadena Cultural Affairs Division,
the City of Los Angeles Department of Cultural Affairs, the Audrey & Sydney
Irmas Charitable Foundation, the Meta & George Rosenberg Foundation, the
Albert and Elaine Borchard Foundation, the Adams Family Foundation, Amazon
Literary Partnership, the Sam Francis Foundation, and the Mara W. Breech
Foundation partially support Red Hen Press.

First Edition
Published by Boreal Books
an imprint of Red Hen Press
www.borealbooks.org
www.redhen.org

ACKNOWLEDGMENTS

Thanks to the following journals where these stories first appeared:

Maine Review 4, no. 2 (Autumn 2018): "Selected Events from Ancient History" and *Story South* 46 (Fall 2018): "The Getting Place."

for Margo

CONTENTS

THE GETTING PLACE

SEA OF TRANQUILITY

House cleaning could whip Eleanor into a white hot fury. Catherine didn't seem to mind so very much. She just futzed and futzed and left all the real grime to her sister. And they both put it off as long as they could. Cleaning forced Eleanor to look at the place, the ratty worn couch and armchairs, the mismatched kitchen chairs, the stains on the rugs, the accrued shabbiness of the place. Catherine would tell her, "It's a camp. It's a camp in Maine. This is what it's supposed to look like." But it hadn't been a camp for some time, had it? It was their home.

Now Stephen and his family were coming, so a deep cleaning couldn't be avoided.

Catherine didn't hear the van pull up, but Eleanor did. There it sat, a gleaming silver lozenge in the muddy, rutted drive. "They're here, my God, they're already here. And this place is still a wreck."

Really, how much could it matter? Catherine nudged her sister aside and ran out onto the tiny portico, down the steps, and reached for the sliding door on the side of the van when it began to open of its own accord. From inside she heard a gravelly voice—Stephen's?—announce, "The Eagle has landed." And the boy, Timothy, jumped from the van into a puddle.

He wore a pair of fat, puffy, silvery boots, what had once been called moon boots—popularly when? maybe twenty, thirty years ago—silvery gym shorts that fell to his knees, and a shirt with a NASA logo superimposed over a picture of the space shuttle. "One small step for man, one giant leap for mankind," he announced. Timothy was nine.

"Well, welcome, strange visitor from another planet."

Stephen came from around the van, hugged Catherine and confirmed Timothy's latest craze, the Apollo moon landing. "Wonderful!" That child. So smart, what was going to become of him?

From the very back seat, his sister, Rhonda, came scowling. Maybe she had been sleeping and had just woken up. Her hair dyed a deep blue was shaved to the skull on one side of her head, and she wore a black tank top that seemed to feature the faded image of a snarling cat. Warning enough.

"Welcome. And how are you, Rhonda?"

No reply.

"She can't hear you through those silly things in her ears," Eleanor said. "Stephen, have her take them off."

"Just give her some space," he said.

"Well, of course, if that's what's needed." But hadn't they just arrived? And was space a time or a place? Or both?

The women waited awkwardly in the driveway when it was clear the van was empty of passengers. The wife—Shannon—was not on board.

The girl, ungainly, horsey, you'd have to say, stormed inside and flung herself down on the couch, pulled out a book, stuck her nose in it and didn't look up.

"The picture of grace," Eleanor said, and thought, she's not really reading that book.

"Eleanor."

"She can't hear us with the headphones, remember?"

But of course she could. And she held the book in front of her face, a force field against her grandmother and great-aunt, against their snooty looks and judgments.

"If that's how she's going to behave, why did she even come?"

Good question. Ask her dad, ask Stephen, who was dragging the bags in from the van. You'd think they were staying for months instead of a week. Which now seemed an age.

After the dinner, which had been horrid—the children held their utensils as if they were hammer and chisel, food spilled from their plates, much was left uneaten—after dinner, then, after the sisters cleaned up the kitchen themselves, and Stephen retired to his bed because it had been a long, trying trip, and Rhonda slumped back onto the couch with her book, which seemed to be some kind of comic book and not a real book at all, after that, the sisters each took a last glass of wine and retreated to the screened porch.

Actions have consequences, their father had often told them. Yes, Eleanor would say to him now, unexpected, unimagined consequences.

■ ■ ■

With baskets filled with blueberries and sketchbooks, the sisters were riding their bicycles home when Donovan pedaled up beside them on a bike of his own: a bike with many gears and outfitted with his camping equipment. His blond ponytail, thick as a dock rope, stuck out from under his little cycling cap. He wore cutoff sweatpants and a dirty orange T-shirt. He was gorgeous. Who had seen him first?

They invited him home for dinner. And he told them he had been on the road these couple months after quitting his job repairing bicycles in a shop in North Carolina. On his way to Nova Scotia, then maybe to Newfoundland. Or maybe he'd jump on the Trans-Canada Railroad. Or maybe he'd just stop and look for work in a bike shop in Nova Scotia. What towns there would have a shop? Because, he told the women, he was a handy fellow.

Instead, he stayed on, sharing Catherine's bed. Though maybe Eleanor slept with him a time or two herself. Honestly, she couldn't quite remember, and such questions didn't invite close scrutiny.

Donovan was right about his claim. He did prove to be a handy fellow, screening in the porch, wiring and lighting the dungeon basement, painting the house, truly just a camp then, but solidly built. Neither of the women (were they women then or just full-sized girls?) would have picked the barn-red color. Yellow trim on the doors and window, though, they'd liked that. There it stands today, faded just the way he must have imagined it, the screens rotting and rusting and needing replacing.

And Stephen a grown man. Who had never known his father. One morning when Catherine was in her eighth month, she woke up to find Donovan's side of the bed empty. His bicycle was gone from the shed along with his panniers and sleeping bag, and himself. The sisters could have taken to the roads in their wonderful old Volvo and found him easily enough.

But. "If that's what he wants," Catherine said, "let him go."

■ ■ ■

"So what do we know now?" Eleanor asked, meaning Stephen's relationship to Shannon, his wife, or maybe his estranged wife or ex-wife.

"I couldn't get much out of him between Timothy racing around counting down, counting up, blasting off, and landing rockets. And those plastic astronauts and keeping them straight."

"Such an odd little boy. We sat in this very house watching those men walk on the moon, remember?"

"Back when we had a television. They say there are things worth watching now."

"Forget it. Tell me, didn't you realize she wasn't coming?"

"No," Catherine said, "no. Maybe I had a feeling things weren't right."

"Hadn't been. You miss so much."

Really, though, Catherine had always hoped for the best from people, from events. For years she visualized Donovan pedaling back up the gravel drive, responding to the tug of fatherhood. Things would come right.

■ ■ ■

Eleanor wrote out a little to-do list on the back of a receipt and placed it beside Stephen's plate at breakfast: Repair/replace screens on porch, new light switch in bathroom, cut weeds on path to shore, unclog kitchen drain.

He gave it a quick glance. "Unfortunately, Aunt El, none of these is in my skill set."

"Skill set? What's in anybody's 'skill set'? You do what needs to be done. That's what I've had to do." She placed a new light switch and a screwdriver beside his plate.

"Please, let's not have this conversation. I've been under a little stress."

Rhonda came out from her nest of balled up blankets on the couch, "Yeah. He's using his vacation to come to nowhereville and hang out with you."

"Hey, cool it," he told her.

"Cool it, yourself," and she slid back into her blanket.

Stephen picked up the switch and screwdriver and headed to the bathroom.

Later, Catherine said, "Am I wrong to blame it on the mother?"

"Well, she's not here, and Stephen is. Face it, you can see who's going to be the principal parent."

"I'm sure he's a wonderful father. He was such a gentle, loving child."

In fact, he had been. But lazy and self-absorbed as well. You take the good with the bad, Eleanor supposed.

■ ■ ■

Rhonda put the silver in wads of knives, forks, and spoons alongside the plates.

"That's no way to set a table," Eleanor told her. "Look," and she began to right the settings, "fork on left, spoon and knife on the right, knife blade turned inside toward the plate."

"Who cares? In our house, we don't worry about crap like that. I mean, we're going to grab that stuff when we need it, so what difference does it make?"

Of course not, who had time for niceties when you have two kids to feed and work brought home in a briefcase—or backpack more likely? You just had to get them fed.

"Your mother should have taught you how to set a table."

"She has a name, you know."

"I know that, I was just using her title."

"Yeah, she has a title for you too. Want to know what it is?"

Good lord. "Shannon, then, should have taught you."

How had it fallen to Eleanor to correct the girl? She could not explain how or why she had become the responsible one. Catherine was older, but somehow she came across as fragile, distracted, unable in some basic way to do the simplest tasks. Since they were teenagers, Eleanor had been the one to make sure they weren't caught driving drunk, who got the pot out of Catherine's purse and hid it away before the parents found it. She took care.

She told Catherine, Catherine sitting on this very porch bawling, "You don't have to keep it," meaning the baby, barely an embryo at that moment. Donovan didn't know yet. It was a sentence she would always regret let fly out of her mouth, not because of violating any moral strictures but because just saying those words made Catherine intent on going through with the pregnancy. Impetuous girl.

An eighteen-year mistake Eleanor would say whenever she'd had enough of caretaking, when she changed another dirty diaper, cleaned up a skinned knee, when she had to be the one to go down to the school and deal with Stephen getting kicked out of glee club, talk him back into school after the firecrackers incident. Both sisters had gone to the parent-teacher conferences, and the teachers soon learned that Eleanor was the one to reckon with. After any bruising encounter, they told themselves, "She's not even that boy's mother."

Just then, Timothy, wearing the same clothes as the day before, raced through, "Dad, preparing to egress for some EVA."

From somewhere in the house, they heard Stephen, "Roger that. Back at 1100 hundred hours."

"Roger." The door to the porch screen door slammed behind him.

And now there were these grandchildren. Eighteen years was only the beginning.

■ ■ ■

Eleanor picked at things. She couldn't help herself. "Don't you some-times think that had we done things differently, Stephen might have turned out, well, more complete?"

"Sister, I don't think we're complete until we die. He's still a work in progress."

"At forty?"

"Do you think we could have staked him like a tomato plant to make him grow the way we might have wished him to be? He was going to become who he was going to be. Very like his father, I suspect."

"Oh God, his father. You haven't a clue who that man was."

"Donovan was loving, gentle, sweet-spirited."

"And good in bed."

"Yes. Good in bed. There's never been anybody like him." It wasn't for lack of looking. Catherine's choices had been odd, risky: roofers, bartenders, sternmen, heavy equipment operators.

Eleanor's men had been more carefully chosen.

■ ■ ■

After dinner, after another messy cleanup, after Timothy had had his bath, after Rhonda had apparently slunk away to her bedroom lair, the sisters repaired to the porch. "Come join us," Eleanor called to Stephen. "Bring one of those fancy beers you're so fond of."

He brought his reluctance with him too. He knew what this would be once the niceties had been dispensed with.

"So, then, what *is* up with Shannon? Honestly, we were surprised when she wasn't with you."

"Were you?"

"Your aunt always wants to think the worst," Catherine said. "She's kind of a conspiracy theorist or something. But I've always liked Shannon."

"She needs a little space, she says."

Space, space, it's all about space. You would think they were living in India or China or someplace. "Well, there's plenty of space here. She can sit on the porch all day and watch the tide come in and out. Nothing could be more tranquil."

"Sometimes she finds it stressful here."

That too, everybody seemed to be under stress. "I cannot for the life of me imagine why." And then Eleanor asked him, "Where is she now? Where is she that is so stress-free?" Eleanor knew how to drive a nail.

"Back home."

"In your very house?"

"We are working out an arrangement."

"And these children?"

"They're fine. They're adjusting."

"I see what you mean. The moon can be such a welcoming place."

Catherine sat up abruptly in her chair, "'We call the moon the moon.' I believe that's from John Donne."

"Sister, that's hardly the best quotation just now, but never mind."

■   ■   ■

Of course it was John Donne. Catherine knew that as well as she knew her own face in the mirror, which these days was showing some strain. So it was that Eleanor found her the next morning with an open book of Donne's poetry. It looked like she may have been crying, but now, fully blissed out, she lay her head back on one of the old stuffed chairs, her teacup on the table beside her.

"Sister, are you stoned?"

"No. Absolutely not. I don't do that anymore. At least I don't while the grandkids are in the house. No, I was just reading." And she began to recite without looking at the page before her:

"'O! if thou die before,
  My soul from other lands to thee shall soar . . .'"

"Please not that." Because how often had Catherine subjected Eleanor to dramatic tearful readings of "Elegy Seventeen"? A poem, by the way, about a guy leaving his mistress and telling her he might be back someday but not to count on it, an irony among many she thought her sister never fully grasped. How often, each reading bracketed by wishes and imaginings that any day Donovan would pedal his bicycle back into their driveway?

"'When I am gone, dream me some happiness.'" Was she crying again now?

"Good lord. 'Think it enough for me to have had thy love.' Let's leave it at that. Now will you get up out of that chair and do something useful in your waking life? You can start by helping me make breakfast for our locusts in residence."

Except the kids didn't like the breakfast Catherine and Eleanor made. Timothy wanted some nasty kind of cereal with bits of marshmallow in it. "Can't I have that, Dad? The usual?"

"No," Eleanor said. "We are not making a special trip to town for junk food."

"Dad?"

"Auntie El says no."

Rhonda said, "See who calls the shots around here, squirt?" She pressed her lips together and let out a burbling spurt of noise, then added, "You need to know I'm a vegan now."

"What sort of food did the astronauts eat on the moon?" Catherine asked them.

"Nasty goo in tubes," Rhonda said. "Baby poop."

"We don't use language like that at the table, sweetie," Stephen said.

"Dad, cut the crap. This is how we talk all the time. Why do you want to fake everything around here?"

Would it have helped the sisters to know the lunar module, the LM as Timothy called it, sailed above the crater called the Sea of Crises before gracefully touching down? Waffles abundant with expensive maple syrup solved this small problem at hand. Apparently, some vegans were OK with butter too. Eleanor rinsed the leftover puddles of wasted syrup down the drain. Brats.

■ ■ ■

Sitting naked on her money manager's bed, having anticipated as always this afternoon assignation—a bonus she granted herself for being the one to go to town and do the shopping—Eleanor found she was not in the mood.

He lay under the covers pulled up to his chin, "What's the trouble with my gal?"

"Don't call me that. And it's that mistake my sister made years ago."

"The kid? I mean, the son? He must be forty or more by now. He's fixed for life once the two of you kick off. Which I must say I hope is a long time coming."

"It's not money. Money is rarely the issue at heart. You have enough, you don't have enough, either way you find a way to make do. We make do."

"Ha. You do just fine."

Eleanor laughed too, "So you say. . . ." But she couldn't let it go, "Poor man, all he seems to do is tap on his computer. It pays him well enough—very well as near as we can tell. His daughter is a mess, and the little boy is a lost soul. For all his astronaut obsession, he might as well be floating away into space somewhere. The man is joyless, and I must say I'm afraid it could be contagious."

"And Catherine?"

"Oh, Catherine lives in a willed state of denial. Will the daughter straighten herself out before she's completely wrecked her life? Will the wife come back into the picture? Will the son ever fit in with any other kids? Of course, of course. Just give it time. All will resolve itself. Everything will fall into place. As if gravity were the most beneficent force of the universe."

"Maybe an orgasm would put you in better spirits."

"I don't think so. Not today." And Eleanor began to pull on her clothes.

■ ■ ■

Her solution was to walk. The tide was going out; the little strip of beach beyond the rocks revealed. Eleanor left the groceries on the kitchen counter for Catherine to put away and went out the door. Dinner? Let somebody else figure it out.

Eleanor and Catherine had never had careers. They took jobs from time to time, receptionists in dental or law offices, attendants in art galleries, saleswomen in boutique shops, jobs where their radiated sense of elegant competence served them well enough. They quit when it suited them, confident they'd find something else when the need arose.

After their parents' deaths work became a nonissue. Still, they might have traveled more, they might have taken up some art, painting, or poetry, or perhaps piano if there had not been the fact of Stephen. At least that was what Eleanor told herself.

When Stephen finished college (a very good college—Eleanor congratulated herself on that), he drifted for a while, never seeming to catch on to anything or anybody. Catherine fretted, but hadn't they done all they could?

It might have seemed that Shannon had saved him. Catherine certainly thought so, but Eleanor was suspicious. There was something cunning about Shannon, something evasive in her demeanor. She never let the sisters draw close to her.

Now here they were, witnessing a marriage gone sour.

She took to the beach littered with wrecked lobster pots, frayed lengths of broken rope, plastic bottles, and those blue gloves all the lobstermen wore. Out beyond the barrier islands the lighthouse stood, but today she couldn't see it. The last of the lobster boats were making their way into the harbor with their noisy diesel racket. A nasty wind kicked up under a heavy sky. Enough.

She started back for the house. They couldn't manage to make dinner.

Up the beach, she could see the child Timothy. He had a five-gallon bucket he must have dragged from under the porch. "What are you doing?"

He looked at her, seemingly baffled that any other person might be around. "Collecting moon rocks to carry back to the LM." Of course, he had traveled to the moon.

"Right, the LM. I forgot." And they walked on together. Surely there was something more she might say to the boy so lightly tethered to the here and now. Though who could say his extraterrestrial visiting wasn't for the best?

Rhonda stood out on the porch, maybe the first time she had been outdoors since their arrival. "Dad's been looking for you, dweeb."

"I told him I would be back at 1500 hours."

"Well, in real people's time, it's 3:30. What slimy stuff have you got in that bucket?"

"Moon rocks."

"Pathetic. This is Earth we're living on. Why don't you pull your head out of your butt?"

"Stick it, blue booger face."

"He knows they aren't real moon rocks, don't you, Timmy?"

"Just so you know, he hates to be called Timmy. Timmy! Timmy!"

Timothy threw down the bucket and ran into the house.

"See what you did?" Rhonda told her.

"What I did?"

"You think you're so smart, so much better than anybody, you can sit up here in your rotten old house and tell everybody how to live. Mom hates you, and she hates Granny Catherine too. Dad's a total wimp, and it's your fault. You made him that way." And the girl stormed away down the beach.

Eleanor thought, I didn't ask for this. But she had.

■ ■ ■

Inside the house, Catherine felt a buildup of static electricity that comes before a thunderstorm and the dread that comes with it.

"Moon walk aborted," Timothy said and went into the room he shared with his father. Maybe forty-five minutes later, Rhonda came in, too, slamming the screen door behind her.

"Have a pleasant walk?" Catherine called to her from the kitchen as the second door slammed, the one to her own bedroom she had given over to the girl.

Stephen rose slowly, the way a person would get up to answer the door when he was afraid it might be a Jehovah's Witness, and knocked on Rhonda's door. He stayed a good while.

When he came out, Stephen went to Catherine in the kitchen. "I was thinking we might have lobster tonight."

"Well, we can, but usually we want to save that for the last night," Catherine told him.

"Yeah, I know. But something has come up at work. Maybe I ought to get back sooner."

"Oh, honey, can't they get along just one week without you?"

"Silly old woman, that's the wrong question." Where had the girl sprung from?

Catherine should do something or say something. But what? In that instant she felt she'd become that very thing: silly, old, and out of place in her own house.

■ ■ ■

The sisters could be said to best rise to an occasion when nothing else could be done. Eleanor raced to the co-op for five shedders while Catherine set the table with the special checked lobster cloth, crackers and pickers, and pails at every corner for the shells. They boiled the corn on the cob, built a heaping mound of coleslaw.

Catherine had insisted Stephen take meals at the head of the table, assume his position as the head of a household no matter how oddly formed, but tonight he would sit with Timothy and help him crack into his lobster. Maybe a picture first with the bright lobsters on their platters. "Everybody look famished," he said.

"I think I'm going to puke. I mean they boiled these creatures to death." Rhonda turned to Timothy. "Hear that, little space monkey? Boiled alive. I saw them do it."

"If that's the way you feel, maybe you should excuse yourself," Eleanor told her, but she said it to the girl's departing backside. "It's not like she hasn't eaten a lobster before."

After trying a bite because Stephen insisted, Timothy wouldn't eat his either. He did eat his corn on the cob and the strawberries and ice cream for dessert.

Eleanor briefly found she'd lost her appetite, but she was damned if she was going to let that girl ruin her dinner. She ate.

■ ■ ■

More waffles, a wasteful end of the good maple syrup, and Stephen making his hands into a megaphone announced, "T-minus four hours and counting."

"And counting," Rhonda echoed with the anguished tone of a person hoping to be rescued from a desert island. The first words she'd uttered this day.

"So get your gear together, all your stuff from outside, under the house, wherever."

"Roger that," Timothy shot back.

"Oh, no, no, no. Stephen, don't you think you can put off whatever it is that is needed at work? We've made plenty of time for you to work here?"

"Dad, we already murdered the lobsters. There's nothing to do. Let's get out of here."

In Eleanor's view, the countdown could not proceed fast enough. Why prolong the agony? How about T-minus thirty minutes? Rhonda huffed and snorted as she went to and from her room gathering her scattered clothes and books and those adult coloring books. She had to do something, didn't she? Stephen tapped on his laptop and made calls. And Timothy flew his LM made of Legos but without the usual sound effects. The sisters could only sit by and watch this disordered evacuation.

Finally, Eleanor said, "Why don't we prepare your moon rocks for their return to planet Earth?" And to Catherine, "Make them some peanut butter and jelly sandwiches for the voyage." She led the child to where the bucket of rocks was strewn behind the house. They washed them in the outdoor utility sink, and Eleanor patted each dry with an old towel, one of the towels the sisters had packed for Stephen when he set out for college. She produced a silvery shopping bag from a fancy Boston shop, and together she and Timothy wrapped each rock in tissue paper.

"A moon rock is worth more than a million dollars," he told her.

"T-minus fifteen minutes and counting, toad breath," Rhonda called from the porch.

"Someday maybe you'll be rich, then," Eleanor told him.

"No, these are fake moon rocks."

"Maybe, then, you'll have to go get some real ones of your own."

"No. I doubt it. Mars, though. I could get some Martian rocks."

Stephen called down this time, "T-minus five minutes and counting."

Suitcases and duffels on board: sixty seconds. Timothy picked up the count in the final seconds, then, "Ignition. Liftoff," and the van began to pull away while Catherine dabbed at her eyes with a tissue. Eleanor saw Rhonda push herself up against the back window. "Was she flipping us the bird?"

"What? I didn't see."

■ ■ ■

Eleanor had picked the uneaten meat from Rhonda's and Timothy's lobsters. She had expected this result when she bought them and determined the meat would not be wasted. She had already planned a cream sauce and cooked up some pasta while Catherine made a salad.

The sisters ate with relish, with a certain relief of a burden having been lifted. Then, as always, carried their glasses of wine to the porch, on this night allowing themselves a bit more than usual.

"The poor child. I do worry," Catherine said.

"He told me the universe is infinite. He'll be fine."

"I meant the girl. She is filled with pain and grief. She's tearing herself apart. You see that don't you?"

"That girl got our goats."

"She did," Catherine agreed. "Yes, she did." She sighed, an uncommonly long sigh.

The sisters sat a long time in the growing dark. Down at the shore, the wind whispered, the waves plashed lightly against the rocks. The clouds had lifted, and a sickle moon hung in the sky. It turned out to be a beauteous evening after all.

SITTING DOWN TO READ
ANNA KARENINA AGAIN

At five thirty in the morning on this early spring day, Mim could read at the kitchen table by the natural light. She wasn't a morning person, but here she sat, an old copy of *Anna Karenina* opened to that first familiar sentence about happy and unhappy families. Which, she wondered, was she living in now?

Outside, stuck against the window was a downy gray bird feather. A red pol, probably, or chickadee had hit the glass and either bounced off unharmed or fell to the deck in a daze where Rocket had picked it off. Though ordinarily she would have felt some remorse for the unlucky bird, she felt nothing now. Rocket was Rocket; he was doing his cat thing.

She meant to read, but instead just leafed through the book. It had been her mother's, evidence of a secret intellectual ambition, an ambition that had passed by the time Mim had grown up enough to appreciate such a book. "Here, you can have this," her mother said one day when Mim was in junior high school and got it into her head that she wanted some adult-looking books for the headboard shelf in her room. "You ruined it anyway." Somehow the book had stayed with her through college, through three moves, the last across country to Alaska. It lay on the bottom shelf of a bookcase filled with children's books, coloring books, magazines on cooking and quilting. Mim took it up this morning with a mixture of embarrassment and determination. She should try to read more. She knew that, she'd meant to. But it was her recent encounter on the late-night plane that spurred her.

Mim thumbed through the rich buttery paper, already starting to fall apart. It was the scattered illustrations she'd ruined, sketches of scenes from the novel, line drawings with color accents. As a little girl, she hadn't thought them finished and went to work with her crayons. Green zigzags crossed Anna entering the ballroom, a tangled ball of blue tied up Vronsky riding the steeplechase. In high school, when Mim actually got around to reading *Anna Karenina* for the first time, she found the sketches irritating and distracting. Nobody looked like she imagined them. Vronsky was too much the dandy, his hair in a pompadour, his mouth a tight red bow. Levin looked like a young Santa Claus, Karenin's hair was curly like a poodle's.

Kenny came padding down the stairs. He looked at her but didn't smile, then went on down the next flight to the basement. This was Saturday; the girls would sleep as long as she let them. After a while Mim could smell the glide wax hot against the iron. There weren't many good skiing days left; Kenny would want to be out there today. She kind of wanted to get in a ski herself. She wondered if Kenny had figured out why.

She set in to reading and got up to the point where Oblonsky came for Anna at the train station. But now Kenny was in the kitchen, banging around making his own coffee. Vronsky was there, too, along with his mother. Small world, she used to think, for a place as big as Russia. She knew all about that now.

■ ■ ■

She'd seen him kissing a woman by the gate for the Alaska plane in Seattle. The woman was tall and thin, cheekbones and smeared blue eyes. Her legs cased tight in black jeans seemed to go on forever, and her black boots made her taller than he was. Jurek wore his usual Carhartts and flannel and an old goose down vest with two duct tape patches on it. As he kissed her, he held his felt fishing hat down by his leg cowboy style. Mim was on the plane with her carry-on stowed and seatbelt fastened before that kiss was over. When Jurek came on, he skimmed his hat into the overhead bin then took the seat beside her.

"Jurek, don't you know what they say? Kiss your girlfriend in the Seattle airport, and it'll be all over Fairbanks before you can claim your suitcase?"

He pulled back a little and looked her in the eyes. "Who's this *they* who does all this saying? I'd like to have a few words with him."

His eyes were black and deep, like gun barrels, like mine shafts, like caves people spent their lives trying to get to the bottom of. Pay attention, she told herself, look out. Then she smiled. She had made a mistake she often made, assuming because she knew who he was, he'd know her. Everybody knew Jurek. He raced on cross-country skis in winter and bicycles in summer and kayaked big rivers and fished for king salmon and always got his moose. Had she ever been to a potluck when he wasn't there? Everybody knew Jurek. "I'm Mim, Kenny Barnhill's wife."

Jurek would have known Kenny. Kenny did all the things Jurek did—the skis, the bikes, the rods and guns—but he didn't do them quite so vigorously. In Jurek's world, that would be a failing. He said, "Mim? What kind of name is that?"

And she told him it was a biblical name, Miriam.

"But shouldn't you be Mir, like the broken Russian spaceship?" He cocked his chin, inviting her to give it a sock if she had the nerve.

She knew he was looking her over. So what, she wanted to tell him, I'm not a hard body. I don't wear Spandex clothing. Mim was one of the moms you saw in the warm-up hut getting the cookies and hot chocolate ready for the kids when they came in steaming wet from their ski. Maybe afterward she'd toddle around the easy half of White Bear loop.

Then he said, "You know Miriam's the one who leads the cheers after Pharaoh's army gets swallowed up by the sea, don't you?" But she didn't, and she didn't much believe him either.

There was more once he got started on this biblical tack. God had given the Children of Israel quail in the desert and then caused them to throw up when they made pigs of themselves. He mooned Moses in a tent. He wasn't a just and angry God, just grouchy, sometimes a little psychotic. Jurek grinned again. "You don't believe this either? It's all in the Bible. How were you raised, dear woman?"

Mim told him. She was raised by her mother in Bluefield, West Virginia. Her mom was a cook at the country club and was out there every Sunday of her life supervising the brunch. Mim grew up watching cartoons on television. All this caused her to remember, with a funny mixture of sorrow and longing, her brave mom who wanted all the best for her, who took her up to the country club and marched her out of the kitchen to meet the members of the school board, the Chamber of Commerce, the Rotary Club, and wasn't satisfied until her daughter went off to West Virginia University on a full scholarship—tuition and fees, even money for pencils.

"You loved her, then," Jurek said.

The word surprised her coming out of his mouth so soft, so fresh. And though she had hardly spoken to her mother for the last twelve years of her life, she said, "Yeah, I did. Sure, I did."

"And how did you come to be here?"

Even though they were probably somewhere in Canadian air space by now, anybody from Alaska would know where *here* was, and everybody would have a story about how. Because of Kenny, that was Mim's. At first her mom had loved him, an engineer. Down in the coal fields engineers were like kings. But then he went and took the job in Fairbanks. It had been almost twenty years ago, during the pipeline construction. And that was OK at first too. They'd get rich and go back home. But they hadn't. Now they were dug in.

"You miss her?"

"Well, she's dead. Maybe I didn't make that clear. She died in a nursing home before I could get there. It wasn't one of the awful ones." But she took that back. There were no kind except the awful ones, were there? By the time she got to Bluefield, her mom's things were piled in a cardboard box, the bed was stripped and the name slot on the door was empty. Where were her dentures? Her wedding band that she wore for over thirty years thinking the man who'd left her would come back home? The people who worked there put on blank faces; they saw it every day.

Here Mim was, telling all this to Jurek, a guy she only kind of knew, trying to explain about the false teeth and the ring. She'd tried to explain it before to Kenny, but somehow she couldn't say it right. Now she felt like she was saying it right. Or maybe that Jurek was really hearing it, hearing it right. And she started crying. The plane was all dark, pretty much everybody was asleep. She sat there crying quietly in the dark, patting all her pockets for a Kleenex. Jurek shifted on his haunch and pulled out a bandana. She let him daub her eyes. "It's all right," he told her, "it's clean."

Sitting in her kitchen, Mim started crying all over again, tears sliding under her reading glasses and onto the open book. She tried to make herself stop; she didn't want Kenny to notice. Against the steam and gurgle of the coffee maker, it took him a while. He came around the table and sat facing her, studying her, then picked up the book and read the title on its spine, "Some kind of story, I'll tell you."

"Oh, Kenny, it's not that."

He gave her a minute and asked, "What, then?"

Mim felt a huge gulping sob come up her throat, then another one. For a while she couldn't speak. She put her face in her hands and could feel the tears leaking between her fingers. "My mom, oh, my mom. I miss her so much, Kenny."

"She's been dead for three years." He didn't mean it cruelly. They had their official family line on Mim's mom: She was cunning and manipulative, wanted Mim back in West Virginia, and blamed Kenny for everything. If Kenny had been one to wonder, he might have considered whether this might be what a little earthquake could do. Up on the surface, things might look about the same, but down deep big plates were shifting.

In some important way Mim couldn't name yet, some things had shifted. She had finally cried just as hard on the airplane, and Jurek had put up the armrest that separated them, and she'd laid her head on his chest and cried into his flannel shirt, cried like a little girl. When she quieted, she lay there listening to his slow jock's heartbeat. Maybe she slept a little that way, she wasn't really sure. But she finally got herself straightened up, took some deep breaths, remembered her manners, and apologized.

"What about your folks?" she asked him. It seemed Jurek hardly had folks at all. His German dad divorced his American mom, and she sent him to expensive boarding schools from fourth grade on, sometimes in Europe, sometimes in the States. Jurek, she said, was just too much for her. But it was OK; he learned to make friends easily. He laughed when he said this, and Mim laughed too.

When the plane stopped in Anchorage, she got off to pee and wash her face; and when she got back on, he was asleep. She studied his wide, thick hands and stubby fingers with dirt under the nails. Cabin life— even some time in Seattle wouldn't get all that out of him. There was gray shot through his droopy moustache and shiny gray stubble on his cheeks, and a bare spot starting to form on the crown of his head. He looked tired around the eyes, but everybody on the plane looked a little rough this time of night. She wondered the things anybody might wonder about Jurek, how old he was, how hard he'd lived.

Kenny stood beside the table and looked at her hard, "You're just jet-lagged. Drink another cup of coffee, and you'll feel better." And he began rushing around getting his gear ready for a ski; if they wanted, Mim and the girls could go later. Wait, Kenny, she wanted to say, there's something we need to talk about. But Mim heard one of the girls in the upstairs bathroom and knew her sister had to be awake too. They always had pancakes on Saturdays, so she got herself up and got started.

Mim let Rebecca and Sarah pour the batter into cookie cutters in the shapes of animals—bears, moose, whales, and wolves. Their excited voices were high and shrill like the birds outside at the feeders. They were still at the stage where they liked bright clothes and stuffed animals and stories and to be cuddled by their mom and dad. Beautiful children with blonde hair and brown eyes. "They're going to break boys' hearts," people sometimes mischievously told her as if this were something to look forward to. As if heartbreak were a joyful phase of life that everybody grew through and out of.

Maybe if you saw her zooming down Sheep Creek Road in her steel-blue Subaru wagon at fifteen miles per hour above the posted speed limit, late for school, late for piano, late for the dentist or swim lessons, you, too, might think Mim had grown past all the phases of romance. She held her mouth pushed closed in a long flat line, her jaw set as hard as a ballplayer's. Her sunglasses weren't giving anything away. Only her right hand resting on the gear shift could tell you she was already planning to downshift to overtake the slow-moving pickup truck as soon as she came to the next straight stretch.

Jurek had shaken Kenny's hand at the airport, then stood a little ways off from them. When his duffle came around on the baggage carousel, he heaved it onto his shoulder and turned to go. At the automatic doors where the inside air and outside air collided with swirls of steamy condensation, she thought she saw him doff his hat. Maybe he had winked. Then he was gone. Since then, she'd seen him on the ski trails a couple times, but he'd not said as much as a howdy.

"Look on the bright side: At least nobody was waiting to meet him on this end." That's what Rachel told her. This was only a week or so later when she met her girlfriends downtown at the Thai place to plan a big yard sale for right after breakup. But they talked about men instead, their husbands mostly. Except for Rachel who had springy red hair and had split from her husband a few years back. All she could talk about was the crush she had on a guy named Steve.

"What is a crush, really, what's that mean?" Mim asked her. She took everything so seriously.

Somebody said, "Oh it means she's got the hots for him, that's about all."

"No, no," said Rachel, knocking her tiny fist on the table for emphasis. She was an elementary school teacher. "No, it's more complicated than that. Maybe that's what it meant when we were kids, but not now, not for me."

When the waitress came around again because they hadn't been ready the first time, they ordered their dishes by the numbers. Wasn't this more polite than mangling the pronunciation? How spicy? Medium, they always said medium. The waitress smiled. Such Americans. Out in the kitchen it must be a running joke, maybe a Buddhist joke. These Americans who have been raised to want everything but are so afraid of their desires. Mim bet Jurek ordered everything extra spicy.

She found herself wanting to talk, to let her secret out, but Rachel wasn't finished yet. She said, "It's deeper than that. You can use a guy to bring yourself off, that's one thing. But then he's still there, still in your head. You think about buying groceries for him, dressing for him even if there's practically no chance you'll see him that day. That's something else, that's real."

Mim probably put too much into Rachel's horny talk. When you taught second graders and lived alone, you had to get it out of your system somehow. But she considered Rachel's situation, having twenty-five boys and girls devoted to her year after year—twenty-five times how many?—who remembered her as their nicest teacher, their prettiest teacher, their best teacher, who if she let them would crawl all over her like a litter of puppies, how, finally, this would not be enough. Right then, Mim should have known she was getting in more trouble.

When the plane had touched down in Fairbanks and the bright lights came up in the cabin, Jurek squeezed her hand and smiled at her. Don't go, she wanted to say like the girls did when they were little, don't let's go. Where had such a wish come from, and what did it mean?

Because it turned out that her girlfriends had lots to say about him once they'd dragged his name out of her. Jurek! They said, my God! They giggled. Jurek! Jurek who went to a therapist and after two meetings ended up dating the therapist. Jurek who one day walked into the warm-up hut and found himself caught in the company of three women he'd slept with in the past year alone. Jurek who'd never left the Dog or the Loon without a woman on his arm, sometimes she was even the one he'd come in with. And the ways he left them: when the kings were in the lower Gulkana, when the reds were running at Chitina, when somebody offered him a seat in a plane for a Wood River moose hunt, or a trip to the Gates of the Arctic just for a hike, or a bike race or ski race in Anchorage. He just picked up and left, sweetly, apologetically; but he left.

■ ■ ■

If Mim had been looking for evidence to corroborate all her girlfriends were telling her, she might have easily found it. Out on the ski trails on the last good weekend, she was making her way in the set tracks, a plodder among the plodders in sweatpants and sweaters, among the ones who couldn't get their wax right and who actually stopped in the trail and ate cookies.

When he overtook her on the crest of a small rise, Jurek appeared to her as a rare and magnificent animal in a black and red skin. His thighs pulsed against the fabric of his tights as he leaned into one ski and then the other; his shoulders flexed and rolled under his turtleneck, his arms drove his poles into the packed trail and sent bits of snow flying out behind him. Human flight seemed a possibility.

"Hi," Mim said as he came toward her. She realized she had been wishing all day long for him, expecting him.

"Passing on your right!" he answered.

Behind those dark back-swept lenses, Mim couldn't make out his eyes. Had he recognized her or not? She couldn't say for sure, but as he disappeared down the trail she felt herself pulled along with him. And throughout the morning, she seemed to see him again and again on the overlapping loops. A large, exotic beast, mythic, elusive, maybe just a figment of her imagination, darting among the birch trunks.

Yet as she sat in the warm-up hut drinking her cocoa, he skied up. He popped his boots out of their bindings and threw his poles down with a clatter. In a couple steps, he was across the porch of the hut and through the door. Mim felt the room fill up with his smoky smell, with the steam of his sweat as he pulled his shirt over his head. He took a towel from his duffle and rubbed himself down, grabbed a fresh shirt and pulled it on. Only then did he slow himself, sit, and begin to unlace his boots. Only then did he seem to see Mim as something other than a fixture of the room.

"'Glory be to God for dappled things,' no?" He smiled; he really was talking to her.

"What?" Mim asked him back.

"Oh, it's a poem." And he sat back on his bench and said it all the way through for her. "I think of it often this time of year when the light brings out the color in the birch trunks and the way the skiers slip between them, fickle and freckles. You know."

Yes, she wanted to say, she did know. She had thought of something like that herself, but she didn't have a poem stored away in her head to go with it. But she said, "You blew me off the trail back there."

"Did I? Well, pardon me. At moments of great passion, we may not be responsible for all our actions. Do you think?"

"I think we're always responsible for our actions."

"Oh, ho. Really, now?"

Somewhere out on the trails, Kenny was poling along, all determination and proper biomechanics. Somewhere down in town, Sarah and Rebecca were at a little friend's birthday party and soon would need to be picked up for the movie that was the next event on their Saturday schedule. "If you had a family, you'd know what I mean."

"Perhaps you could explain to me sometime." He smiled. "Over a cup of tea." But just now he had to rush off to grab a sauna and shower at the university locker room.

Later that afternoon, Jurek would make his way home where he'd make a pot of the tea he liked so much, put on a heavy sweater and sit out on his cabin porch, take in the sun and read, read with the time to savor every word. This evening? Mim couldn't guess where he might wind up and whether he would spend the night in his own bed or not. He owned a cat, but any cat of Jurek's would have learned to live off voles and squirrels when it had to. Mim wondered whether to envy such a cat or not.

■ ■ ■

Every morning Kenny got up and made his own breakfast before Mim and the girls came downstairs, made a big pot of strong coffee, poured half in his thermos, left the rest for Mim, and was out the door. Sometimes he called from work, but rarely. She would see him when he came home in the evening.

When the pipeline construction wound down, Kenny had taken a job with the state Department of Transportation. It was a cut in pay, but he hadn't much cared. While everybody else was pissing their money away on trips to Thailand and Bali, on cocaine and big-ass trucks, he and Mim had socked theirs away. They'd built their house out of pocket, paid cash for cars. They weren't rich like the truly rich, but they were still doing all right

What Kenny brought home was a briefcase he never opened and his empty thermos and a sour sort of gossip. Mim knew the familiar names but not the faces. Ross: the guy who spent his days going from drafting table to drafting table working up elaborate and expensive sports pools. Dwight: the guy who everybody knew laid out to go fishing and hunting with his pals. Jordan: the one who hit on the secretaries, D.B. and Cal: the ones whose projects went over time and over budget.

Now that Kenny was a section chief, he didn't spend much time out on sites, which meant he didn't have to work long summer evenings, didn't work weekends. And maybe it really meant he'd lost his passion for engineering. Mim guessed that'd been true for a long time now but didn't want to ask. Kenny always said, "Don't ask a question unless you want to know the answer." Engineer talk, talk that was all about being so sure of things.

Sometime back, she had quit asking. In the hillbilly world she grew up in, there seemed to be only two ways of being. You could have a life made up of hollering resentments and recriminations, of door slamming, plate-throwing fights, and, for a while anyway, the passionate kiss-and-make-ups that went with them. Or you could have the life she'd surmised the country clubbers led, the life of please-and-thank-you, of intact family units, of mothers who bent their heads like flowers attentively listening to their children's silly chatter. If this is what she had wanted her life to look like, it pretty much did. Kenny kept the house and cars shipshape. He put up a swing set for the girls, made them a playhouse in the trees, and clapped at the right times at the piano recitals. Mim knew she should be more grateful to Kenny for having such good sense. Why wasn't she? Even now, she saw Kenny's formula was right. Here was a good question, but she wasn't sure she was ready to listen to the answer.

■ ■ ■

If he had the money, Jurek would fly to Hawaii to do his taxes. He thought it might be better to suffer the indignities of a semi-public accounting of the most private aspect of his life in a warm climate. Instead, he sat down at the kitchen table and took out his spandoflex file and set in on the long and complicated job.

You'd think his tax situation would be simple, but Jurek's father who couldn't be bothered to raise him had set up a trust fund and let it go at that. And Jurek, while briefly declaring majors in religion, English literature, anthropology, and physics, had tried some economics as well. When he came of age, he had taken charge of his money and placed it in various stocks and bonds and mutual funds. Usually what he earned was more than enough for the way he chose to live. In a bad year, he might take a job on a fishing boat or with work gangs on the railroad or at a construction site out in the Bush. But mostly these jobs were Jurek's little experiments in working life, experiments in what he called real people's life.

Living the way he preferred in his snug cabin with a loft, a cabin he'd built himself, keeping a big garden on a sunny southern slope, and making sure the freezer on his porch stayed full of meat, he really didn't need much walking around money. He could even help you out if you needed a plane ticket in a hurry or wanted to buy a rifle or new pair of skis or even a river boat. You could get the money back to him whenever you could; one of his rules was never to remind anybody of the money they owed him.

He only had a few rules, but he stuck to them: Buy only good knives and keep them sharp. Eat what you kill. Loan just about anybody money in a pinch, but loan nobody his tools, equipment, or books. Love the women who might come his way, but never get caught making long-term promises. How much better it would be if men such as Jurek were made to post their private rules on a small white card on the inside of their cabin doors like in a hotel room. Then women like Mim could be fairly warned.

Standing at that cabin door, she misread his dislike of close financial reckoning and the Internal Revenue Service as having everything to do with her. "I came for that cup of tea you offered." His eyes were hard and dark as lumps of coal. Why should she take one night on a plane when they were both strung-out and jet-lagged as anything more than Jurek's way of passing the time, of entertaining himself at her expense? She would like to tell him how much this drive out to his cabin had cost: Her surreptitious snooping that got her his address off his ski bag. Her poring over the maps in the phone book with a magnifying glass and not being able to find his little self-named road. Her roundabout asking. Who, exactly, was she fooling? That there were at least two dozen Subarus in Fairbanks the same color as hers did not stop her from feeling like she was being spotted, clearly identified, and regarded with suspicion as she made her way out Rosie Creek Road toward his cabin.

"Come in," he finally told her, "you're letting in the cold." Don't waste fuel: another of his rules.

To Mim, Jurek's life looked so imminently portable—two pickup truck loads, and he'd be out of here. The big room of his cabin had a table and a couple of chairs, a futon made into a couch, and a stuffing busted armchair. A full bookshelf ran around the top of the room, and there were a couple of plants on the stereo speakers. Above all, the cabin was neat; there was just enough room for everything, and everything was in its place. You might think Jurek lacked for nothing, and you would be pretty close to right.

As he started getting the tea things together, Mim could feel his mood lifting a little. He took a large brown teapot edged with gold from among a half dozen off the top of the refrigerator. It was an antique, he told her, only used for special occasions. Probably Elizabeth Barrett and Robert Browning took tea in Venice from this very pot.

"I should know who they are," Mim told him. She had wanted to major in English but had wound up in elementary education thinking it would be more practical. Around Jurek she felt she didn't have an education at all.

"A love-struck couple," Jurek told her, "in love against her family's wishes. Very messy business."

He brought out a pear, a block of cheddar cheese, and sliced them up. He brought out some smoked salmon strips. "These are made from silvers, sweet ones. Taste." He offered her a piece on the tip of his knife blade. "You get these from the old German guy in Nenana." Jurek had to admit that he had never been able to make his own come out as good.

He brought out two small china cups with saucers. As he poured, he announced, "Lapsang Souchong." It was his favorite tea. He preferred it as an after-dinner tea, but for her he would make an exception.

When she stood up from the futon to take her cup, she reconsidered her choice and took the stuffed chair to sit in. The big arms made her feel warm and protected. She liked that; she liked his making a fuss over her even though she didn't like the creosote taste of the tea at all. "You've got a wonderful view," she told him.

He admitted it was true. Out the window was the still-frozen and snow-covered Tanana River glowing white and beaten hard as a high- way by snow machines and dog sleds. Beyond it stood Denali in all its pink and lavender glory. "You can't see it every day," he told her. Maybe, Mim was thinking, you wouldn't want to, maybe that would be too much beauty. You'd only get used to it. Maybe it was better just to have every now and then.

There were some ways Tolstoy had planned out for a woman's life that she only recently was coming to understand. Mim considered that her first time through his book; she read it like Kitty would have—a big rollercoaster ride of love and pain and loss. She remembered sitting on her mother's ratty couch with an afghan wrapped around her legs looking up into the gray winter light out the window, crying and crying over Anna's taking Seryozha his birthday presents and having to sneak into her own house. Anna wanted it every which way, her little boy, her place in the St. Petersburg social world, her handsome officer, and true love too. Who was Tolstoy but some avenging angel coming to say, no she couldn't, no you can't?

She'd skipped school to read the way her girlfriends skipped to watch *Days of Our Lives* when it was going to be really good. She had read all day. Now it was pitch dark and who knows how late? The little coffee table in front of the couch was covered with balled up Kleenex, empty soda bottles, and cracker crumbs. Mim felt wrung out, empty, like she would feel two years later when she broke up with her boyfriend to go off to college. Anna's death had broken her heart, as Tolstoy must have known it would, and Levin and Kitty's marriage was not enough to make up for it.

Up at the country club, her mother would have been sitting in the kitchen with the other cook and the dishwasher and a couple of waitresses waiting for the last of the card players to leave. She would bum a Kool from the dishwasher. When the last of the men went out, they would slip into the club room and pour themselves drinks from the bar. Mim was in college before she walked into that stainless steel kitchen and caught her mother laughing, tipsy, with a cigarette hanging off her lip, a tough old bird. She still had plenty of life in her. And for the first time Mim wondered: All those years of wearing her wedding ring, of hoping, hadn't she ever given up, given in to a man? Somebody who Mim could picture hanging around, waiting while her mom locked up and stuffed the wad of keys in her purse?

Mim's tea was cold in her cup; Jurek had eaten most of the snacks he'd meticulously laid out on a patterned china plate with a chip in it. He'd stoked up the woodstove and the cabin had grown close. She felt herself relaxing into the chair. The smell of the wood smoke, the salmon, and tea made her feel she could burrow in like the girls' gerbils napping in their cedar shavings. She could almost take a nap.

Then she'd asked to see up in the loft where there was another futon on the floor and lots of books stuck in wooden boxes turned on their sides, a smaller table with a desk lamp and a chair. Jurek kept a journal, another way he surprised her. But when she considered she was in what amounted to the bedroom of a man she scarcely knew, she bolted.

Who could say what might have happened next? To put it in Kenny's language, inertial mass had not reached the point of inevitability.

She realized Jurek had given her a way out, a way to just say it was a mistake, to slip down the ladder of his loft and go. Her head filled up with all sorts of matter, Kenny, the girls, their gerbils in their spinning race. She pictured herself crossing her arms, taking the waistband of her sweater and pulling it over her head, reaching behind herself, un-hooking her bra and letting it slide down her arms. She felt her nipples pucker as she imagined the chill of the room against her bare skin. She had never done any such thing, not even with college boys when she was a little wild. Where had she gotten this picture? Out of some mov-ie, she guessed.

When she got home, there sat Kenny in his favorite chair, working on an extra hard Sudoku, from a book of many extra hard Sodokus, muttering to himself, his extra fine pen point clicking in and out as he worked out the numbers in his head. Wanting his dinner, of course. Neat in his khaki pants and oxford shirt. His same uniform from col-lege days. She almost felt sorry for him.

Driving her girls here and there, making the family's dinners, she let her thoughts—aching, scattered, aroused—run away with her. Lucky she didn't crash into somebody or catch the kitchen on fire. It wasn't what had not happened at Jurek's cabin, but what could have. She wondered if her actions, maybe everybody's actions, were like a novel, a swirling whirlpool as the water drained out of the bathtub, everything funneling down, inevitable, irreversible.

■ ■ ■

Nothing happened. Spring stuttered on in its frustrating way. The snow went. Ski season was over. Jurek did not ferret out her phone number; he did not secretly call; he did not rattle by their house and park his ancient Suburban a discreet distance down the road and wait.

Weeks passed. She went with Kenny to a potluck dinner for bicyclists though she didn't own a bike. These were Kenny's friends, not hers, and his friends of long standing, but she had trouble keeping their names straight. More men than women and a terrible spread of food, lots of chips and Doritos and beer, gobs of pasta all stuck together. Guys didn't care; they dug right in, talking their baffling bullshitty talk about ball teams and scores and who bought this bike or took this ride. Mim thought she might have to go into the bathroom, lock herself in and cry.

When Jurek appeared, it seemed that everybody in the room turned to him like pathetic sun-starved plants on the windowsill turned toward the light, as if his arrival was a confirmation of whatever reason they thought they had to be there. He laid his caribou stir-fry in its beautiful hand-thrown bowl on the community table and people swarmed to it. There he was, slapping men on the shoulder, hugging women, flashing his big white teeth, offering a joke or knowing comment for each of them.

Of course Mim had hoped he might turn up. That was her reason for coming. But hadn't she hoped he would turn up everywhere? The grocery, the post office, the credit union?

She wished she could have said there was something special in

Jurek's greeting for her. How was it that some people had this magnetic gift that pulled others to them, that held them in thrall. So easy to like, to admire, to love even. Few people had that gift, most of us would have to work at it. Mim knew she would drive out to his cabin again.

How had she let a wild emotional impulse roll over into a self-conscious willful act? She, a grown woman, not a girl who didn't know the difference?

■ ■ ■

Jurek's journal was not the story of his life but a collection of his thoughts, thoughts not always connected to his actions. If the world was a disordered place—as it surely was—where else was order to be found? He used his journal to write epigrammatically instructions to himself. "Kill animals gently and with respect, like the Natives do," he told himself. "Sleep no longer than necessary." "Seek to know beauty." Jurek's heroes were the stoics, the epicureans, the cynics, all philosophers who'd given up on the greater good and struck out on narrow paths of their own. So had Jurek. He did not vote because it was pointless. But he often volunteered at the Rescue Mission; he gave them money too. He did not love the name of Jesus in the way the Mission staff did. The Golden Rule: there was a good idea, but who could honestly expect people to come up to that? You'd have to believe in miracles. In this systematic, disciplined way, Jurek wrote spare entries in the journal on his tidy desk. He did not believe in miracles.

Kenny had a little desk too. It sat in the corner of the family room, covered with some fly-tying stuff he'd lost interest in, some fishing magazines and back issues of *The Master Skier*. Could it be that Kenny had lost interest in the world as well as in engineering? If Mim looked at Kenny from outer space, what would she see? An ant. An ant creeping along doing its duty. Which was admirable. Why was that not enough?

■ ■ ■

She had arrived without warning; she had come to repay him for his treat of pears and cheese and too-strong tea. And she had in her car a shopping bag containing two ripe cantaloupes, grapes, chocolates, and a bottle of white wine—which she hoped to chill by sticking it in the snowbank made from the spring slide off Jurek's roof. Furthermore, she had come to finish their business from that other day, a business she was not altogether sure Jurek was disposed to.

Here is something Mim had noticed about him, how his cabin and his storage shed were neat as a pin, while the back of his Suburban was full of all sorts of junk. Some of it was Alaskan junk, a come-along, flares, a tow chain, an axe and a bow saw, an old sleeping bag. But some of it was seasonal too. And as winter gave over to summer, she saw how his many pairs of ski boots and Sorels gave over to breakup boots and river sandals, bike shoes and running shoes, well-greased and well-used hiking boots.

So she was not surprised to come upon him on his porch with his waxing bench set up, ironing a last coat of wax into his skis, this last little bit of the season, before storing them away on the rack he had fashioned for them in his shed. So many, so like a quiver of arrows in their bright colors. And so like him to take such care. She liked this about him and found a way to tell herself that it was different, not like Kenny's anal engineer's way of wanting nothing more than neatness. Jurek believed in beauty. His every gesture was about beauty. She told herself this. She felt strung taut, aware of her skin inside her sweater and jeans, aware of the cool moist air of snowmelt, aware of the quiet.

He smiled at her when she pulled into view—straight white teeth, he'd probably never had a cavity in his life. She realized she needed that smile. But when she got out, her grocery bag split open in her arms; a cantaloupe went rolling down the bank, the bottle of wine behind it.

Jurek strode directly off the porch in one giant step and, in his breakup boots, always in the right footwear, went to retrieve them. Mim bent to pick up the rest and burst into tears as she tried to clean the silty mud away.

"Hey, hey, what's this?" he said, sounding put out, mystified.

"I was hoping to surprise you, that's all."

"Well, you did surprise me."

Not in the right way, she was thinking. But he took the bottle of wine and seemed to know what she'd hoped to do with it, scoured it off with a handful of snow and buried it in the bank. Then he took her into the house and sat her down in the same chair she'd been in before and began to clean the grapes, cut the cantaloupe, and filled two plates. She had lost her advantage.

Outside, his waxing iron was smoking, and he dashed out to see to it. Once again, she had a sense she had intruded on his orderly life. Maybe, she thought, that's all she could do. Jurek would always name the terms and conditions. And if she had continued to sit and sniffle in his bro-ken-down easy chair that would have been the end of things.

Instead, she got up and took up the knife, cut away the seeds, and sectioned the cantaloupe, cleaned and broke off a bunch of grapes, and opened and arranged the chocolates. She took the plates outdoors. "Why don't you finish that up?" She could tell that's what he wanted to do anyway.

They were talking about nothing; they were talking to fill up the space of time. Leaned against one of the spruce posts that held up the porch roof, Mim was watching, though; she was watching for the last pair of skis. She was playing the kind of tricks on herself you play when you are a kid—after the next blue car, then such-and-such, after I count to fifty. . . . So as the last ski of the last pair went onto the bench, as he dribbled the wax down the ski, as he began to iron it in long even move-ments, she said, "You know I came out here to seduce you."

He glanced at her. She wanted to think he blushed. "It's not that hard to do."

"So they say." She herself was blushing. She could feel beads of sweat come up between her breasts, could feel her own pulse.

"Who's this they?" He smiled. He'd asked her that before, hadn't he? "Never mind. I can probably guess." And he unplugged his iron and un-

clamped his ski. He went back in the house and came out with a corkscrew and glasses for the wine.

Mim worried for a minute they might be plastic. They needed to be
glass, to be a little elegant if this were to work. And they were, they had
twisted glass stems and a ring of gold at their lips. And the wine was
cool. He gave her a glass and went to sit across from her against another
porch post. She slipped off her wool socks and threw them over by her
muddy Birkenstocks. The night before, she'd painted her toenails red,
and now she wiggled them in the sunlight.

"What's that all about?"

"So when you take my clothes off, you won't have to bother with my
socks. I never know what to do about the socks."

"Thought through every detail, then?"

It was true; in some way she had. She had let herself grow brazen.
This was what had stopped her the last time: Now she knew that she
could. She knew then as she knew now that she could pull her sweater
off and unclasp her bra (though she had worn one this time that opened
in the front because she wanted Jurek to do it for her, had woken up
in the night thinking about wanting him to do it for her). Now maybe
what she knew was that she wanted. In this way she was alert to him.
Her nipples were hard; she felt them. But she held herself in check and
knew she couldn't let herself go until he touched her. That was what it
would take. He would have to do something so she would know to let go.

He took her into the house and kissed her as the door swung shut
behind them. He kissed her gently and slowly, with consideration and
respect she thought. Then he kissed deeply and long, kissed her neck
and ears and her mouth again and began to slowly stroke her back. Then
he pulled her sweater over her head and undid her bra.

Neither of them had their shirts on now. The room was cold. He held
her away from him and took a long appraising look at her. She imagined
the kind of women he usually undressed had small firm breasts. For an
instant, she actually thought about apologizing.

"What is this? What is this between us," he said, "ether? Some kind of special substance? What?"

Mim looked down too and thought she could see the air between them, that it was a purplish blue the way it can get on a long spring twilight. "What?"

"This."

"Love." That's what she said, but it wasn't an answer or another question, it was a sound, the sound the word made.

■ ■ ■

This, Mim saw, is why Anna Karenina sat and cried after Vronsky took her on her parlor floor. Not because of shame as Tolstoy may have thought. But because she suddenly no longer knew who she was. She was no longer just a wife and mother and could not go back to that place in her heart no matter how hard she tried, no matter how hard she might want to. But who was she now? A woman who had just wrung herself out through wanting, through pleasure. A woman who had allowed a man to see her naked and coming in broad daylight, who'd opened herself to him that fully. Now she must wonder who he really was, whether he understood and was capable of understanding.

■ ■ ■

"Girlfriend, are you out of your mind?" This was Rachel talking, blurting really, but Mim had to tell somebody so she called up Rachel and asked her to meet for breakfast at Sam's Sourdough.

"I did. I slept with him."

"How could you?"

"He gave me fruit to eat."

"Jesus God," Rachel said. "Fruit to eat! That's all it took? There's a Bible story you might know about that trick."

Mim did know that one. She knew the devil had something to do with it too. What could she say? Rachel did it all the time, or at least acted like she did. But Rachel said that was different. She had no kids; she had no husband. Well, she had one, but she got rid of him. In fact, that was why she got rid of him because she knew she was one to want to fool around. "It wouldn't be fair."

"Not fair," Mim said pushing her eggs around her plate as if the idea was new to her.

"Are you going to eat that or not?"

"Not, I guess."

"Does Kenny know?" Before Mim could answer, Rachel said, "Of course he knows."

"How?"

"How? Look at you, girl." Rachel leaned in and said this in a big stagey whisper, "Look at you. You look like you spent all night fucking. You look like you just came down from the biggest orgasm in your life."

People in the next booth turned around to look. And they saw Mim with her hair strewn wildly around her pink face, her irises going like pinwheels, her mouth hanging half open.

"And the girls? Where's their momma right now? Not home dishing up their oatmeal is she? They don't know what, but they know. Everybody knows."

"Everybody," Mim said like she was receiving a verdict, irrevocable, but in her dream state it didn't seem to matter so much.

"Look out the window." Out on the sunny sidewalk, a guy pushed a shopping cart full of assembled junk, a couple of cyclists glided by, some joggers, a girl and a dog. "This is Fairbanks. Everybody knows everything about everybody. Or did you forget?"

Mim had forgotten.

"Well," Rachel told her, "it's kind of like those kayakers Jurek likes to play with down in Nenana Canyon. Once you're in, you're in. Try to enjoy the ride, stay out of the soup, and maybe you'll find a good place to eddy out."

Really, nobody knew anything yet. Rachel would take care of that soon enough.

■ ■ ■

Mim had never been a particularly imaginative person, but now she found she had to be, inventing a new life wherein she was much more social, much more in demand than she ever had been before. Suddenly, her girlfriends wanted to meet her for lunch dates all the time. They went on girls' nights out too. She volunteered. And she went to board meetings of organizations that Kenny had never known her to take much of an interest in. How did she come to be on their boards?

Driving into Jurek's place where her car would be safely obscured by trees, she felt a tremendous sense of relief. She had allowed herself to become lackadaisical. She believed, or needed to believe, that she had taken an evasive route, she had escaped detection.

There he would be. Maybe putting in his garden, maybe splitting some of next winter's wood. Maybe sitting on his porch in gym shorts or nothing at all reading a book or sketching the view. Wherever he was, she would grab him by his hand and lead him into the cabin as if he were a little kid being led off for punishment. Inside, she would pull their clothes off and have at him.

For those few moments—excitable as she was, they didn't last long— she was free from the worries that nagged at her. Later, lying on his couch or bed or on the worn rug on the floor, she would ask, "What's going to become of us?"

This was a question Jurek was reluctant to answer. "The Greeks had a word for it: Olbos. Satiation. You have all the happiness you need, so why ask for more?" He didn't tell her the rest. How in all the myths, nobody could stop right there.

■ ■ ■

For years Mim had carried around this image of Tolstoy. Maybe she'd seen him sometime on TV, wandering around in black-and-white footage with Walter Cronkite explaining things in voice-over. Could that be right, could there have been movie cameras when Tolstoy was still alive? She remembered a doddering old man with a big white beard and messy white hair, what was left of it anyway, and he wore something like a white nightgown. Sort of like the Mr. Natural guy you saw on truck mud flaps for a while.

That man, grown into a wispy kind of saint, had another kind of guy in mind for women like Mim, for every woman, she supposed: Levin. There were some of those types around. Steve, the psychologist at Rachel's school who biked to work in all weather, his bike covered with flashing lights, its tubes wrapped with bumper stickers, "bikes not bombs," "work for peace," "love your mother" with a picture of our earth as seen from outer space. Mim imagined he saw himself saving the planet one pedal stroke at a time. A Quaker? A Buddhist? It seemed he was a little of both, and did yoga too.

"You should see his abs," Rachel had told her. Rachel had seen them up close.

"So what's going on with Steve?"

"Steve?" Rachel made this look that said Mim had said something completely off the wall.

"Your crush."

"Oh him. He's gone, he's toast. Who's that guy you were telling us about the other day? In that book you're reading?"

"Levin."

"Yeah, Levin. Deep, spiritual guy, the one who goes out and cuts hay with the peasants and gets it in his head he's at one with them and the universe and everything else? Steve was like that. It just goes to show."

"That?"

After a few weeks of environmental meetings, peace meetings, social justice meetings, she had had enough; after hours of his earnest do-gooder talk, and more talk. "I just wanted to yell, 'shut up and screw me.' I mean, I like the earth well enough, but I'm not going to ride a bike to school at forty below just to let it know."

"Her," Mim said, "earth is a her."

"God, you should see his abs. But I thought we were going to have to say a prayer or something before we got down to doing anything. All this incense and candles and crap. Enough."

Mim felt like she had to defend him—Levin, not Steve. "Levin is supposed to be the hero of the book; he's the guy who seems a little kooky at first, but he turns out to be the real deal." But she knew she had not believed it herself, not even when she was a high school girl. She knew all about those drippy guys who other girls said were so deep. Who needed them? After she tried a few wild ones, she had settled on Kenny, not deep, not wild, just plain old Kenny. "The thing about Levin," she told Rachel, "is that he's so spiritual. He's trying to get past the material world. Know what I mean?"

"No."

Mim watched Rachel swirl her tea bag in her cup. That was the trouble with Sam's, they only gave you one tea bag no matter how many times they filled up your little teapot. It came to Mim that weak tea was it, the whole problem in a nutshell. That was the life we walk around in, watered down, diluted, if we let ourselves. She surprised herself by saying, "That's Tolstoy trying to fix everything up for you, making you think there's something better if you're just patient and stay away from locomotives."

"Those are the choices? Getting creamed by a train or getting religion?"

Instead, Mim pictured herself naked in bed with Jurek. Potentially painful, but not regrettable. Not regrettable.

"Seriously," Rachel said, "that kind of guy is not a real option," meaning Steve or Jurek or both.

What kind, then, was? Because as weeks rolled on, Rachel, still willing to meet her at the coffee place on Geist, a dangerous place, a gossip mill, said, "Sister, you have fucked up bad."

"Why?"

"Look, everybody colors out of the lines every once in a while. But you have to cut it out. You're going to ruin your marriage, mess up your kids. Everybody's going to hate you."

"You do crazy shit like this all the time." Crazy shit, listen at me. This is the way I talk nowadays, Mim thought.

"Yeah, but I don't have a Kenny."

"You'd be bored stiff with Kenny."

"For sure. That's why I don't have one. But you do. You've got a Rebecca and a Sarah too."

■ ■ ■

The last time she'd driven out to his place, Mim saw the signs Jurek had posted seeking help locating his cat gone missing. She never could have guessed he would care. But he did care, was fretful, angry with himself, almost grief-stricken. "He could still be alive," she told him. That was true, and it only made matters worse.

Today, when Mim pulled into Jurek's narrow drive, she found his Suburban gone. She had no means of communicating when she might come, so she just took her chances. She sat in front of the closed up cabin and read her book. She considered herself lucky when she found him home. But just being in his yard, being in his world, was a small reward. She read and waited, "'He has the right to go when and where he likes. Not only to go away, but to leave me. He has all the rights, and I have none.'" Ugh. Poor woman. She put the book aside and looked out over the river where the Mountain was nowhere to be seen.

Out of nowhere, Jurek roared into his drive. Unshaven, in grungy clothes, he had been off for two days of trout fishing south of the Alaska Range—an undisclosed location, of course. He was randy and cheerful, and she thought happy to see her. "It's not locked; it's never locked," he told her as he led her to the cabin door.

That's when they saw the cat, still alive but mauled, probably by dogs. Though Jurek had made a cat door so the cat could come and go at its pleasure, something had gone wrong. It had made its way back to a patch of ground off to the side of the porch where it lay panting. There was no point, he said, in taking it to the vet.

Jurek went inside, came out and sat by the cat gently stroking it. When it managed to purr for him, he reached into his pocket for the small pistol he had retrieved and shot the cat in the head. Then he discharged the remaining rounds from the gun into a nearby spruce tree.

The suddenness of the gun scared her, pulled her breath out of her. Just then, Jurek had, too, his hardness, his violence. "You can't blame yourself," Mim told him as he went to his shed for a spade—words to soothe herself more than him.

"I don't. I gave him the freedom to come and go, and this is how it worked out. Still, he was the best kind of friend; we didn't ask too much of each other."

Clearly, though, he was distraught, and Mim thought she might comfort him by asking, "So you will get another one?"

"Oh no. This one came by the cabin one day and decided to stay. Another may present itself someday."

"Are you never lonely?"

"Often I prefer to be."

"Have you ever wanted children?"

"I was a child myself once, but outgrew the condition."

"I could get pregnant."

"You're too smart for that. I have nothing against children. But I have nothing for them either." He made a smile hardened by irony that could not be pushed through.

What had she expected? Only that Jurek swept away by this passionate love would throw over his cabin life, would put his knowledge of books and authors, of philosophy and even physics to some higher use. Where had such a notion come from? From the runaway train of her lust.

Sex with Kenny had quickly become hurried and perfunctory well before the girls were born. His thoughts always seemed to be elsewhere, the same wherever engineers' thoughts went when they stared absently into space at the dinner table, or didn't pay attention to what you were saying when riding in the car.

"No. I was an unwanted child, so maybe it's a genetic trait."

"I have kids, you know."

"I do know that."

Her girls, Mim had thought too many times, would fall in love with Jurek just as she had. That he would not care to love them back had not occurred to her.

Jurek gathered into himself, nursing the grief for his dead cat privately. Instead of becoming vulnerable, he managed to make himself less so. The spark of desire that had caused her to drive out to his place in the middle of the day faded. She got in her car and drove home.

Hadn't her mother raised her to have good sense? She was, Mim learned early on, the very model of what a single mistake might cost. Love? Maybe Mim's mom would agree with Stiva Oblonsky: love was nothing more than a misfortune best avoided. No, she had never told Mim she was a burden, never complained about the hours she stood on her feet in a kitchen cooking better food than she could afford to give her child. Mim had absorbed the lesson by osmosis. Despite her high school boyfriend's best efforts, Mim went off to college a virgin.

■　■　■

Kenny should have figured it out sooner if he'd known how to look. Dinner late, Mim just not there when he tried to talk to her. They'd gotten out of the habit of talking seriously, but this was a little worse. Instead of just not listening to him, now it was like she was listening for some far away music.

When he did figure out what, he didn't know who. Around the office, guys were kind of smirking, having conversations over by the coffee pot that seemed to come to an abrupt halt as soon as he got close. He came home and here she came, following him back up the driveway. Where had she been, and where were the girls? Errands she told him, and the girls inside playing with their Barbies. Except they were fighting, Sarah yelling that Rebecca had taken her Little Mermaid and would not give it back.

"All right," Kenny told her, "things are falling apart around here, and I've got a pretty good idea why."

Mim had imagined this moment many times. And when she did, she imagined herself in a calm, measured voice, a voice an engineer would recognize, telling Kenny she had fallen in love with another man, that she wanted a divorce so she might be with him. Now she burst into tears, now she said, "I wanted to tell you, but I didn't know how." She knew it sounded corny even as she said it. And she knew she'd avoided saying it because she hadn't had the nerve.

"Who is it then?"

When Mim told him, he only said, "The fucker." She had never heard Kenny use that word before, and in light of what he, what everybody, knew of Jurek she could see how right it might seem. But she wanted to say, this is different.

In Kenny's student days, his intro to structural engineering professor began the first day of the class with a slide show, one slide after another of collapsed bridges, broken tramway towers, cracking apart buildings. This was the cost of miscalculation. Pull a boner like that and you would have it hanging around your neck the rest of your career. That something like this could happen to him, that it could happen when he thought he'd done everything right, made all the right calculations, made him feel so defeated, he just sat in his favorite chair and stared. There was that feather still clinging to the window. Where was that fucking bird-killing cat?

■ ■ ■

Up to now, Mim's life by comparison to those of her friends had stayed on a well-ordered path: College, marriage, marriage to the same guy, kids, kids sweet and good-natured. And farther along, expectation for kids to do what they would—continue their piano, maybe move from creative movement to ballet, play a sport, make good grades, go to college themselves, then off into their own happy married lives. It was not as if Mim had scripted these developments. They had occurred as naturally as the turning from one season to the next. She needn't do anything but get up in the morning and do what needed to be done. The group yard sale, she remembered. That's what needed to be done. She called Rachel to ask about plans.

"Oh," she said, "it's this Saturday."

"Why didn't anybody tell me?"

"Ha, ha. We thought you'd be too busy."

At this moment, the arc of Mim's life had begun to curve in a way a man like Kenny with technical inclinations might appreciate, in the way geography might resolve into geometry and then into algebra: Something as formulaic as a parabolic curve, its apogee realized, now bent on its downward course. Seen from his perspective it might look that simple.

■ ■ ■

All that followed was Mim's idea: She pressed Jurek for more time, thinking it was only time, specifically not enough of it, standing in their way. She asked for a whole night together, and he had agreed, but it would be a fishing trip to one of his secret spots, a night not in his comfortable cabin but on Thermarests and in too hot sleeping bags. Though among her friends some looked at tents and saw erotic possibilities, Mim begged to disagree: sleeping on the ground, discovering unexpected roots and rocks in the most unpleasant places, crawling out to pee in the woods and hoping to get back in without an army of mosquitoes following behind.

To pull the trip off, she had told her boldest lie to Kenny, that she and her gal pals were going on a quilting retreat at the hot springs. True enough, some of her pals were going on just such a retreat and ordinarily Mim would have been with them. She counted on Rachel to cover for her. She thought of this trip as a kind of test.

"Oh joy. To test what exactly? How far you can bend over backwards?"

Mim knew her way around a campsite, had set up plenty of tents, made fires, and cooked on them. But she had never held a fly rod in her hands, and it did not occur to her that Jurek would hold her to the same standard as he might any other fishing partner. He grew impatient quickly with every back cast she snagged in the bushes, with every lost fly, every knot he had to tie for her.

As they crossed a low place in the river, shallow but rocky and swift, Mim in her uncomfortable and unfamiliar wading boots felt her feet go out from under her. As she fell forward, she dropped her rod and put out her hands to catch herself. Jurek grabbed her by the suspenders of her waders and picked her up like a kitten. "You," he said, "are outside your limit."

"Well, sure," she said, "this is all new to me." Of course it had occurred to her that the boots and the waders in a woman's size had been worn by others before her. Was part of the test to pretend not to notice or pretend not to care?

"Let's get you back on land." He led her back to the bank and went back to retrieve the rod.

"Oh, I've ruined your fishing rod." She was trying to sound sorry.

"Nonsense," he told her, though the tip dangled loosely from the line on the end. He looked at her appraisingly, "I should never have brought you here."

"Really, I'm OK."

But despite Mim's expert cleaning and scaling the fish, despite the tasty herbs she'd thought to bring from home, Jurek's mood did not lighten.

What had she imagined? That Jurek, like Prince Vronsky, would become a new man through the force of love alone? That this man who had never bothered to register to vote would become a civic activist?

That this congenital loner would readily take on an instant family? Out in the woods where everything was peeled back to the most basic choices, Mim saw how slight a bit of Jurek she'd managed to take hold of.

■ ■ ■

She went home to an empty house. Kenny's pickup and the girls were gone. All she found was a cryptic note written in Kenny's angular print with mechanical pencil on a sheet torn from his notebook, "I have girls."

Now it was her turn to stare out the window. Which is where she sat until the phone rang. It was Rachel. Kenny had gone to the hot springs. The girls were with him. He'd asked for her.

"What did you say?"

"What could I say?" He was angry in a way Rachel had never seen him. "I was scared."

"Oh God, oh shit."

"I tried to tell him, get real. This is the real world. Stuff like this happens. You just have to get past it. Go home and talk to her."

"And?"

"He said, 'Ain't going to happen.' I think he meant it. Are you alone? I mean, where is Kenny now? Where are the girls?"

"I don't know."

"Well, you've got Jurek, I guess."

"I don't think so."

"That, too? Well, now's not the best time to say I told you so, but. . . ." Was it possible to feel glee coming across a phone line? "What are you going to do?"

"I don't know."

If Mim could have summoned the energy just then to be reflective, she would have tried to piece together how quickly her life had arrived at this irrevocable moment. A moment when she felt there was no ground beneath her feet? A moment when her actions, actions she couldn't explain to herself even though she'd gone and done them, done them willingly, even joyfully, began to crash against one another.

■ ■ ■

Mim has grown used to hauling the heavy jugs of water up the narrow path to her own little cabin, has gotten used to showering at the school where she works as a teacher's aide while trying to work her way back into the system as a full-time teacher. The girls like spending time at the cabin; they even think the outhouse is a funny novelty. It took a while to get to this place. Kenny holed up with the girls in a motel for a few days after his angry trip to the hot springs. After a while he relented, unable actually to take care of them himself, and allowed Mim to negotiate for a divorce with joint custody. Mim cried a lot. Why she did is puzzling to her still. Maybe she had really wanted Jurek, but finally she understood she just wanted out.

There are still very many things Mim does not know, beginning with who she is and what she hopes for. She's trying to figure herself out, admittedly a lifelong project. And she does think of poor Anna Karenina from time to time, thinks how her own—or anybody's, really—life can seem to be like a book or a story. Some things happen, may happen in unexpected and undesirable ways, happen whether you want them to or not.

Sometimes Mim can still be pretty damned miserable, but that doesn't mean she sees the path of her life as inevitable. This wasn't a lesson Tolstoy could teach her, something she sees he was all wrong about. Instead she realized she'd learned all she needed to know from Ann Landers, that wise lady she'd read as a girl every day in the Bluefield paper. Over and over again, Ann counseled the confused and broken-hearted that a person didn't go looking for love with somebody else if everything was OK with the one she was with.

Today as she races to town, late again, she gets caught by the tourist train at the crossing just past Annie's Greenhouse. The heavy blue-and-yellow engines roll by, each one shouting, "Alaska! Alaska!" The tourists sit inside their special cars at tables with linen cloths and bud vases or come out onto their porticos and wave at the waiting cars, smug in their assumption that they know something of this place and the people who live here. Most assuredly, they do not.

While she waits, Mim watches the hypnotic sway of the cars as they rock along, listens to the lull of their clanking rhythm. But to throw herself under the trucks of a passing rail car? It never enters her mind.

As for Jurek, Mim never thought to ask him if he, too, had read *Anna Karenina*. Of course he had. Silly people, Anna and Vronsky, especially Vronsky. He was vain and self-absorbed, often rash and reckless. He loved himself too much and the world not enough. How else to explain that nonsense: shooting himself and then going off to the Crimea? Foolishness, all of it.

PATIENCE, JACKASS

A figure in a polo shirt and baggy short pants comes to the gate where a sign reads, "Swim at your own risk." From a distance his spindly legs make him seem a boy in early adolescence, but his blond hair, lank and in need of a trim, is shot through with gray, and his face is a tired face. He calls to the lone woman sitting in a lounge chair on the concrete apron beside the pool. "It's dinnertime, Mother," he says. Inside before a television set blaring the evening news interspersed with remedies for a variety of digestive ailments, the table is laid with their meal, Dinty Moore beef stew, tater tots, some green beans, and a wedge of iceberg lettuce with orange-colored dressing poured over it. The man's name is Kyle Schuller. But wait a while before you judge him (tater tots, for Christ's sake), whether to pity or to scorn.

■ ■ ■

Kyle was at Boy Scout camp, the same scout camp he went to every summer. But this time he was on his own. The other boys in his troop and his scoutmaster would come another week, which was OK. They all hated Kyle, and he hated them back, so no big deal. When a boy didn't go to camp with his troop, he was put with the other strays in a cabin and assigned a provisional scoutmaster to look after them. They were supposed to have a counselor in their cabin, but for some reason they just didn't. Which suited Kyle and the other boys fine. The provisional scoutmaster dropped by and told them he was confident they were mature enough to handle things on their own. Besides, then he, their scoutmaster, could stay in the lodge with the other adults, where there was a stove, hot and cold running water, and maybe a sip of whiskey before turning in.

Right away Kyle decided he didn't much like their scoutmaster. The man was tall and thin as a razor, but somehow you knew he could throw an eighty-pound pack on his back and hike all day and feel self-righteous about it. He wore the same uniform as the boys, shorts with khaki knee socks and garters to hold them up. Only his garter tabs were intricate beadwork. He wore patches on his shirt from Philmont Scout Ranch and the most recent national jamboree and talked about *scouting* as if it were a kind of religion. That was enough to make Kyle hate him, but mostly he hated the man because he bore a striking resemblance to Kyle himself. He could see the other scouts looking at him and looking at the man—Paul Perkins was his name—and wondering.

The first night after lights out, the kids in his cabin stayed up late talking and joking. It didn't take Kyle any time at all to figure out they were pathetic, a bunch of hicks from McDowell County. Rubes. When they started talking about shooting squirrels, Kyle realized that was really what they meant.

Maybe over the years Kyle had come to believe the things he subsequently did at scout camp were conscious decisions. That would be wrong, though. He was a boy completely governed by a smug, angry impulse, though by the end of the week that would change for good.

His provisional scoutmaster was the waterfront director too. Kyle would try for his swimming merit badge. It should be a snap; he'd been taking swimming lessons at the country club ever since, as his mom liked to say, he was old enough to pee in the pool. As they hung on the rope between the deep and shallow water while one of the older scouts demonstrated the breaststroke, Kyle turned to the kid beside him and said, "That's not how you do the kick. Nobody does the kick like that anymore." The kid took a quick look at Kyle and edged away farther down the rope.

Paul Perkins heard him, and said, "Smart guy, you want to show us how it's done?"

"No," Kyle told him.

Paul Perkins looked at him hard, fixing Kyle's features more permanently in his mind, "Aren't you one of mine?"

Kyle knew well enough what he meant, but he said, "Yours? I don't think so."

That evening as they formed up to march down to the field to strike the colors, Kyle lingered close enough to Paul Perkins to hear him telling another scoutmaster what happened down at the lake. He didn't call him by name, just "this little shit." Eavesdropping was a life skill Kyle learned from his mother.

Things went downhill fast from there. Kyle sat stone-faced while Paul Perkins prowled the dining hall, keeping time with his pumping fist and leading the boys in campfire songs. "I've Got Six Pence"? Come on, what kind of song was that? He refused to practice the breaststroke kick as Paul Perkins taught it. He produced several packs of firecrackers from his duffle bag and began slipping out of the cabin at night and setting them off around the camp.

It wasn't very hard to catch him. As he stood snickering in the dark just out of the switched-on light of a cabin full of hollering, scrambling boys, he felt a heavy hand come down on his shoulder, "Easy there, cowboy." Two of the senior counselors had been trailing him all along, pleased to make use of their Indian-like stealth to capture the troublemaker. Nobody hit Kyle, but they pushed him around causing him to lurch and stumble on the dark path as they dragged him to the lodge.

Paul Perkins may have tried to act angry, but secretly he was pleased. "I guess you'll be going home in the morning," he said. But he was wrong. Kyle's father probably owned half the coal in McDowell County where his cabinmates' fathers worked as miners. Kyle's father owned his hometown paper and had his fingers in every money pot in town. Who could guess how many people called Kyle's father boss? Sometimes at dinnertime or in the evening, the phone would ring. There would be a problem at the paper. At first Kyle's father, a short, red-faced man always dressed in a business suit from morning to bedtime, would talk in a growly insistent voice into the phone, then he would shout and cuss, his words spilling out in explosive balloons of expletives like Mr. Dithers's in the funny papers. Finally, he would storm out, back his car into the street, and slam into drive with a jerk and a squeal and be gone. His mother would light a cigarette as she and Kyle looked out onto the empty street, "Why on earth did I marry that man?"

It wasn't Kyle's father but his mother people were afraid of. Kyle heard them say more than once she was a piece of work. She wore her hair pulled back against her skull, twisted into a knot and held in place with whatever was at hand, a pencil, an elegantly lacquered wooden stick (it was a chopstick, but so few people in this town had ever seen one, how would they know?). Probably she dyed her hair, but she had it done out of town so nobody could say for sure.

When he first heard somebody say that—"a piece of work"—Kyle, even though he was too young to have any experience of sex at that time, imagined it had something to do with sex. In a way he was right. His mother sat by the poolside every sunny day from spring to fall, baked as a brick, the straps of her swimsuit pushed down, her breasts almost fully exposed to the world. When she blew the smoke from her Salems in two thick streams out her nose, she radiated a kind of predatory sexual magnetism that got golf pros and towel boys fired from the country club.

That was her favorite line, "I'll see you fired . . ." for slow service, snippy remarks, mistakes in the order, any kind of mistake, really, the biggest one being not knowing instantly who she was.

Paul Perkins was new around here, though, and he didn't know. Before he got too far along in giving Kyle a pleasurable chewing out, the camp director intervened. Kyle would get a second chance.

The next day it began raining. It rained through the day with no let up. The boys went to the crafts shed, the first-aid tent, lazed around in their cabins. Just before supper, Paul Perkins stomped in wearing his official Boy Scout slicker. Skits, he told them, each cabin would make up a skit for after supper tonight since there would be no campfire, no outdoor games. "OK," he said with that same horseshit enthusiasm he put on when he got all the boys to sing stupid songs, "who's got an idea?"

Nobody said a thing. Who would, knowing Kyle would mock them as soon as Paul Perkins was out the door?

"Well, then, here's one." Paul Perkins produced a length of grungy yellow rope from under his slicker. "You," he said, pointing to a pimply boy on a bottom bunk, "who are you?"

"Joe."

"Joe, buddy, you're going to be a prospector in this skit and," he hesitated dramatically, "and Kyle here is going to be your burro."

"Oh, no," Kyle said.

"Oh, yes," said Paul Perkins. He went over to Kyle, tied a bowline in the rope, and looped it around his neck."

The way the skit would work was that Joe would lead Kyle—crawling along down on all fours with the rope around his neck—into the middle of the room, put his hand to his forehead, and scan the distant horizon for God knows what. Kyle would ask in a plaintive voice ("Can you do a plaintive voice, Kyle?" asked Paul Perkins), "How much longer?" And Joe would say, "Patience, jackass." This exchange would go on a dozen times or so until finally another boy planted in the audience would holler, "How much longer?"

"See, Joe?" Paul Perkins asked him. "What's your line?" Joe sat on his bunk looking stumped.

"Jesus God help us," Kyle said. "Is that the line?"

That night Kyle made his voice sound like his pissed-off mother's when the check was slow at a restaurant. Then when the plant delivered his line, Kyle was the one who hollered back, "Patience, jackass."

"Hey," the camp director said over the laughter to Paul, "that's a new one. That's a nice twist." Kyle looked at Paul Perkins who was pretending to be pleased but was mad as hell instead. Things were going to be even harder for him now; he might not even pass his swimming merit badge. He decided he had to try to get the hell out of here.

After the skits were done, Kyle walked down the camp road, across the wooden bridge over the creek, up to the camp caretaker's house. The wife was a big motherly kind of woman, the kind of woman Kyle could wrap around his finger as he spilled out his sad story about his very sick mother and needing to make a call. Even though it was just over the mountain, it was long-distance. The wife didn't hesitate for a minute and led him to the phone. A boy and his mother, after all.

While the country boys slept heavily and loud, Kyle silently packed his duffle and stole out of the cabin. Just on the other side of the creek sat a car waiting for him. It was a low black car, a 1953 Oldsmobile to be precise, all its chrome removed, a skull with green illuminated eyes on the back window shelf, a placard in place of the front license plate that read, "Cannibal."

"Good deal," said the driver when Kyle slung his duffle into the back seat and climbed in. He offered Kyle a drink from his pint of liquor, and Kyle took it straight. Whatever it was, it burned like hell. Kyle knew a little about liquor; he'd been pilfering from his dad for some time, but he'd always cut it with soda or juice. This was different; he couldn't say better. They started to pull away and out of the camp, but Kyle said, "Wait, let's do something."

The boy driving the Oldsmobile was Lynn Porter, but everybody called him Groundhog. He was a big, thick-bodied boy with black hair combed in a heavy jellyroll up over his wide forehead. He wore a motor-cycle jacket covered with multiple zippers, epaulets, and tin stars, cool if it hadn't been made of some kind of plastic. In a school where football was everything, where boys crashed against each other daily so that they finally might wear maroon sweaters with cream varsity *B*s on them, where girls lived to make subdeb and wore their hair permed just like their mothers', Groundhog sat in the back of the room with his greasy black boots stuck out in the aisle for other kids to trip over. There he was, living proof of an alternate universe, one Kyle would gladly blast into.

"Tough car," Kyle had told him one day as everybody was spilling out of school, when the kids with cars and their pals were all piling in to go to the drive-in. Kyle himself was not yet old enough to drive. When he got his license, his mother promised him he could have a car or a motor-bike provided he made Eagle Scout. Kyle thought if he worked it right he could get both out of her.

"What do you know about it, boy?" Groundhog said out the window and romped the engine so the car rumbled and shook.

"Nothing."

"That's right. Get in and I'll give you a little lesson," and he opened the door from the inside since the door handle on the outside had been removed and the holes filled so a guy might never know a handle had ever been there.

Inside, the panels that should have covered the doors were missing so Kyle could see the gears, cranks and levers that operated the windows and doors and locks. Inside, the car smelled of rusty car parts and motor oil, of must and mice turds. The seats were covered with surplus wool blankets from the Army-Navy store. Once they had inched up the school drive to the road, Groundhog turned to the left while the other cars went right. He spun a rooster tail of gravel, shifted into second gear with a squeal, and then another into third. Kyle's head snapped back over the seat. The car swerved from side to side but managed to stay in its lane. "Wow," Kyle said.

"Wow? All you got to say is wow? You think this is a comic book?"

They took a left and another left, went rolling up a narrow road Kyle had never known. The car swayed through curves, bounced its frame down on the roadbed as they crested the dips. He had no idea how far they had gone or where they were. They pulled off at a country store. "You got some money, boy? We need gas."

So far Kyle and Groundhog had not palled around too much. Groundhog, it seemed, always needed gas and Kyle always had money. Only once had Groundhog pulled into the drive at Kyle's house. There, his Oldsmobile dense as a stone seemed to pull in every bit of nearby light and snuff it. Groundhog blew the horn and waited for Kyle to come out. "Nice little friend you got there," his mother told him.

Usually they bought Dr. Peppers and bags of peanuts when they stopped for gas. Groundhog showed him how to pour the peanuts down the neck of the bottle, real people food he called it. They didn't talk much, just drove, but sometimes Groundhog would be moved to speak: "See that car?" he pointed with his Dr. Pepper bottle at a powder-blue Mustang going down the road. Mustang was a brand-new car that year, the very kind of car Kyle was angling for. He would have said, "Tough," but before he could get it out, Groundhog said, "That's a pussy car."

And once they went to the garage where Groundhog sometimes worked, a garage connected to a salvage yard where Groundhog's job was to pull useable parts off wrecked cars. The floor was black with grease, worn tools splayed all around, rags and various crusted small car parts lay on the workbench. Guys on creepers slid in and out from under cars like snakes and spat on the floor. Kyle kept his hands in his pockets.

Since school let out, Kyle had not seen Groundhog at all. He had a phone number scrawled on a grimy piece of paper in his wallet, that was all. What was there to lose? He dialed that number from the caretaker's house. He asked for Lynn. It took a while for Groundhog to come to the phone. "Nobody calls me that," he said, but he agreed to come.

Kyle already had it planned. The two boys slipped over to the lake where they launched every canoe and rowboat with a good strong push, took the paddles, oars, and life vests from their pegs and threw them into the water behind them. For good measure, Kyle went to the car and dug a pair of his scout shorts and a T-shirt out of his duffle and left them on the pier. It gave him no end of pleasure to think of all waterfront activities suspended the next day and the camp counselors practicing their best lifesaver techniques, forming a line and surface diving again and again in search of his body. It had to be down there somewhere, didn't it?

The next morning just about the time reveille would be sounding over the mountain at camp, Groundhog dumped Kyle and his duffle on the corner just down the street from his house. Kyle dragged in through the living room, passed his mom in the breakfast nook as she was having coffee and her first cigarette of the day. "Don't even ask," he told her, one of her own lines he'd heard her serve on similar occasions. He went to his room, pulled off his shoes and shorts, fell down on the bed and into sleep.

He woke up when the phone rang. It was the scout camp, of course. He heard his mother tell them, "He walked. That poor child walked over that mountain." He heard her speak again, "I have to wonder what you did to him." Another pause, "No, what *you* did to *him*." Her voice did not go higher but lower as the conversation continued. His dad's lawyer was mentioned several times. Then the house got quiet again.

Kyle did not fall back to sleep. He felt like shit. He tried to put the night together, but he didn't remember much. He could remember certain things but wanted to get them in order. He was sneaking up on naming the one thing. They'd driven around, bought gas of course, more booze, but then: He knew what happened. At that age he only knew one way to say it. Groundhog, Lynn, had fucked him in the ass. He asked him not to, told him not to, but was too weak and too drunk to stop him. Then, maybe, he thought he puked in the car. Good. Good, if he really did that. He felt like he had to puke right now; he got up and made it to his bathroom.

That's where his mother found him passed out again. How did he get home, really? When he wouldn't answer, his mother said, "Just try not to do anything that your father will have to keep out of the paper."

The rest of the summer, Kyle rode his bike. It was a French-made bike his mom had bought him. It broke all the time, and when it did, he didn't even know how to fix it. Every day when he made his way to the country club where he suddenly felt safe and at home rather than bored and annoyed, he listened for the sound of a glass-pack muffler and looked around for a place he could hide. He hated the bike. He hated his life.

"It's not the end of the world, you know," his mother told him. What did she know? He acted out at camp. He somehow slipped away from the camp and had himself a little adventure. Those scoutmasters needed to do a better job. Boys at Kyle's age get bored tying knots, identifying leaves, and making lanyards. On the other hand she let him know his car was hanging in the balance. It was up to him to get back in those scout people's good graces.

Kyle felt like the wind had been knocked out of him. He sat on the other side of the pool from his mom, his eyes hidden behind a pair of his dad's Ray-Bans. Was he a queer or something? Or did he act like a queer and didn't even know it? He looked at the girls sunning themselves, lying on their bellies, their bathing suit tops undone. Something was wrong with all of them, butts too big, calves too thick.

He had taken his dad's *Playboys* out from between the mattress and box spring, flipped the pages of naked girls, and waited for his penis to do something. It was not especially cooperative. And he remembered, he had come, too, in that car, come despite himself. What did that say about him?

And Lynn? Because Kyle would try not to ever think of him as a groundhog again—a groundhog was a funny animal, a happy animal, the kind of animal that might be the star of a Saturday morning cartoon. Groundhogs were vegetarians as far as he knew. Lynn was just what he claimed he was, a cannibal.

There was one girl, though, a girl who came to the pool as often as Kyle these days. He knew who she was, a daughter of one of his dad's employees. And he knew her parents could not really afford to be members of this country club. She, this girl whose name happened to be Lynn, too, swam lengths of the pool with a dogged determination. "Poor thing," Kyle's mother said, "that's all she's got going for her." Lynn, and her parents, too, had hopes she might earn a swim scholarship to a good college, to any college really. She was a tall skinny girl with flyaway hair grown a little green from all the chlorine. When she walked to and from the dressing room, she stooped a little and folded her arms over her chest, her dark goggles already in place over her eyes. But when she practiced her butterfly, her long legs flipped behind her, her head and chest rising out of the water as her arms—spread like the wings of a big bird—pulled her along, she was like a great sea creature, exotic and rare.

So as she stood at the shallow end breathing hard, her workout over, her goggles up on her forehead, her eyes rimmed red, Kyle made a considered decision. He raised his Ray-Bans and said, "Hey, you're pretty." She laughed. She blushed. She had been made fun of before. "No kidding, you're beautiful."

She heaved herself out of the pool, got up, and walked away. Kyle rushed into the men's dressing room, threw his clothes on, and found his bike leaning against the cyclone fence, actually glad for once nobody had stolen it. When Lynn appeared and set out on her girls' three-speed, Kyle followed, followed right on her fender for a while and then began to swoop up alongside her and finally to ride circles around her. "Beat it. Get lost. Go home." She talked to him like he was a dog chasing after her.

She rode her bike into her parents' carport, threw it down without bothering with her kickstand, and ran in the kitchen door. Kyle pushed in behind her. She turned on him, came toward him, took hold of his hair, pulled him to her, and kissed him fiercely. "Is that what you want from me?" she asked him. Before he could answer, she kissed him again. The second kiss lasted a long time, and as it did, its character changed, became more gentle, more giving. Then she said, "You'd better go, my mom's coming home soon."

That night he found his penis more cooperative. Patience, jackass.

The next day the girl Lynn slid out of the deep end of the pool and left without looking at him. When he rushed out through the country club to intercept her, he found her climbing into her mother's car. For days to come, she contrived ways to avoid him. Through it all, while Kyle hunted the girl Lynn, he feared the guy Lynn and nursed a hate for Paul Perkins. Lynn, a mutant groundhog standing up on his hind legs like Godzilla, a destroyer, was too big for hate, with him hating didn't even count. Given a chance he would waste Kyle without giving it a second's thought. Paul Perkins, though, was the identifiable cause of all this, no swimming merit badge, no other merit badges Kyle had planned to knock out in an easy week. Paul Perkins who stood between Kyle and his car, some kind of car not a Mustang. Paul Perkins who made it so Kyle had no choice but to ride off into the dark with Groundhog and who was the cause of everything that followed. Paul Perkins who made a living as an eternal Boy Scout, who had no idea who he was dealing with. "I'll have you fired." Kyle practiced saying this out loud in a variety of voices to Perkins in an imagined showdown in the camp director's lodge. Probably his father had that kind of pull. He worked himself up to the point he jumped on his bed and threw punches into his pillow. "Fire his ass!" he shouted, and shouted it again and again riding down the street on his bike, "Fire his ass!"

Here she came. Just like that Kyle was riding along no hands when Lynn the girl came around the corner on her bike headed straight for him. As soon as she saw him, she turned the other way and started for her house. When he caught her quickly enough, she was panting and laughing. Laughing. She let him in the kitchen without a fight, and as they stood one step inside the door making out, she said, "Wait a minute," and pulled her sweatshirt over her head and undid her bra. "You, too," she told him. Her breasts were soft as air.

"I don't know what you see in that girl," his mother told him.

It was a funny kind of game they played, Lynn always trying to hide from him or run from him, but more than willing once he caught her. He liked it; he was a schemer anyway. Tangled with her on the couch in her parents' living room, he said, "Let's get your dad's liquor and put it in some Cokes."

"We don't drink alcohol," she told him.

He considered for a moment, then said, "OK, why don't you take off your pants?" She stood and in one motion peeled off her Bermuda shorts and panties. Her pubic hair was so pale and fine as to almost not be there at all. He took in her long swimmer's body and thought at this moment she might really be beautiful. When he tried to go inside her, she said, "That hurts. You're hurting me." But he did not stop.

As he rode away on his bike, Kyle remembered how Groundhog had acted like he was reaching the little pint bottle over to him but had taken hold of him instead, put one big hand in his chest and with the other and pulled his web belt loose and began to work at his shorts. Kyle's only thought was how to get loose. Yelling out into the empty dark, "Let me go. Leave me alone," he squirmed around and tried to pull himself out the open window of the car. He got himself halfway when he felt the button on his shorts pop and his shorts slide off his butt. He could feel Lynn's liquor breath in his ear and his thick arms coming up through his own arms and locking behind his neck, Lynn's weight pushing his chest down against the window frame. "I got you now, boy, holler all you want," Groundhog told him. And then Kyle thought maybe he just gave up. He was crying. It hurt like hell.

These days, Kyle lives with his mother in one of those flimsy townhouses that just went up behind the Food Lion. His father drank himself to death years ago. The coal mines ran out of coal, the circulation of the paper shrank to nothing, and then he sold it to a chain for a not very good price. Maybe he had never really been a clever businessman, or maybe it was the booze.

Kyle went away to a good college and wasted no time in flunking out. He finished at a nearby college that once aspired to be second-rate. Then he went to work in the job his dad had waiting for him. There had never been any work to do, and one day there was no job either. For a while he'd managed the Save-U-More until the security camera caught him with his hand in the till. His ex-wives left the area and don't keep in touch.

Groundhog Lynn disappeared from Kyle's life. He quit school that summer, and Kyle never saw him again until he saw his obituary in his father's paper. Lynn Parker walked into the Vietnam jungle and came out in a body bag, finally destroyed by something bigger and meaner than he was. Kyle hoped he knew what hit him. A week or so later in a different section of the paper, there was a photo of Kyle receiving his Eagle Scout badge with his mother and father looking on, his tubby scoutmaster, too, and presenting the award, Paul Perkins, representative of the Appalachian Council, Boy Scouts of America.

Kyle got his Mustang. Even though it was black with a red interior, it would always be, he could never manage to forget, a pussy car. He drove the shit out of that car; he ruined that car, and it gave him no end of pleasure as he did. Too bad, he might think, it would be worth something nowadays.

And Lynn the girl? She was that weird girl skittering down the halls at school with her many books pressed to her breast, not looking at anybody, especially not Kyle. He thinks of her from time to time, her sleek swimmer's body revealed to him in the shadowy light of her parents' living room. Does he think of her sorrows? Her pain? Her wishes and joys? Whether she has ever known love from a man or a woman? Whether she has children and whether happy days stretch before her? No, not really.

And his mom? After a life of having sex with men she barely knew on golf greens, massage tables, the back seats of various luxury automobiles, she remains oppressed by her still unsatisfied ardor. Her skin the texture of a dried locust husk, her eyes hidden behind dark rhinestone-accented glasses, here she sits at the tiny kidney-shaped pool behind their Executive Towne Home development with a gin and tonic, and waits. "Honey," she tells him, "whoever thought life would be so goddamned long."

■ ■ ■

That afternoon years ago, Kyle rode his bike up a narrow road until it turned to dirt, then got off and pushed it up to a radio tower enclosed by a cyclone fence. It was dusk, and the heavy wet air was settling into the valley below him. He felt the evening's chill coming on. The hills were cast in purple and green. Kyle was reminded of the scout camp. Just now would be the time for evening colors, bringing down the flag, all the boys saluting at attention, and the camp bugler playing "Retreat" on his silver horn. The sound rolled and echoed between the hills before dying away. He loved that ceremonial time of day. But what did it have to do with him, with anything in this world?

In the houses down there, lights were coming on, families were sitting down to dinner. Though he was never given to deep thought or reflection, he wondered who they were, what they were like. Really, were those families any different from his? Were any of them, down deep, any different than he was? Was the life he was living the only kind of life there was? He took his bicycle from where it leaned against the fence and rode home in the deepening dark. Here he stands. He knows no more now than he did those few long years ago.

HER ONE NIGHT IN A TENT

1.

When the plane landed, the locals pulled their frayed and dirty duffles and backpacks from the overhead bins, the raisins grabbed their small carry-ons, and all filed into the terminal. It was nicer than Alexis had imagined. A few stuffed animal heads hung on the walls, a few more stuffed animals, bears and musk oxen, in Plexiglas cases. Something to gawk at while the bags were barfing out from the hole in the middle of the baggage carousel. Then the locals climbed into the waiting pickup trucks and rattletrap Subarus, and the raisins in their brand-new Reebok walking shoes and elastic waist slacks followed their designated college kid out to the appropriate tour bus.

Nobody was left except Alexis and one guy at the rent-a-car counter. He had a smile like a hungry wolf and introduced himself as James, consultant on questions of environmental impacts for the oil companies. Then he asked which motel she was staying in. Alexis had no answer. She figured she'd drive into town and find something. James made a suggestion, Sophie's, the same place he was staying.

Done with the paperwork for her car, she went to the curb to wait for the shuttle bus. James was already there. Sophie's? Anywhere but, she thought.

When she got the complimentary Fairbanks map featuring tourist attractions, she saw there were chain motels across town, as near as she could tell about as far from Sophie's as she could get. Here she was, in her room, plastic, predictable, across a multilane road from the same familiar big box stores she could find in every town in the Lower 48. It had been a long, tedious flight. Leaving Seattle, the pilot had promised arresting views of mountains and glaciers, but all she had seen was cloud cover. She lay down on the bed and fell asleep.

When she woke up two hours later, it was still light. Of course, this was Alaska. She went out and made her way at some risk across the road to a chain restaurant where the food was no worse than it would have been in the restaurant belonging to the same chain in her hometown. She sat there after her plate had been cleared drinking a second glass of wine and wondered, why in the hell was she here?

Maybe she should try to look up Curtis. She had clicked the "contact me" link on his website and written a short message, dates she'd be in Alaska, maybe they could get together for a drink or cup of coffee. He didn't write back, which was about what she expected.

She took her tourist map out of her purse and circled the attractions she would try to see: the university museum, Alaskaland (what on earth could that be?), the ice museum. Maybe she would drive to North Pole and look for some Christmas presents in a place where she was assured it was Christmas year-round. That about covered Fairbanks, and she had booked her trip for two weeks.

Curtis had been easy enough to find. When she Googled him, he came right up. He even had a website, Spinach Creek Clay Works. She clicked on his site, and there he was, older, more worn around the edges, but definitely the Curtis she had known. He leaned forward, his big brown eyes staring right out of the computer at her, his hands cradling a large serving platter with fish swimming around its perimeter. She had to admit, it was a handsome piece if you liked that sort of thing. Honestly, she didn't, preferring more polished work. The website, though, featured more of Curtis's pieces, most all of them with blue-green glazes, presented against black backdrops. Carefully done, elegant even. He always had had a good eye; she knew this. But his website showed a degree of professionalism she didn't think he was capable of. Though that was the Curtis she knew a good while ago. People do change, though, don't they?

Alexis was well traveled, having been to the major European capitals as well as to Australia and New Zealand, to Moscow (technically a European capital, she supposed, though she found it seedy and dirty), Tokyo, even Beijing. She loved cities, she loved culture. She thought of herself as an adventurer. But, really, she hated the woods, hated getting bug bites, hated mud and rain. So why was she here sitting in a coffee place around the corner from the ice museum. No kidding, it was full of ice. She had flown five thousand miles to see some corny carvings made of ice?

There was a Google pin drop on Spinach Creek Clay Works, there were even posted hours for the "showroom and shop," whatever that might mean. She told herself she might as well go see.

Spinach Creek Clay Works lay well off the beaten track, the pavement having given over to a washboarded dirt road some miles back. She remembered she'd signed something back at the car rental desk promising not to drive on certain unpaved roads. ("Nobody takes that seriously," James had assured her.)

If Alexis had a notion of what Curt's place looked like, it went something like this: A neat little cabin, smoke curling out of the chimney, a grassy yard and flower beds lining a neat flagstone walk. Laura Ingalls Wilder lite.

What she got was a tall, narrow house, some squared-off logs nailed into place halfway up its plywood walls, the rest covered with Tyvek except for the places where the Tyvek was pulled away and drooping. Around the yard were piles of assorted shapes and sizes covered with blue tarps. An older red pickup truck with a yellow door and fender was parked crookedly in front of a high wire enclosure, skinny wooden poles holding it up. Behind it was a garden, nice and orderly. In the weeds sat the better part of the donor yellow truck. Its bed, cut away and made into a trailer, was parked nearby with a full load of logs.

Up a little hill stood a cabin, a small, neatly finished cabin with a porch and a slab of clay above the door, clay formed into a ragged mountain chain and deeply gouged with the name, Spinach Creek Clay Works. Alexis went up the steps and peered in a window. The place looked dark and disused. Somebody was around though; she could hear the excited squeals of children from behind the house. She started in that direction, past huge piles of wood stacked to the rafters of flimsy sheds and what must be Curt's kiln under another more substantial shed.

The girls, maybe four or five years old, ran laughing back and forth under a hose held by a woman who must be their mother. A cat, probably startled by Alexis, shot out from behind one of the woodpiles and ran past the mother and children. The three turned all at once to see, their eyes wide as if they were a family of wild creatures standing in a clearing in the woods, taken by surprise. One girl's hair was long and blonde, the other's raven black. Their mother's red hair flared in the light as it cascaded down her shoulders. All three were thoroughly naked.

"Go put your dresses on," the woman told the children who scampered up to the rickety deck and pulled their dresses off the railing. "We didn't hear you come up." She took up her carpenter's jeans and a sweatshirt from the ground, and she took her time slipping them on, not wanting to take her eyes off Alexis.

"I was looking for Spinach Creek Pottery."

"Wednesday," she said, "he's at the farmers' market. He'll be there Saturday and Sunday too. Look for him there."

"OK, I will. But would you tell him Alexis came by? I'm an old friend of his, an old friend from grad school."

"I'll tell him."

"Thanks. Sorry to interrupt your fun."

"We needed to get busy anyway." The girls came down from the deck and stood a little behind their mother. Their little cotton dresses were dirty, so were their faces, their hands and feet. Alexis saw they had flecks of chipped purple polish on their nails. So did their mother. At least Alexis supposed she was their mother.

She tried once more, "Universität Wien," the lettering on the shirt washed out almost to the point of illegibility, "Did you go there?"

"Go where?"

"You know, the University of Vienna like it says on your sweatshirt."

"This? It came from Value Village."

It turned out there was a pretty good restaurant downtown. The kid at her motel desk put her onto it. After a nap, she showered and did her hair and put on linen slacks, a nice shell, and an understated silver necklace. As she did her makeup, she considered her skin, pale delicate skin, carefully maintained, her nails manicured and polished with clear lacquer, her eyelids neatly tucked. Nobody could tell. And she considered that naked woman, a girl really, her full breasts, her flaring hips, and her sturdy muscled legs. There wasn't a tan line on her anywhere. Alexis tried not to imagine the implications. Sick of the clunky hiking shoes she'd bought just for this trip, she put on her sandals and went out.

"Seen all the sights already?" James had slipped up on her from behind.

"No," then, "yes." What was the point?

"Been to the Park?"

The Park, the Park, everybody said the Park. It took her awhile to get what they meant, the big National Park south of town. "No. I mean, not yet. I'm supposed to, I guess."

He didn't ask, just pulled out the other chair at her table and sat. "You should go." A waiter glided up. He ordered a beer and asked if she'd ordered her meal.

She thought about lying and just walking out, but she said, "Yes. The halibut."

"Good choice. I'll have that too."

So she found herself back in her motel room, a little tipsy, having agreed to go to the Park, the goddamn Park, leaving off at eight the next morning with James, who she did not much like. She picked up the remote for her TV and began flipping through the channels, looking for news of the real world, but it was three in the morning eastern time; the real world had come to a pause. The farmers' market didn't reopen until Saturday.

There were mountains out there, James assured her. And there were vistas. At a point on a hilltop, James pulled over and invited her to take in the view. What view? A bunch of puddles stretched out in an endless boggy landscape. Majestic mountains coming. Though this time of year the Mountain was rarely out. There it was again, the Mountain, the Mountain, as if everybody ought to know what of all the mountains Alaska claimed to have, people were talking about. And then they said Denali, which wasn't the real name of the Mountain at all.

They were too late to get a bus all the way to Wonder Lake and took one to the visitors' center instead. All the way, people on the school bus hollered for the driver to stop. They had seen some animal, or at least thought they had. With no binoculars, Alexis was never sure anybody ever saw anything. Finally a wolf sauntered down the road. It looked emaciated and sick. Big, big deal. Seeing a wolf was very special their driver told them. At the visitors' center, artwork by locals was on display. Not exactly Uffizi.

"Sorry we didn't make the bus to Wonder Lake," James told her. They were eating a barely warm pizza they had waited forever to arrive.

"Don't be," she said.

"Har, har," he barked. He really laughed like that. Nobody except cartoon characters laughed like that, did they? He pissed her off, and the more this whole adventure went off the rails, the more annoyingly cheerful he seemed to get. "What did you expect when you came here?"

"I don't know. Something like Banff, something like riding the Canadian National Railroad through the Rockies."

"Tablecloths. Stemware. Wine cooling in a sterling silver bucket."

"Precisely."

"How long have you been divorced?" His tone was psychological.

Alexis felt her face grow hot, as much from anger as from blushing. It didn't matter, the visual effect was the same.

"You know, single women of a certain age don't just up and come to Alaska alone. Young ones, yes, wide-eyed backpackers. Old dodderers like were on the plane. Lots of those."

If this had been an old movie, Alexis would have slapped his face, stormed out to the highway, and hitched a ride with a dashing adventurer who would reveal mysteries of the world and wonders within herself as yet undiscovered. But their bus driver and the Alaskan men she had encountered walking around downtown Fairbanks had bad teeth and bad hygiene.

"What are you? Forty-five? Fifty?"

She wanted to lie, but whether to adjust it up or drop it down? Either way, she would step into a trap. "Forty-seven." Which was the truth. Just as James said, divorced, on this trip in part to take her mind off her ex and his sweet young thing doing the continent, doing the museums. He would be impressing her with all he knew about Renaissance art. Alexis had been an art history major.

"A lovely forty-seven too."

"Oh, cut the crap, James." Who knew what the hell time it was around here? Maybe seven o'clock, maybe three in the morning. "Let's just call it a night."

On the drive down, James had warned her there would be no hotel rooms available near the Park, but it wouldn't matter. He had a friend who owned a cabin, and they could stay there for free. Just down the road from the pizza place was a little wooden gate, the kind of gate that might lead to a Hobbit house, with a rock leaned against it to hold it shut, a little gate that led to a secret world surrounded by all the garish tourist draws. And down a narrow path was a cabin perched on a cliff above the tumbling river below.

James felt along the top of the door jamb until he found the key and opened the door. He led Alexis right out to the deck where she had a clear view of the drop to the river, to the gnashing rocks. She was not charmed. A person could die down there.

"I don't like this. Does your friend know we're here? And where are we supposed to sleep?"

"He doesn't know we're here right now. But it's OK. I can use this place." James began opening big black trash bags and pulling out bedding of different sorts—quilts, comforters, blankets, and sheets. He loosed a slipknot on a rope around a foam mattress, and it sprung open onto the floor."

"Great. Where's mine?" Silly girl. "You thought we would sleep together." Sillier still.

"You thought of that too." Yes, she had, but that thought had run down its own little fanciful path and had not wound up at a place anything like this. "Sometimes it can actually be better if you don't like the other person very much."

She took her clothes off. It's what people in Alaska seemed to do.

■ ■ ■

"So, James," Alexis was pushing the last of her sourdough pancake around her plate, chasing the last bit of syrup, and since she already had been completely exposed to this man, this stranger, she thought what was there to lose? "I was wondering," and she told him about her drive out to Spinach Creek Clay Works and the naked woman and her naked children and how she had been received.

"Har, har," he interjected throughout her story. "This is a crazy place, you know. These hippie types come up here, and they just think they can commune with nature and all that stuff. I don't know how they handle the mosquitoes."

"But why didn't she like me?"

"Like you? What did you want from her?"

"Nothing. I mean I was just looking for Curtis."

"There you go."

At least James paid for their breakfast. And when he dropped her off at her rental car parked at an all-night supermarket, he told her, "I need to do a little work up on the Slope for a few days. Try to parley with the bunny huggers and see if we can pump a little oil. But when I'm in town, you can find me at Sophie's."

Alexis leaned her head on the steering wheel and closed her eyes and muttered over and over, "I will not cry, I will not cry." It wasn't James, or if it was, it wasn't because she'd slept with him. He was an emissary from the world of hard facts. Her husband had ditched her for a younger woman, fresh out of law school and in his firm. He'd seduced her the same way he had seduced Alexis herself many years ago, stopping by to chat with a cup of coffee in hand, then bringing a cup for her, too, then suggesting they go to a little place around the corner for coffee. Then the rest. Maybe that young woman had left a marriage or a boyfriend too. As Alexis had left Curtis. Curtis, who was supposed to be making art while she worked on her dissertation when instead he was getting stoned and shooting hoops with his pals.

It had been ugly. "Shit," and "Fuck," Curt had yelled, throwing his pots and bowls against the walls of his workshop, a celebration of self-destruction, as Alexis had seen it. Go ahead, she thought, wreck things so thoroughly there could be no going back. "You don't even like to fuck," he told her. That much was true. Maybe that accounted for James and a couple of others since the divorce. Maybe she could still learn.

It seemed like she had made this trip on the thinnest of threads. She could always change her ticket and fly home now, today. Or she could stay and go to the farmers' market in the morning. It wasn't a question of money. The divorce had left her with plenty. And time.

2.

When he saw her making her way from produce stand to craft booth, picking up this and that—mittens and hats made from spun dog fur, say—and dropping them back as if they might be radioactive, Curtis knew it was Alexis. She would never have any of the handmade wooden geegaws, mugs and pots, potholders and aprons on offer here. He had always suspected that was how Alexis had regarded his own stuff all those years ago. No doubt she still did. In his experience people didn't change much.

As he watched her make her way toward his booth, faking a disinterested curiosity, angling in to make sure it was him, considering whether he was worth actually making the contact or not, he felt a hot surge of anger. It surprised him; he thought he'd worn it out. He let himself revel in it.

Except: Her shining blonde hair, cut short, but perfectly moussed. Her hands, her long elegant fingers, her long legs. She wore some kind of expensive blue jeans that cupped her cheeks, not baggy-assed things like Alaskan girls wore. He'd forgotten her ass. Mostly, though, it was her legs he'd loved and held in his memory and wished he could get a look at, better still wished them bare and wrapped around his head buried in her crotch.

She walked up to his booth and took it in in a single panoramic sweep. "This," she said, "is nothing like the stuff on your website." If she was looking for something to say that would provoke him to respond, she had done it.

He looked at the ranks of coffee mugs, the teapots, the trivets, all seemingly shattered by a sentence. "Yeah? Well, this is what sells."

"What if a person wanted to see those other pieces? The ones on your website? Maybe come to your 'showroom and shop.'"

"No. No. That's closed for the summer." His eyes ran laps around the market, looked everywhere but at Alexis. Fuck, fuck. Bobbi had told Curtis about this prissy lady who had come around. Prissy. He thought she pretty much nailed it. So why couldn't he tell her to just fuck off? "Look, this thing shuts down at four. Give me a half hour to get closed up, and we could go somewhere and catch up."

Curt watched her wander through the crowd and out of sight. What did he think he was trying to do? He should have blown her off, but he wanted to teach her a lesson. Still, he'd have to make up some lie. Dumbass. Bobbi was quick to jealousy. And he was eaten up with dumbass. He ought to bust everything in his booth to pieces.

That time before when he'd destroyed all his work, he'd thought he was through with clay. He'd come to Alaska, run off, really, from his life in the Lower 48, without finishing his graduate degree. He'd taken a job teaching in the Bush. Anybody could get hired to teach in some districts out there. And he had done OK for a while, did something useful, did not become a drunk, but it wore him out, and he got lonely as hell.

He came back to town; eventually everybody teaching out there did. And he dug into his considerable savings, bought his piece of land, and began building his place. His still unfinished place. And he was making good headway until he wandered into a craft bazaar at a hippie music festival down in Talkeetna. There it was. Clay, clay formed into the most pitifully clichéd and boring shapes he thought he'd ever seen. "God," he told a guy standing behind a table of such mediocre shit, "this stuff sucks."

"You think you can do better?"

"Absolutely," Curt said, and before he wound up in a fistfight, he went back to Fairbanks, got himself into an undergraduate class so he could use the kiln and a wheel, and started over.

■   ■   ■

Though Curtis rarely drank a beer during the day, and never at a bar—they couldn't afford bars—he took Alexis to a scuzzy place down by the river where a few regulars carried on a mocking banter with the bartender and watched Fox News. He took some pleasure in watching Alexis examine the upholstery of the booth before sliding in.

"Nice atmosphere."

"Nothing contagious," he said. Well, hell, she probably hates me, too, he thought, but changed his mind. Why else would she come here? "So you want to buy some of my pieces?"

"I do. Yes. I was coming to Alaska anyway, and I found your website, and I liked your stuff. And besides, it would be a way of apologizing. Sort of."

"Sort of." He let the line lay between them for a while and drank his beer. "I'm not sure I've got a pot that could do the job."

Now she turned red in the face, and she started fidgeting just like always when she had something she wanted to get out. Not that she didn't have the words for it; she had plenty of words, hard and sharp. He saw that her hands were bare, none of the rings she wore back then, flimsy things bought from college town street vendors. Of course she would have outgrown them. Just a wristwatch thin as a dime. Probably cost more than his truck. No wedding band either. "Curt, don't make this be hard."

Poor woman. The men at the bar leaned out of their drinks and into the insistent current running along in the booth behind them. Better than that political bullshit on TV, and she was pretty, not the kind you usually see around here. "Hard," one of them pretended to whisper, "I got something hard."

"Let's leave." Curtis knew she meant they should walk out the door and each go, just go. But he insisted she drive and had left his truck at the farmers' market. Even though it looked like a setup, it wasn't. Or at least it wasn't supposed to be. It's just that everybody knew his truck, and he could be in deep shit if word got around he was seen going to a bar with a pretty blonde woman. Sometimes he thought Bobbi wasn't too smart, but she could add.

There they sat, parked in the farmers' market parking lot, empty except for their two vehicles. He should've gone on home, but he wanted to see this through, maybe have his version of the fight he wished they'd had twenty some years ago.

But it was Alexis who spoke first. "I was expecting to see something original."

"Yeah, well, little kids cost money. Little kids grow out of their clothes, wear out their shoes, get sick, eat. You would be amazed how fast they wear out their shoes. And who could have guessed they could eat so much."

"So?"

Curt had started over with this idea about himself. He thought he could be one of those guys like Sequoia Miller or Mark Shapiro, the kind of guys who get articles written about them. The kind of guys who just throw their pots, do their work while people come looking for them. He threw some amazing shit. Alaska museums own some of his best stuff; people who paid attention own some.

"When I met Bobbi, things changed a little." And until this day, until this very fucking day, he had not minded so much.

"Are they your kids?"

"No."

"And is she your wife?"

"No."

Marriage doesn't mean anything these days, does it? Alexis of all people ought to have known that. Her ex was handsome, is handsome, she supposed. And there was money. She had made a project to decorate her house just so, and the yard and flower gardens too. Somewhere along the line, they made a deal. He would have his small affairs, and she would have the rest. Not the best deal, then it wasn't a deal at all. And then what was there left to do?

Curt had thought he would just leave Bobbi out of this, but he found himself explaining, justifying really. One day—one day—just saying it makes him see how fast his life had made a hard right turn. One day he had come out of the art department at the college; he wasn't taking classes, he was through with that, too, maybe he had decided that the whole academic proposition was working against him, against his creative impulses. And here was this woman with the hood up on her beat up old truck looking at the motor.

"Need a jump?"

"No," she said.

"Need a lift to a garage, maybe?"

"No."

"Somebody on the way to help you?"

"I don't need help."

She had all this red hair spilling out of the hood of her crummy parka patched with duct tape. Inside the cab sat two little girls huddled up under an old sleeping bag. A feral cat and kittens.

"Look, it's cold as shit out here, and you got two kids in that truck. Let me give you a jump."

She didn't say anything, but she let him pull his rig up beside her. It worked. The truck fired right away.

"I'm guessing your battery won't hold a charge," he told her and got her to follow him to the parts place down the hill where they could test the battery.

When it turned out he was right, she finally opened up a little, "What should I do?"

The parts guy jumped in, "Nothing you can do. You got to get a new one." And they followed him into the store where there were batteries displayed for different prices and guaranteed for various lengths of time. Bobbi picked the cheapest one.

"You buy that, you'll be in here this time next year," the parts guy said.

"You're just trying to sell me something."

"No," Curt said, "he's right. Get the good one."

She looked like somebody had punched her in the belly. But she got out a credit card, and the guy ran it. And it went through.

Even though there was a sign forbidding working on cars in the parking lot, the parts guy made an exception considering the situation. It only took about ten minutes to change the batteries out. Curt said he'd take the old one in so they would get the rebate, and she said, "I guess you think I owe you something now."

"No, not at all."

"Well, I thank you," but it seemed hard for her to say it. She drove off. Back inside the parts store, Curt had the battery charged to his card.

"So," Alexis sighed loudly, ran her long fingers around the rim of her steering wheel. Curt's story, tiresome, predictable, made her want to throw him a lifeline, "You're letting your career go. You see that, don't you?"

What gave her the right, the right to be the one in charge, who made all the big calls? Because that's how it was, and now it has happened again.

Curt climbed out of the rental car and into his truck, mad as hell. Well, he didn't have to see Alexis again. But he wanted to.

This was the thing about clay, its messiness, its viscousness, its invitation to dig in up to his elbows. And to find that zone, that place where he went when he was working on the wheel where nobody else could find him. Back in the day, he used to toke up before working, but then he came to a place where he saw no need to. He could find the place he was looking for on his own. Right there on his tractor seat in front of his wheel, but not there, not anywhere he could name, this place where he slipped outside time. Surprises happened that way.

He'd forgotten. Because now there was always something else in his head, time or money, or the way the two of them got tangled up. He meant what he said about the girls. He loved those girls, or thought he did, and he loved Bobbi, too, or said he did. Right now, he wasn't sure about those things.

Driving out to his place, Curt caught himself singing along to an indie band playing on the college radio station, the same song he and his buddies used to sing along to after a good night in the studio, or after playing ball to the point of exhaustion, or after getting high, "I think I think too much," in a monotonous stoner voice. A kind of mantra he had decided he could live by.

■ ■ ■

It was Fairbanks. Sooner or later the woman in the red truck with the yellow door and Curt would cross paths again. When they did in early spring, she pulled crossways, blocking him in where he was parked in the Fred Meyer lot, and jumped from her truck. She was plenty mad, took money from her pocketbook, twenties, wadded them up and started throwing them at him. "Take your damned money. I don't want nothing from you. I never asked nothing from you."

Curt laughed and that made her even madder. She came at him and pummeled him with her balled up fists. He grabbed her by the wrists and held her still. "Look, it was a favor. You seemed to be in a bad way. I thought I could help out. I didn't have any ulterior motives," and he knew that was a lie when he said it.

Why didn't she? She calmed down. "All right. But I do owe you something now. Come to my house, and I'll cook you a dinner. But that's all."

It turned out she squatted in one of the old cabins on Happy Road, only wood heat and a gas cookstove with two working burners. The food was good, though, moose meat and bunches of vegetables, a blueberry pie. Yes, she was proud to say she kept a garden, and there was a root cellar and an old refrigerator, and an Alaskan freezer—an old footlocker out on the porch.

Curtis had brought a bag of kids' books from the library. Those girls hadn't been read to much; they thought it was special and cuddled into him on a couch—it had to have come from the transfer station. And Curt discovered he could read in different funny voices.

Once he broke through her thin protective anger, she was pretty much guileless. Two kids, two guys, both who split pretty quick. The cabin and its shabby contents, just as he'd supposed, straight from the transfer station, the truck and the rest of the junk buried in the snow in the yard was all she had to show for a life waitressing, cleaning other people's houses. She made do on food stamps, gifts of fish and game here and there from her neighbors who weren't much better off than she was.

So, then, who took advantage of whom? Curt, a horny guy, got laid, and one thing led to another. No danger of thinking too much there.

"You been with that woman," Bobbi told him.

"Who?"

"Don't lie. I know. I see it on your face."

But he did lie and kept on lying. What the fuck, she'd get over it.

The next morning, Curt told Bobbi he needed to glaze and fire some

of his greenware so he could take it down to a bluegrass festival in Girdwood next weekend. He would have to bust ass all week to get ready, but
then, "You could go."

"No I can't. I'm not traveling all that way in that truck with the girls
and sleep in a tent. No way."

He knew she'd say that. He knew he asked her because he knew she
would.

Alexis did not show up at the farmers' market, and Curt kept looking around for her the whole time. Maybe he'd guessed wrong. And
when he got home, he just found a note, "I know you been with her
again." Well, hell, Bobbi'd done that kind of thing before. It didn't take
much.

He knew where she and the girls were, out in her old squatter's cabin.
Fine. Let her stay there for a while, remember what it feels like. Besides,
he had lots of shit to do if he was going to have enough stuff to justify a
trip to Girdwood.

3.

When she got back to her motel room, Alexis found a message on her
phone from James. The hot springs, would she like an outing? "No, no,
no," she was saying those words when the phone rang. Don't pick up,
who else could it be? She picked up.

"These people," James said, "they want all this oil money, but they
don't want to muss up their tundra. I keep telling them they can't have
it both ways, but what can a guy do?"

"James, I didn't think to bring a swimsuit. Alaska, you know."

"Hey, you can buy one at Freddy's—not Calvin Klein or whatever
you're used to—but a perfectly acceptable swimsuit."

She stood there holding the phone, hoping maybe enough dead air
would do the trick."

"You ever been to Odessa?"

"Texas?"

"Actually, I meant the one on the Black Sea, but either will do, I suppose. I've been to both and in this respect, they're the same. You want to see some people who should be made to sign a blood oath never to appear in a swimsuit in public? This is the place. Smelly hot water. It has a certain perverse charm."

"Do they have accommodations? Or would we stay in another friend's cabin?"

No, he promised this would be a day trip, back in her own room safe and sound for the night.

"All right, then." In his odd way, she decided, he could be amusing once you got used to him.

■ ■ ■

Back in James's enormous rental SUV, Alexis slid down in her seat. Enough screaming kids doing cannonballs into the indoor pool, enough gun toting, moose shooting chitchat in the outside Jacuzzi where it seemed to her that Alaskans' notion of an appropriate distance from a stranger in a bathing suit was much too close.

Halfway back to town, James said, "This restaurant isn't half bad," not a suggestion, but a stop on an itinerary he had privately worked out in advance. She was wrung out and felt she might molt. To get back in her room, take another shower in less offensive water, and slather herself with Clinque. But she said, "Whatever you say." She did have to eat.

"You do have to eat," he told her.

The food was good, but Alexis quickly realized she had drunk too much wine. She was dehydrated, and it had gone straight to her head. James ordered another bottle. "No," she said, but he filled her glass anyway.

Of the two, he was worse off. When they stood to leave, he jostled the table and stumbled against her. "Maybe you'd better drive."

And in this way, even though there were two double beds in her room, Alexis found James peeling off down to his T-shirt and boxers and climbing in with her. "Come on, get in the other bed."

"Just a little cuddle. We're lonely animals after all." And he fell asleep instantly, his heavy arm thrown over her. And she, tipsy, tired, went off right behind him.

In the morning, bleary eyed, she slipped out of bed and finally into the shower. That man in her bed, a bully, a sneak, a manipulator, how much did she know about him, really? Because he had this rapid-fire patter, jumping quickly from this thing to that, rolling up huge swaths of the landscape, whole categories of people into mocking generalizations. "Did you see that one in the flowered suit with the little flouncy skirt? Honest to god, why do they think those things are going to cover that much real estate? This guy who owns the place," meaning the hot springs even though by then it had been rapidly receding on the road behind them, "he's into all these alternative energy ideas. I want to call him up and say, 'Have you ever considered renting one of those little cabins to a plastic surgeon?' I mean, he could make a killing on liposuction and then use that blubber the way the Eskimos did, to light lamps and such. Har har."

"Funny," she'd said because she didn't think it was. That only egged him on and on until she found herself in the same bed with him again when she still had no idea who this man really was.

"Hey," James said, stepping into the tub, "can I take a turn?"

"Sure." And she climbed out the other end and began slathering herself with lotion. Oh, oh, a relief, until James appeared behind her and offered to put some on her back. Why not, get it over with, get him out of here. But he began to gently massage the lotion in big sweeping motions, then working his hands down her backbone while she leaned on her hands against the vanity. She liked it; she'd always had a weakness for back rubs. Then he worked down to her bottom and slipped his hand through her legs and began to fondle her. "Hey!" Though she wasn't altogether surprised.

He entered her from behind and brought his hand around and kept manipulating her. She was taller than he was; she bent a little at the knees and hips and began working with him. She watched herself in the huge bathroom mirror, watched James's face, surprisingly weathered, gray stubble apparent in this harsh light. But it was her own face she couldn't look away from, a look that went from perplexed to what some might imagine to be tortured. Her orgasm was explosive.

"Oh, my." She felt she might faint, but she leaned on her elbows, and took some deep breaths. Dazed, her face gone pale, she wondered, who is that woman in the mirror?

"Har. Pretty damned good. Now throw some clothes on so we can get downstairs before they close the continental breakfast."

When James left, she went back to her room, put the "Do Not Disturb" sign on her doorknob, stripped down to her underwear, and lay down. She had thought she might sleep, but she couldn't. Her life, she thought, had been built from cultivated skills. She was the hostess whose table linen was elegant, flower arrangements tasteful, who could pivot dinner conversation from guest to guest so that even the dullest among them felt affirmed. She was gracious even when her husband's latest was known to be in the room. Her life had been a series of calculated progressions. Even when the outcome was unsatisfactory, it made sense. When her husband left her it was just the final step on a path they had embarked on a decade ago, maybe longer. His affairs became more involved, more public among their circle. Her solo trips abroad grew longer too. The divorce was a necessary step; expected, it had not hurt so very much. That life was gone.

And in this strange place, her skills were valueless. She did not hike or ski or fish, could not skin out a moose or dress it. In fact, the idea of "dressing" a dead animal had been foreign to her until she overheard those people at the hot springs. Her gardens were filled with perennial flowers, not vegetables.

Alexis considered her options. She could become one of those women, those women who drank to moderate excess, who contributed to select worthy causes, who, then, reserved the right to offer cutting remarks and get away with them.

If James had used her, and she admitted to herself he had, she had let him. But what bothered her was that he had accidentally revealed a woman who did not seem to be her. That woman in the mirror. When she traveled to this odd town, such a revelation might have been what she thought she wanted. Now she wasn't so sure. She couldn't think of what she should do next, next in this day, next in her life. If she'd let herself, she might have had this thought before she bought a ticket for Alaska. But here she was.

She got up, dressed in her blue jeans, her hiking shoes, in the polar fleece top she bought when she bought her swimsuit. She headed for Spinach Creek Clay Works.

4.

This was totally fucked. This. Everything. Curtis hadn't slept, hadn't been to bed at all. And now he looked off his rickety deck into his yard grown full of the kind of bullshit Alaskans seem to be magnets for. Fifty-five gallon barrels, an old hot water heater, metal shelves he'd dug out of a dumpster, old gym lockers salvaged from a school remodel. He had something in mind for this stuff but lost sight of whatever it might have been. That truck transmission covered with a tarp, those woodpiles under sheds, woodpiles under tarps, lumber, sheets of mildewing plywood, the three-sided logs cut and ready to be fitted against his cabin walls. What wasn't undone was half done. Whatever wasn't ruined yet would be soon enough. If only all his crap could be pugged, ground up, and rendered back to some sort of useable form.

How had he let things get this way? Chasing a sweet piece of ass. That would be Bobbi. Chasing her like Wile E. Coyote after the Road Runner, running from mesa to mesa, doing fine until he happened to look down. And now he was tired of it, tired as hell. He let himself look down, and now he was trying to figure out how to pick himself up and, like Wile E. Coyote, spring back to his original shape.

Sometime last night he decided there wasn't enough time to fire his greenware for Girdwood. It was stupid to even think so. He couldn't get the kiln up to cone and keep it there without sitting it all night, without a little help. And even then, not enough time to fire and let things cool. He was stuck. Suddenly he had some time in his life; suddenly it'd come as a useless hunk.

So he'd gone out into the yard, began pulling the sectioned logs off his trailer, took up a maul, and began splitting. He worked for god knows how many hours and was now so damned tired he could hardly stand up.

The last thing he needed was to see Alexis pull up in her rental car. He watched her as she took in the split wood scattered every which way. He'd not bothered to gather and stack it, and he knew she was thinking up some dismissive remark about it as she approached the house. She'd not seen him peering around from his deck, and he had half a mind not to acknowledge her knocking. Didn't he tell her not to come here?

But he answered the door, thinking even as he did that he looked completely strung out like maybe he's been doping, like Alexis would assume he's been doping. "It's not what you think," he told her.

"Maybe this isn't a good time."

Bullshit. Bobbi and the girls were away for the day he told Alexis. And she didn't ask where, which was a good thing, because Curtis couldn't think of any place they might have gone. Away, just fucking away. "You're here."

"Can we look at the things in your studio, then?"

The studio. Well, there you have it, Exhibit A. Dusty shelves, burnt-out track lights, a few random pieces here and there. Curt did have some very strong things wrapped in newspaper and stuck away in cardboard boxes under the counter. He pulled them out, unwrapped them, and laid them out for display. This was just about the money, he decided. They could use it.

There was this video Curt had watched again and again about these Japanese potters. There was an old guy and his sons—at least Curt thought they were his sons. Together they made these incredible pots. And the old guy, a dodderer in the movie, probably long since dead, had gotten to be a national treasure. They fired a traditional Japanese wood kiln, the four of them looking like something out of the Middle Ages. Curt had tried to peer into the background of this film and find some evidence of the here and now—a car, a refrigerator, a radio—but there was nothing. So they did this incredible firing, and the old guy came along and he inspected every pot, and most of them, maybe three-quarters of them, had some little flaw or another and the old guy broke them. He seemed to break them with a weary resignation. This was what great art cost.

"Fucker," Curt yelled at him once, yelled at the video running on the grainy TV screen. "What do you know about Happy Meals and Barbie Dolls?" Because he could work that way, too, busting up everything that was even the slightest bit off perfection. He could. But he couldn't.

Alexis had taken up a large sky-blue platter with three large black ravens spiraling into the center. The ravens looked rough and crazy just like ravens actually look. They had a scary energy that jumped right off the plate.

She took up a long narrow piece with silvery-gray fish racing up against grayish-blue water—dozens of fish, violent, determined. "Curt," she said, "these are good."

"Fuck yeah, they're good. What did you expect?"

"Well, this *is* what I expected. But it wasn't what I saw at that crafts fair or whatever it was."

He wanted to say he didn't owe Alexis anything, especially not an explanation. But she was the only one who might understand. He told her about the Japanese potters, told her about a pursuit of perfection. "But, you know, sometimes you can care too much."

"I don't get that, Curt. I don't get caring too much."

"Because there's more to it than that. I'm crazy about those little girls." And he thought, once he trucked out to Bobbi's squatter's cabin and went through his apologetic ritual for something he'd not even done, and she accepted, his reward would be a three-day fuckfest.

"I don't understand your choices, Curt." Alexis stepped with her long legs right over the fact of the girls and into the mess in his yard. Choices.

It wasn't that he had been lying, but he was. There had been a point when he made choices, and then a point when things just happened and he let them. "I have to go to this music thing down in Girdwood this weekend, and I really don't have enough stuff," he told her.

"Will you take these?"

"No. People who go to those things don't want to spend money on ceramics. If they have any money at all, they're going to spend it on food. Or drugs. It's bullshit. It's a trip out of town, that's about it. Some of the bands are OK."

"Will your girlfriend, partner, whatever she is, go with you?"

"No, no she hates those kinds of things."

"I could go. It would give us some time to talk."

"No," he said, but he knew he would take her.

5.

Curt didn't tell Bobbi he was going. He did not go out to the squatter's cabin and make up. He let it go, let her stew a little longer. They could straighten things out when he got back from Girdwood. Probably this was a mistake. No, it *was* a mistake. Fuck it, it was done. But driving down the highway in his truck not so full of pots and cups and vases felt funny, felt like he was driving this road for the first time, like his familiar world had grown different and unsettled.

All Alexis had said so far was the sleeping bag and pad he'd insisted she buy were more expensive than she would have imagined. When would she ever use them again? But Curt refused to lend her a bag. Bobbi would smell her on it; she was a little animal, her senses had not gone obsolete from disuse like theirs had. Yes, Curt insisted, she could even smell when he was horny.

People didn't talk this way in Alexis's world. People did not say words like *fuck* and *shit* as a matter of course. Maybe when they broke a champagne flute, or on some other extreme occasion. "Curt," she said, "use your words," the line she'd heard a young mother trying on her squalling kid in the airport.

"What?"

"I mean you talk like a middle school kid. You're educated, you're articulate. Why have you become so lazy?" But he was anything but lazy. "Intellectually lazy, I mean."

"Because it doesn't make a fuck's worth of difference. Talk is talk, that's all. It's not what you say, it's what you do."

"What are you doing, then?"

"Me? I'm driving to this damned music festival in Girdwood where I am not going to sell enough shit to pay for my gas. I know what I'm doing. What are you doing?"

"Don't call your work *shit*."

"What are you doing? What are you doing in my truck right here, right now?"

Yes, what? Outside, the road ran over hills around curves past woods and more woods. Every now and then a broken-down little store appeared along the road, then it was gone. Here is a great empty place, and she was emptied out too. Alexis, she thought, use your words, make something out of your words.

Then there was the same gray river, the big hotels and junky little shops signaling the approach to the Park. The pizza place. But where was that little wooden gate? Alexis couldn't find it along the walkway full of tourists in their expensive once-in-a-lifetime adventure togs. She wished she could have dreamed it.

Again, no Mountain was to be seen, only more gray river, more trees, and empty woods. And that noise, a high pitch squeal, what was it? At first Alexis thought something must be wrong with Curt's big old truck, but then she decided if he didn't notice, it must make noises like this all the time.

In fact, there was something wrong, and Curt was trying to ignore it. But by the time they got to Wasilla—nothing but a long strip mall of a place—when the noise was persistent and much louder, there wasn't much choice. He pulled in at the Chevy place. "Just wait here," he told her, leaving her and walking into the service entrance. After a while, a mechanic followed him out. "Why don't you wait inside," the guy said. "There's free coffee." So she sat among the tattered magazines, all featuring a dead animal of some sort presented to the viewer by a grinning man on the cover. It occurred to her that Curt might dump her in this place and just take off in his failing vehicle.

He came in, sat down across from her on another dusty couch, and said, "This bites. We're talking a transaxle. Not new. He wants me to take a loaner down to Anchorage and get one from a junkyard." Curt looked kind of shell-shocked.

"I could go."

"Yeah, you could." And she did, but Curt was silent the whole way there and back, running the figures in his head. Totally fucked. He should have never started on this trip, should have never allowed Alexis to come along. The mechanic would have to keep the truck until the next day. The loaner turned into a rental. But, "Hey," the mechanic said, "nice hotel up by the lake. Get a good meal, give yourselves a treat."

Fuck that. Curt pulled the tent, sleeping bags, cooler, and other assorted stuff out of the truck, and threw them into the rental car. They stopped at a grocery store, and he grabbed things off the shelves and threw them in his buggy.

"Want me to get this?" Alexis asked him.

"No. Shit no. I don't want a single fingerprint of yours on this trip."

This place, a rutted dirt road leading down to a creek, looked like the perfect place to murder somebody. Just brain her with a big rock and leave her for a bear to eat. How well did Alexis know Curt anymore? He'd had a bad temper; maybe he still did.

Instead, Curt stomped out a place off the road and in the tall ferns, pulled the tent out of its stuff sack, and began setting it up. When she went over to help, he flipped her a little plastic bottle, "Bug dope. You'll need it." Then he went on setting up the tent, and she tried to follow his silent lead.

He cooked them a dinner on his stove the size of a coffee can and poured up wine for them both from the bottle he'd bought, a good bottle, but he had no corkscrew and snapped the neck of the bottle off against a rock. "Pretty clean break, but watch for glass anyway." Alexis ate her canned spaghetti off a tin plate, drank her wine from a Dixie Cup. The sound of the highway was audible through the trees. To pee, use the woods, and no toilet paper. "Just air dry." This, she thought, was Curt's Alaska, the Alaska he wanted her to see, to feel like the small hard rock she sat on.

Alexis crawled into the tent and changed into her long underwear; she tucked her bra and panties into one of the mesh pockets. There was a certain unavoidable intimacy in a tent. Maybe that was a good thing. But she zipped her sleeping bag up to her neck. Curt came in and began to peel off his own clothes until he was fully naked. He slid into his own bag, leaving it unzipped, and folded his arms behind his head. "You don't have to clamp your knees together; I'm not interested."

His armpits were smelly, and she had no pillow. "Use your pullover," he said, "just ball it up."

"So this Bobbi? Is she a ceramicist too?"

Curt snorted. "Bobbi? No, hell no. When she met me she didn't even know people made pots. She thought they just came from the store that way." He lay there for a while, then said, "She never finished high school." He shouldn't have told her that.

"My God, Curt, what's she do?"

"Do? She takes care of the kids, the garden. She helps me fire the kiln, helps make sure it stays at cone. Stuff like that." The truth was Bobbi couldn't hold down any kind of real job. She had issues that made her not too reliable on a daily basis. Sometimes Curtis thought he understood why the guys she'd got her kids with had cut out, not that it was the right thing to do. He just came to appreciate the impulse.

Outside, mosquitoes drummed against the netting. Alexis took a long breath. "Curt, do you ever wonder how we came to this place and time? I don't mean this very place, or this very minute, but in some larger, more cosmic sense?"

"No, Lexi, I don't." He didn't mean to let that pet name slip out. He was tired, tired from loading his truck, tired from making camp and dinner, tired, mostly, from thinking about the dent that transaxle was going to make in his thin reserves.

"I mean, things do happen to us, things we don't necessarily plan on, but they do. And then there are things we can actually make happen. Even now."

"You mean, 'I fucked up my life, and now I'm trying to fuck up yours.'"

"No."

"Yes."

"No. I mean you have a special gift. You had it when we were in graduate school. I saw it then, but I started to think you'd never get yourself together. I admit I gave up on you. Then when I saw your website, I thought you had done it."

Time to tell the truth, Curt thought, because what he had planned was to fuck her brains out and then treat her mean, pay her back, teach her a lesson. Then the truck broke, and though he did not believe in anything like divine intervention and doubted Alexis did either, he had to think something had happened that made him tired of the whole business. "Everybody has some special gift if you look at it the right way. Which means nobody has a special gift. What difference does it make?" He wanted nothing more than to beam himself back to Fairbanks, to go find Bobbi and straighten things out, maybe read the girls a story and put them to bed. Let Bobbi crawl in bed naked beside him, a little nookie and then off to sleep. As if any of that might be a live option.

"Still, you want to try your best. You owe yourself that." Alexis heard her voice come out squeaky and wheedling. It seemed ridiculous to imagine she might have saved him, but she still thought she could have gone into the Alaskan wilds and brought back this prodigy whose fresh eyes might startle some gallery owners awake. After that, other things might happen as well.

Curt didn't say anything.

"I mean, life is so short." She felt like she was saying the kind of things somebody in a movie said in a groveling voice to try and stop the psycho-killer with a gun held against her temple.

"Jesus pussy. Leonardo, Michelangelo, Caravaggio, every one of those guys you put so much time into studying, you'd say even they could have done more. I'd say, they all died anyway." All that stuff, all that bullshit about the primacy of art. That movie where the Japanese guy broke vessel after vessel, all those stories he used to tell himself about suffering for art. Maybe what it came down to was making everybody around you suffer for your art. "Believe whatever you want, but nothing I've made or will make is going to get me the money for that transaxle when the credit card bill comes through." He lay back and closed his eyes.

After a while Alexis said, "You're wasting your life, you know."

"No, I'm just living it."

She tried again. "If you focused on that large-scale work, those elegant designs, your blue-green glazes, you could build a body of work that would get you some attention. Put yourself forward more, exhibit outside Alaska, get some pieces featured in magazines." She went on in this vein as if these were thoughts he'd never thought before.

But it seemed Curt had fallen asleep.

Alexis could not sleep; she knew she had to consider what she might make of the rest of her life, and she did try, but just now she was too tired to come up with anything. In her sleeping bag staring up through the fabric of the tent as the light faded then grew stronger, Alexis passed the short Alaskan night.

THE GETTING PLACE

Listen to that, that wicked cackle and pop when Bruce let off on the throttle. He had been working on his Fat Boy in the shed all morning, and now he had it: washed and waxed, gleaming chrome, and that unmistakable Harley sound.

He was running a little late now, running up Shear's Road into town the back way. He was supposed to be at Katie's soccer game, well, a while ago. Now he was coming up Fieldstone Drive toward the middle school, and right there on the street in front of the Presbyterian Church sat this car, probably some church lady in there fixing the flowers for tomorrow's service. And what did Bruce spy with his little eye? Her purse right there on the car seat inside the open window. Before he knew it, Bruce had hooked it onto his finger and was sailing up the road with that purse sitting right in his crotch.

Under the portico outside the school, he went through the purse and took the money and the credit cards out of the wallet, then put it back in the purse. He could hear the little girls squealing at their game behind the school, could see all the parents' cars in the parking lot. Everything just like it always was only better. He rode across the street and flung the purse into an open dumpster behind the high school where it rang like a gong when it hit. Sweet.

Bruce already knew what he was going to do. He rode up to the main drag and walked into McDonald's, ordered, what, three dozen, five dozen Big Macs? How many kids were there on a soccer team anyhow? Then he went across the street to the Get'n'Go and bought Cokes and Dr. Peppers and Gatorade in all different colors. He asked for extra plastic bags so when his burgers were all ready to go, he could load all he'd bought into the bags, hang them off his handlebars and speed his way back to the middle school. Sometimes it amazed him how things could fall into place.

The soccer game was just now getting over. The little girls, their uniform shirts so long they were like little tunics, were cheering each other. Who won? Nobody really cared, did they? Not with munchkins like these. They just herded up and down the field chasing a ball that looked to be waist high. Little cuties. He waded into them, into Katie's team, the Pink Panthers, and began handing out his sodas and hamburgers.

"Daddy!" Katie hollered at him. "Did you see my goal?"

"Sure, honey, it was great."

Kids were taking the pops and carrying them to their moms and dads to twist open the tops, tearing into the hamburgers.

This lady was coming at him. Terrific legs in her little runner's shorts. "Hey," she said. No tits. That's what's wrong with those woman runners. "Hey."

"Hey yourself," Bruce told her.

"Did you bring this," she hesitated a second, "this crap down here? This soda and all this?"

And then he saw Cindy up in the bleachers, and he saw that she was glaring at him too.

Later, standing by Cindy's car, he admitted, what the hell, who knew hamburgers and pop were bad for kids these days? He would have killed somebody for a Ronald McDonald hamburger when he was their age. Yes, even when he was their age and all there was was the shitty Whataburger, Bruce knew there was a bigger, better world out there. The only question was how to get there. Then he said, "What did you do to your car?" Because the plastic air dam down below what would be the front bumper if cars had bumpers like they used to was all smashed up and half missing.

"Oh, that? I did that on one of those concrete thingie-doos at the Harris Teeter parking lot. I was wondering if you could fix it for me."

"That little piece of plastic is going to cost you six or seven hundred dollars. You got that kind of money?" Bruce was sorry as soon as he said it. Now Cindy would just come back on him about child support. Which she did. Ruined his day, but if that's what she wanted, OK.

Suddenly there was this goofy-looking little guy standing in the middle of their argument. He had on a white dress shirt and blue pants that looked like they went with a suit, and he was skinny as a stick but with a round tummy that hung over his belt. His sandy hair stuck out in funny ways all over his head. "Hey," he said, and before he could say anything else, Bruce said, "Bug off. This is a private conversation here."

"No," the little guy said, "I just wanted to say that was a fine thing you did back there, those hamburgers and soda."

"Sure," Bruce said.

"I mean, it was real Christlike, you know? You know how Jesus fed the multitudes?" When, if ever, had anybody ever said Bruce was like Jesus? He began to feel better about this guy. Validated, like Cindy was always talking about. "Vern Hart," the guy said and stuck out his hand to shake. "That's my team down there." Faith, that was Vern's team. The league patsies in their yellow T-shirts somebody's mom dyed for them and their iron-on numbers and blue gym shorts that came from the Army-Navy. Christians.

"Listen, Vern, we got to finish this little talk, OK?"

"Bless you just the same," Vern said. "My church is out on the bypass, the old Carpet-for-Less place. If you ever feel the need, you know." And he was gone.

"So," Cindy said, "where'd you get the money for all those hamburgers?"

Bruce smiled. "The Getting Place." The good old Getting Place, where all sorts of surprising things come from.

Down under the big maple tree that stood in front of where Bruce grew up, up on the Mill Hill, Bruce and Ronnie Hayton played with their Hot Wheels, taking two fingers and making roads in the dust. It seemed like every day Ronnie had a new one. "Where'dja get that red Corvette?"

And the answer was always the same, "The Getting Place." Bruce got this picture in his head, a big old tree, maybe with a tree house where a boy could live in it all by himself, but with a big hole in the side of the tree for sure. And inside that hole would be all the stuff anybody could want: toys, bikes, tennis shoes, money, hot dogs, and soda pops.

Until one day Bruce said, "Let's go to the Getting Place, let's me and you go get some new cars." And they did go, up on Main Street, into the old-fashioned kind of dime store they don't have any more, full of bins of rubber balls, bubble stuff, baby dolls and their clothes, and up on the shelves model cars and airplanes, little bottles of paint and brushes, and a whole rack of Hot Wheels in their plastic packaging.

"Which one you want?" Ronnie asked as they spun the rack. Bruce said a black race car with yellow wheels and a stripe down the middle. "OK," Ronnie told him. "Go tell the man up there you got to pee and where is the bathroom." Bruce did, and the man led him back behind a little curtain and watched him into the bathroom. When he came out, Ronnie said, "Let's go," and outside, "here's your car."

See how easy that was? Bruce and Ronnie got other stuff from that store and stuff from the grocery store—candy bars, those chocolate cupcakes with white icing squiggles down the middle. As they got older they moved on to packs of cigarettes, from rubber balls to softballs then baseballs, fishing lures, and tools. Sometimes they got caught; sometimes they ran like hell. But nothing that bad ever happened to them. They had to pay for stuff, to stay out of a store like forever, but they always went back after a while to one Getting Place or another.

They swore: The Getting Place was just between them. Bruce had never even explained it to Cindy, not even when he thought he was in love. Ronnie moved away somewhere, and somewhere out there Bruce knew he still had his Getting Places. Now a guy in his late twenties, Bruce did too. Stealing wasn't as much fun without Ronnie to go along, or at least to tell him about it, but it was fun enough even if he didn't need what he stole. He stole a golf club once, stuck it down his pant leg. He didn't know what kind it was. Probably it was still out in the shed somewhere, good for killing snakes or something like that. He wished he could show that to Ronnie.

Stealing stuff made him feel good. But he'd never been blessed before, though, like that Vern guy had said. All brand-new, Bruce rode around on his Harley for days soaking in his blessing. Except when he got home one afternoon, there was a cop car in front of his trailer, two wheels up in the yard, two in the street.

"Hey," he hollered when he shut off his bike, "you're ruining my lawn." This was supposed to be a joke, his yard being a pounded piece of red dirt with a dog tied out back. A mean dog, too. But it was only Alvin Beale, his old buddy he'd sat the bench with back when he was trying to play football. That coach hated him. "Alvin, buddy."

Alvin kind of smiled. It had been a while, maybe. He said, "You got all your paperwork up to date on that scooter?"

Bruce said he surely did, and he sat himself down on the front stoop beside Alvin to shoot the shit for a while. Football, fishing, cars, and dogs, they covered that. Then Alvin said, "You know Mrs. Martha Maclelland?"

"Who?"

"You know, Mrs. Mack, Mrs. Raymond Maclelland? Our sixth grade teacher?"

"Oh yeah, shit yeah. Lie, lay, swim, swum. Mrs. Mack."

"Anyhow, somebody stole her pocketbook from out of her car right on Fieldstone Drive. Chalkeye found it Monday morning in the dumpster behind the high school." Chalkeye had been the school janitor long enough to know lots of good things might be found in a dumpster if you only took the time to look.

That's what Alvin told him, and then he said again as he was climbing in his cop car, that he sure hoped Bruce had the paperwork up to date on his motorcycle since the word was coming down to be checking on all the bikers now that the weather had turned nice.

■ ■ ■

Well, shit. Now here he was sitting in the jailhouse hoping somebody would go bail for him.

Alvin Beale came in, and the guard let him into the cell, then left them alone. "God, Bruce, I just about told you they were on to you."

"You didn't, though."

"Guy's got to keep his job, you know?"

Bruce hadn't looked at the name on that credit card, and neither had the help who swiped it through the card machine and let him scrawl some squiggle on the signature line. And if he had known, would he have done anything different? "How's it going to go down?"

"They got you on both surveillance cameras."

"Shit."

"You got a little rap sheet going. You might have to do some time."

"Aw, man." Bruce started rubbing his hands up and down his pants, looking around as if up in some corner or under the steel cot he was going to find a clue to get him out of this mess. "You could be a character witness for me," he told Alvin.

"Bullshit."

"I know, I know. I just got to think."

"You should have done some thinking last Saturday."

"Fuck you," but as Bruce said it, the guard was letting somebody through the big door at the end of the hall. It was that preacher in the same blue pants but wearing a yellow Banlon shirt. Talk about a character witness.

"How you doing, preacher?" Bruce said, and Alvin said he had to be going. Alvin out, preacher in, was that bad to worse or what?

"You know," Preacher Hart started—he put on this world-weary voice Bruce had heard his whole life from teachers and principals, "you disappoint me. I had you figured for a good man, a family man."

"I try to be," Bruce said, putting on the same voice he's always used with the same teachers and principals, full of crocodile contrition.

"That's not what I'm hearing. I hear you took that money. I hear you are not a good father, you weren't a good husband. I hear you're about a year behind in your child support."

"That's Cindy talking. There's two sides to every story." Bruce was getting his back up now.

The preacher let out a sigh and cut him off. "You know what? I want to believe in you. I want to believe that whatever made you buy those children hamburgers and sodas, that goodness that made you do something for others and not just yourself, that goodness is in you. In you trying to get out. Am I right?"

Bruce admitted to the preacher he was right, and he felt a wave of warm light pass over him just like after the soccer game.

Then without any preamble the preacher offered to go his bail without Bruce even having to ask. On the condition Bruce be in his church on Sunday morning. Well, all right, then. How hard could it be to put up with a little church music, a little preaching?

First things first, though. He got on his bike—fuckers impounded it and he had to pay a fine and get an inspection to get it back—and rode straight over to Cindy's place. There was little Katie slamming her soccer ball against the side of the building, kicking the hell out of it, right foot, left foot. "You're the best," Bruce told her.

"Daddy, why did you lie to me?"

"Lie to you how?"

"You didn't see my goal, did you?"

The storm door banged open and Cindy said, "Honey, get in the house. Your daddy and I have some business to discuss."

"Right here on the street?"

"Right here. Everybody knows anyway, so what difference does it make?"

"Knows what?"

"Bruce, you shame me and shame Katie too."

"Hey, last time I checked we're divorced."

"I've still got your name. So when it's right there in the *Tribune* for all the world to see. That preacher was over here. I thought I'd never get rid of him. God."

"Preacher Hart? He's my man. He went my bail."

"You could have rotted in there for all I care." But that wasn't exactly true. Vern Hart was going to do some things for Cindy, or so he said. He was going to talk to the judge, make sure Bruce didn't do jail time in return for Bruce promising to catch up on child support and alimony. And when he said that, Cindy felt a little glow of hope come up inside her.

■ ■ ■

Right away Bruce didn't like the looks of the place. The big plate glass windows had been painted over with pictures that were supposed to be Jesus and his disciples doing this and that—riding in a sailboat fishing, eating dinner at a big long table, handing out picnic baskets to gangs of people—clumsy, goofy drawings like maybe kids made them. Inside there were more paintings on the cinderblock walls and Bible verses on felt banners. A mess of mismatched chairs lined up in uneven rows.

A big Black man approached Bruce and announced himself, "Leroy Walker. Man, how you been keeping, Bruce?" Leroy Walker—Bruce had not seen him since high school. And here he was in nice, neat britches with creases in them, a sharp shirt with palm trees swaying all over it, and still looking like he could break a guy in half. At football practice, Leroy Walker had come close a number of times to breaking Bruce in half.

"I'm OK, OK. Nice place."

"We try, man. All in Jesus's name."

"Right."

"So, preacher wants you right up in front." Leroy had Bruce by the elbow and was steering him up the long aisle, probably passing all kinds of other people he'd known in high school. Bruce didn't want to look. There at the front was an empty bench, a bench just like the one Bruce had sat on for all those football games, and Leroy steered him to it.

"What the hell is this?"

"It's all right. It's just the sinners' bench. We all been on the sinners' bench at one time or another."

But it wasn't all right. After the singing, some rocking out with electric guitars, which wasn't too bad, Preacher Hart got down to business. "Friends. Brothers and sisters in Christ, we have a sinner come among us—as we all are sinners, we know—but Bruce has come among us. Stand up, Bruce, if you will." And Bruce had to stand, wishing he had pounds of rocks in his pockets to pull him back down, wishing those rocks could pull him right through the floor. "Bruce is a thief. But those crucified with our Christ were thieves, too, and we know of those two, one repented and found grace. Jesus visited grace upon him even as he was dying only to live again."

And so on. Forty-five minutes of preaching with Bruce as Exhibit A—the repentant thief. Except when the altar call came, Bruce did not answer. He sunk his head between his shoulders and felt like buckets and buckets of cold piss were being dumped over him.

At last the preacher gave up. Some five or six other souls had rededicated themselves to Christ. That haul would have to do. Bruce told himself, put up with a little more singing, and you're out of here.

There stood the preacher handshaking one and all as they left. Bruce tried to go wide, but the preacher intercepted him, took his hand, and looked earnestly into his eyes. "You fucked me over, man," Bruce told him. And he tried to get himself out of the parking lot as fast as he could without running anybody over.

■　■　■

That warm glow? It went away. So what, Bruce thought, he didn't care. Besides he got what he wanted, got out of jail and got his bike back. Parked in his yard, the engine still pinging as it cooled, that old hog put the wind back in him. As he lay back on his stoop and nursed his third cold one, he watched sideways as a gold-colored car rolled slowly down his street passing one trailer house and another. It looked like a stalking lion, low, its exhaust making a deep-throated purr.

The car stopped right in front of his place, and Leroy Walker climbed out. He was wearing a dress shirt and tie, sharp polished shoes, a gold pen stuck out of his pocket. Simple enough: He'd heard what Bruce said to his preacher, and now he was coming to beat the living shit out of him.

Bruce sat straight up and took hold of the top step with both hands to keep himself from running off into the stand of scrub pines behind his place. Be a man, he thought. Be cool.

"Bruce, buddy," Leroy said in a low, even tone.

"What you want with me?"

"Bruce," Here was Leroy sounding like Bruce had hurt his feelings.

"I ain't scared of you."

"No, man, it's nothing like that. Jesus is all about forgiveness."

"Why'd Hart put me up on that bench?"

"We all been on the sinners' bench. I was on it weeks and weeks before I let Jesus in. Preacher praying for me; Yvonne praying for me. And me nothing but a balled up knot of pride. Finally I let go. I had to let go. You. You got to let go."

Bruce laughed a little, "I thought you were coming over here to kick my ass."

"It don't work like that."

"You used to."

"Bruce, football—that's a game. That's the object of the game. We're talking about real life here."

"Real life." Bruce let the words roll around in his head. Looking at TV, drinking beer, riding around on his scooter, trying to score a little nookie—if that wasn't real life, what was?

"I want to see your ass on that sinners' bench this Sunday, hear me?"

Bruce nodded.

"Praise Jesus," Leroy Walker told him, and he let his powerful hand fall onto Bruce's shoulder.

■ ■ ■

You know those little do-hickeys they got these days? You just stick this hose down in a gas tank and rattle it around and pretty soon gas starts to spurt out the end. Beats sucking on some old piece of garden hose. They sell them in all the hardware stores. Bruce got his at Morrow Brothers, that old-time hardware on Main Street, slipped it under his jacket while the old guy was in the back cutting a piece of glass for a customer.

Now he slipped it under his jacket again and rode out into the dark. He was looking for that preacher's place, but he couldn't find it, couldn't find anybody around his silly-ass church, couldn't get a clue as to where to look, couldn't figure how such a man might live a normal life.

Leroy was another matter. Down Shear's Road at that new development with big brick pillars with a fancy name—Runnymeade, whatever that was—on big golden plaques set into the brick, down in there where every house looked like a little castle. Leroy Walker lived in a castle. Who would have guessed? And there sat his fancy gold car pulled up in front of his place looking just like an ad in a magazine, the kind of magazine about people Bruce had no use for.

Bruce cut the engine and coasted up silently alongside Leroy's car. The damn thing had a latch on the tank that could only be opened from the inside like all the cars did these days. Bruce was ready for that, and he easily pried the cover open. Messed it up, flimsy tinny shit even on a high-end car.

It wasn't cool to steal from friends or neighbors; Bruce knew this. He wanted to keep the peace with the people around him. Which isn't to say he'd not stolen his share of gasoline, a tank full here and there in a lonely parking lot at night, maybe from a car left behind a shop to be fixed in the morning.

Just then Bruce didn't care. Everything about Leroy pissed him off. His house, his car. Where did a Black man get off owning shit like this?

That Leroy had come over to his place and made nice made everything worse. Sinners' bench? No chance of that.

When his tank was full, Bruce started his bike, opened the throttle and tore off. Would Leroy notice? Would Leroy know who? Oh, yeah. For sure.

Bruce sported around for hours on that tank of gas. One thing you got to say for motorcycles is they get good mileage. Still, he couldn't help but believe Leroy had rolled out of his comfortable bed at the sound of Bruce's engine and was out hunting him right now. Or maybe sitting outside Bruce's place waiting. So Bruce went by Cindy's place instead.

He stood outside rattling the flimsy storm door, knocking on the glass, knowing she knew that if she didn't get up and let him in he'd start hollering.

A light went on in the front room. Cindy appeared in one of his old worn-out shirts. She opened the door but didn't unlatch the storm door. "We've been through this, Bruce."

"Been through what?"

She gave him a flat stare.

"What?"

Which was worse, let him in or let him holler and cuss while she called 911? After the last time, Alvin Beale caught her on the street and told her to get a restraining order. Except, she'd said, Bruce was all right most of the time. "Everybody," Alvin said, "is all right most of the time."

There he sat in Cindy's living room, on her busted-down couch covered with a throw, she in a porch rocker brought in just so she and Katie would have chairs to sit on.

"That preacher," he said.

"Don't tell me. I know all about it. Honest to God, Bruce, you want to pick a fight with everybody in this town. The man's trying to help you, and I wish you'd let him. I don't like the way he looks at me when he comes over here."

After protracted negotiations, after being turned away from her bed yet again, Bruce slept on Cindy's couch. Always a sound sleeper, Leroy

Walker lay with Yvonne in their king-sized bed, at peace with the world, secure in the bosom of the Lord. Preacher Vern Hart did not sleep.

■ ■ ■

Preacher Hart tossed and turned while his heart let in his own private iniquity. It was lust that ate at him. For the longest time, the object of his fantasies had been Yvonne Walker. Beautiful as she was, she was a real lady of the church, modest in dress and behavior. And her husband was a pillar of the church, not to mention a former all-state football player in two different positions. The combination encouraged the preacher to exercise restraint.

Cindy Webb, Bruce's ex, was another matter. When Preacher Hart had gone to her door, he had roused her from sleep even though it was after ten o'clock in the morning. She stood before him, behind her locked storm door, wearing a man's shirt partly buttoned. Perhaps that was all she wore; he couldn't say for sure, though he had since often wondered about it. When she finally let him in, she went off and came back wearing sweatpants to conceal her fine long legs. As they talked about Bruce and what could be done for him, the preacher could not keep from noticing her breasts moving loosely beneath the fabric of the shirt, noting the cleft between visible inside the carelessly buttoned garment. It was as if the woman had no regard for his position.

Preacher Hart had never made love to a woman. He had never fondled a bare breast, had never felt a breast covered by a brassiere and a blouse except by the merest accident. Pure in act, but not in thought, he suffered an unrelenting erection thinking of Cindy Webb. He imagined himself opening her shirt; he imagined the soft treasures waiting for him there. He imagined Cindy Webb inviting him to do more in language no church lady would ever use. He relieved himself with his hand.

In a world fraught with beatings, robberies, rapes, murders, famines, pestilence, and wars, you might think, in the grand scheme of things, no biggie, just one poor lonely preacher getting his rocks off. But

Preacher Hart lay on his sweaty and stained sheets filled with shame and self-loathing, farther from sleep than he had ever been, still unable to let go of the image of Cindy Webb's breasts dancing inside her shirt.

What could he do to make things right? What could he do to undo his secret sin? Still unable to sleep, he went at himself again. Then, tired and sore, he slept.

Is this how a man in this day and age might be reckoned to wrestle with an angel of the Lord?

■ ■ ■

"Preacher." It wasn't the voice of the Lord, but the basso profundo voice of Leroy Walker on the phone. Six-thirty in the morning, and Leroy was in no mood just now to talk about forgiveness. Leroy had been trespassed against, pure and simple. And at this moment, he was ready to go Old Testament all the way. No turning the other cheek, but having been smitten, ready to smite somebody back.

"Listen, let me handle this," the preacher told him, suddenly returned to himself and filled with higher purpose. He appreciated once again how God worked his plans in mysterious ways. He would have another go at Bruce's soul straight away.

■ ■ ■

Bruce had a job though most people might not have thought so. He worked over at the Honda junkyard in Rowan County pulling parts off wrecked Honda cars. His daddy worked out there before he died, and he got Bruce on when the last textile mill left town. Don't go out there looking for a left front fender, you'll be making a long drive for nothing, most busted up part on a car.

But this man who was coming along the road wasn't looking for any parts for any car, though Lord knows, his rattly old van could use some help. Big old sixteen-passenger thing, beat to hell, exhaust blowing blue.

Somebody had painted the word FAITH in big yellow letters on the sides and across the stubby hood, only there it was backward like on an ambulance so if you looked in your mirror you'd see FAITH coming up behind you. Preacher Hart liked the idea of that.

Bruce's boss man sat in a busted-up La-Z-Boy all day, sending his boys out in the yard for parts, taking in the money. The boss man, name of Henry Snipes, had a microphone hooked up to a PA so he could just pick it up and holler out to get somebody to fetch a part: "Get me an alternator for a 1999 Accord. I think there's still one in that green car back of row six." Damned if he wasn't right. Hadn't been in the yard for ten years, but he had a handle on every car out there. Bruce didn't much like his boss, but he'd never had a boss he liked. At least this one paid in cash.

The man hollered at the preacher as soon as he got in the door, "Ain't got nothing for you. Honda car parts, no Honda motorcycle parts, nothing for no other kinds of cars. You'd think people these days don't know how to read."

The preacher kept on coming, "I'm looking for a man."

"Who would that be?"

He asked for Bruce, and the man said, "You not from the government or nothing?"

All around the greasy room sat assorted parts with little pasteboard tags identifying model and year. The walls were covered with old calendars advertising different car parts and services, each featuring a woman in an alluring posture with her clothes sliding off her. Everywhere he looked, the preacher saw women leaning across the hoods of cars as their breasts tried to slide out of their skimpy tops, or women with impossibly long legs in tight tiny shorts pushing their firm butts at him. These women, mouths wet and welcoming, eyes full of eager promise, would not turn him loose.

Preacher Hart, feeling himself growing red in the face, said, "Preacher," in a mumbly way, a kind of way that might make a man wonder if he was ashamed to admit it.

"You don't seem like one." But Henry called for Bruce on the PA.

The preacher moved toward a calendar with a clear celluloid sheet covering a girl. When he pulled up the sheet, her bathing suit went with it. There she lay naked to the world.

Henry Snipes had sidled up behind him. "Quite a sight, ain't she? Old enough to be your granny by now I expect. But still a sight." He made an appreciative sigh, and the preacher heard himself sighing along.

From out on the road came the sound of a Harley-Davidson running through the gears. The boss man chuckled. "That would be your boy. I guess I'm going to have to dock his pay today."

■ ■ ■

Leroy sat before a cup of coffee made the way he preferred it, strong and black, just like him he always said. Yvonne tried to settle him down before he headed for work. "You can't let that Bruce get to you. He's a weak-willed man, a little man, you see that."

Leroy grunted.

"And you been so good, walking with the Lord."

"Good," he said as if he was unfamiliar with the idea.

"It's just a car."

Yvonne was sorry she said that. Leroy loved his car; he loved his house and his suits and the gold pen in his shirt pocket. He earned these things, and besides, didn't the preacher say blessings came to those who loved the Lord?

■ ■ ■

They keep all the high-end stuff at Walmart in a kind of corral. A challenge, but Bruce was up for it. He could make things right at least with Katie if he could cop her one of those video games she kept hollering about. What was it? Farmville? Something like that. First he cruised through the produce section and grabbed a banana, ate it as he went up and down the aisles and stashed the peel in the hunting and fishing department, hung out there for a while looking at the guns locked in their glass cases. He always thought it'd be good to have a nice nine millimeter like the cops on TV. He'd get one soon enough. But just now that wasn't his mission.

Once in the electronics section, Bruce realized he didn't have a clue about any of this computer shit. There was this guy, gray Carolina Panthers hoodie, black jeans, cheap running shoes, and a grungy ball cap, flipping through the heavy metal CDs. He asked him.

"No, man, can't help you. If I had a computer I'd be downloading this stuff like everybody else, you know?

Bruce didn't know. He didn't own a computer either. Couldn't ask the help for sure, so he wandered over to the computer games. There were a few with cartoon characters he didn't recognize on the cover of the plastic box. Even if he didn't get the right one, he was sure he could get something Katie would be happy with. Surprise her.

In one slick move, he made like he was hitching up his butt-sagging blue jeans and stuffed in the games using his own baggy hoodie to hide them. Then he fooled around flipping through the CDs, waiting until the lady at the cash register was busy with two different people asking some kind of complicated bullshit, then slipped out through the security gate, which started dinging real loud. He held up both hands above his head to show her, and she said, "That's OK. Sometimes it just does that."

Relaxed, so damned pleased, Bruce had just straddled his bike when the guy in the Panthers hoodie was right there beside him, "Let's see what you got under your shirt, partner."

"Fuck off," Bruce told him.

Then the guy flicked out a little wallet with a badge in it: only a security cop. He saw what Bruce was thinking. "Don't you do it. I made the call when you went out the door." And sure as shit, here came a Crown Vic with all its lights flashing.

"Goddamn, Bruce," Alvin Beale told him. "Get in the car." Bruce sat there locked in the backseat while Alvin did his incident report, writing down the names and prices of the games, then stood around shooting the shit with the store security guy for another fifteen minutes.

"You and him asshole buddies?" Bruce said as soon as they pulled out of the Wal-Mart parking lot.

"Leave it alone," Alvin said. "You got enough trouble right now."

■　■　■

Owning a junkyard does give a man plenty of time to think. Henry Snipes popped the lever on his La-Z-Boy and put it into full recline mode thinking to catch a little nap. Business was slow just now. Instead, he found himself thinking of the preacher who'd come in the other day looking for Bruce. Poor ol' boy, there he'd stood frozen stiff in front of that girl. Looking at those raccoon eyes, like he'd been up half the night pulling his pud, you'd think he'd never seen a naked gal before. Maybe he hadn't.

This place, Snipes often thought, was this the kind of place where a man might go hunting for his heart's desires? Not some big-assed desire like winning the lottery but some little thing that would make him feel like his life was complete in some necessary, manageable way. That missing wheel cover, the hatchback to replace the one that kept leaking after getting rear-ended. To be able to sit in his car waiting for the light to change and feel like he was one of the tribe of clean, decent people who didn't go around in cars with their air dams duct-taped to the fender and a rag in place of a gas cap.

And what is wrong with that? We're only simple animals, after all. Henry knew nothing of Bruce's Getting Place, but if he had, it would have made perfect sense. Down in the basement of our brains there are all sorts of raisin-sized glands that make us do what we do. We want, we lust, we crave this and that. We can't help it. A man could ruin himself, beat himself to death fretting over what comes naturally.

■ ■ ■

Preacher Hart thought otherwise. He sat parked in his van outside Cindy Webb's apartment building trying prayerfully to find some excuse for what he'd do next.

People are no damned good, and that's a pure biblical fact, starting with Adam and Eve. Actually, starting with Eve. It was her, wasn't it? That Cindy Webb who couldn't keep her shirt buttoned. The preacher found himself growing angry. A just and vengeful God, that's who he was thinking of now. And the preacher began to consider, if perhaps only elliptically, his role might come to be the instrument of his will.

Sometimes he was filled with envy, envy for the preachers from name-brand religions, those Baptists, Methodists, Presbyterians in their tall brick churches with stained glass windows. Someday, he thought, he would build his church, if not on a rock, on a foundation of just such bricks. He would leave the prefab Carpet-for-Less building, where once a customer could choose from hundreds of carpets and remnants in dozens of colors and designs, all outgassing a myriad of petrochemicals, the smell of which still hung in the air.

But that wasn't it so much. Jesus was probably OK with Vern Hart's ambition, to want a Crystal Cathedral. And a television audience was good, too, right? To fill stadiums and have saved souls running down the steep steps like rivers to his altar call represented the church triumphant? No sin there.

His lust, though, was another matter.

Some higher purpose, he told himself, had called the preacher to Cindy Webb's townhouse. He wanted to believe that. He turned off the van and went up to Cindy's door. He could hear her through the storm door talking on the phone.

"Why are you calling me? I don't have the money. Guess why not. Rot in there for all I care." But after she hung up, she thought, maybe that preacher could still help her out, maybe he could get Bruce to pay up.

And almost by magic, there he stood. When she let the preacher in, she wished she was wearing a bra under her T-shirt.

Preacher Hart looked to be in considerable pain. Cindy offered to get him a glass of ice water or some sweet tea. Maybe a couple of aspirin.

"No," he said, "it's just that. . . ." He took a step toward her and buried his head between her breasts. It took her a moment to realize the noise she heard was his sobbing.

Cindy worked at Big Daddy's Barbeque nights and cleaned people's houses three or four days a week—whenever she could, actually. She could see what that preacher was thinking, coming over in the middle of the morning, and her still in some old cutoffs and the T-shirt she'd slept in.

It would be nice, wouldn't it, if Cindy knew about the Getting Place, knew a place where little girls' soccer shoes grew on bushes waiting to be picked and computers sprouted right out of the ground? Pick one as soon as it ripens and next year come back and get another one when that one goes out of date and doesn't have all the new software and won't download the newest games.

Some people claim the devil can only come through your door if you invite him in. Cindy didn't know that, though she should have thought of it by now considering the men she'd let cross her threshold. Shouldn't have let this one in the door, she thought. Well, live and learn.

She gently pulled the preacher's head away from the thin fabric of her dampened T-shirt, set him down on her couch, and began to stroke his hair and speak to him in the same tender voice she had used to calm Katie when she was a tiny child. Making sure he kept his hands to himself, she promised him, "Everything's going to be all right."

■　■　■

A small corner of the Honda junkyard is reserved for Acuras. Acura, a kind of Honda for finer folks; you'll rarely get such people out to a junkyard parts hunting. But every so often, one will come through the door.

This fellow, a big Black man, filled up the whole damned door when he walked in, and Henry Snipes wondered if he hadn't seen him somewhere before. Black folks didn't come to the Honda junkyard much, but that's a different story.

The very place was unclean, and Leroy Walker felt a need to gird himself up in his old headgear and pads for protection. Was it the lewd pictures of the half-naked women or was it just the grime, because Leroy had been fastidious long before he ever found Jesus.

All the man wanted was the lid for his gas cap. Not so easy, is it, since even on a high-end car that cover plate is welded into place, not screwed? Yeah, Henry had one but Leroy would have to come back tomorrow or maybe the day after. Just now he didn't have anybody in the yard who he'd trust with a cutting torch.

The preacher had gotten Leroy into this. And now maybe he was trying to get him out. He had arranged for another deacon of the church to fix the cover plate, match up the paint, make it just like new. All Leroy had to do was run out to the junkyard and get one. It didn't matter, unclean was unclean. And this place was unclean.

Out in the clear air, Leroy took a deep breath. There sat his car with the lid to the gas cap mangled and bent. The things of this world are fleeting. Indeed, they are, but did it have to be a little pissant to teach him that?

■　■　■

Some few days passed.

Then didn't what happened next have to happen?

Hadn't Henry Snipes's wife told him as much? All day she sat at home drinking coffee and chain smoking her Salems working out some poor woman's horoscope. Casting, she called it, and she got paid good money for doing it, making these little pie charts with goofy symbols all over them. Then the customer (she might prefer to call herself a seeker) came to the house and sat with his wife at the kitchen table and shared a cup of coffee while they went over the chart. The crazy thing was people believed in those charts. They saw in them the story of their lives, past, present, and what could happen on up the road. After today, maybe Henry would start to believe a little, too, because she had told him as he stepped out the door: Today looked to be an inauspicious day for him. Beware.

When Bruce came in, Henry didn't say anything about his skipping out. The boy was bad to pitch a drunk, but at least he wasn't a meth head. In his line of business, you took the help you could get.

That talk about the gas cap cover being welded in place? That was a lie. All it took was a ten millimeter socket and a little wiggle to pop the thing loose from the paint. Henry just wanted that Black man who thought so well of himself—he could feel pride rolling off the man, that gold pen in his pocket and all, probably a pimp—he wanted that man to have to make another trip out to the ass-end of the county. He sent Bruce out into the yard to fetch the cover.

If he had been thinking at all, Bruce would have realized the part he was retrieving was the very piece of Leroy's car he'd ruined. But he was as he always was, a tangled wad of contradictions not tied too tightly together: Mad as hell and yet somehow pleased with himself at the same time. Bailed out of jail a second time, but sure that for all the shit piling up around him that he would continue to live his life pretty much as he had been. Maybe a little time in the work farm, but hey, three hots and a cot for a few months. Beat working in a junkyard. To anybody else, that life might look like a cascade of fuck-ups, but wasn't it the way his daddy before him and his daddy before him had lived? And hadn't they done OK? Sticking it to this one and that, hanging with your buds, always watching out for number one, but still managing to come out, well, OK. If his job at the junkyard was gone when he got out, he would find something like it. So OK, OK, what the hell.

■ ■ ■

Think of some kind of cartoon where an anvil is falling off a big old building toward some poor guy walking along all innocent. Until a hero of some kind swoops in and grabs it at the last minute.

The preacher had seen that cartoon before, and he knew he had to be Underdog, Mighty Mouse, that small unlikely and unexpected hero, who saved Bruce and Leroy from each other and themselves and from whatever ugly outcome might follow. Maybe Cindy would hear about what he'd done and love him for it. He tried to take back that last thought.

Leroy Walker always drove the speed limit. Yes, he was once all-state at two positions, he had a college degree from a pretty good school, he was in Rotary, but he was still a Black man driving a stylish car. And maybe his caution was a good thing since on this day, while he took his time and checked his rearview mirror often, Preacher Hart sped along as fast as his van, with poor compression that hit on only five of its six cylinders, would go to reach the Honda junkyard before Leroy.

■ ■ ■

Beware? What the hell was that was all about? This morning was looking to be not so different from every other day, a slow business day. Henry Snipes stretched his recliner to its fully recumbent position and glided into a happy dream where he cruised along in a 1972 Cadillac El Dorado with a calendar girl come to life at his side. She took his hand and placed it on her bare thigh.

Henry woke to a ruckus. Here was a fellow—now who the hell was he? It took a minute to register. That damned preacher. And what was he doing? He was all in a sweat with tears running down his face ripping Henry's calendar collection off the wall, throwing each of them into a pile on the greasy floor.

Preacher Hart hadn't planned to do it; he was a mild-tempered man. But the sight of the women, inviting him, tempting him even if it was only to buy a particular brand of spark plugs, all of a sudden became too much. He had to do something to ease the knot of passion tying up his heart. He didn't have time to think, wasn't able to think.

But, really, wasn't it like Jesus driving the money changers from the temple? In some cases, then, may wrath have its justifications? Except was the preacher's wrath about pin-up girls or his own sorry self?

In an instant, Henry forgot he had a bad back, pulled the lever on his La-Z-Boy, and launched himself into the room. He had not laid his hands on another man in anger in twenty or more years, but now he took the preacher by the front of his shirt, cocked his arm, and let his fist fly.

A booming voice—for just an instant the preacher thought he might be hearing the voice of God himself—said, "Turn him loose." There stood Leroy Walker, so big he blocked out the light.

Unfortunately, as Leroy had learned back in high school physics class and had made a career of proving on the football field, objects in motion tend to stay in motion so Henry's fist continued to follow its projected path. The little preacher's head snapped back and blood squirted out of his nose.

"Old man, you're going to pay for that." You'd think the voice was thunder calling down lightning.

Though Preacher Hart never had the chance to witness the full measure of Leroy's power, he said what he knew he must. "No, don't you do it."

Bruce knew a thing or two about that power. Here he stood just inside the backdoor to the shop with Leroy's gas cap cover in his hand, every nerve ending in his body flashing, telling him he should run like hell, but he was stuck, frozen in place.

Henry or Bruce? Both at this moment seemed equally deserving of Leroy's fury.

Leroy had made all-state as a fullback and linebacker. When the option play came around the end, he had to choose: take out the quarterback or the pitch back? What if he got it wrong? Better, he learned, to act decisively rather than not act at all.

That was some time back. Now he discovered his ferocity had abruptly abandoned him. He stood looking from Henry, to Bruce, to the preacher.

And Henry, too, saw the preacher standing across from him, maybe saw him clearly for the first time, saw him in all his frailty. Pitiful. He picked up the cleanest greasy rag from a box on the floor and handed it to him to staunch the blood running onto his white shirt. With Leroy standing on his left and Bruce on his right, each stuck in a weird kind of suspended animation, Henry considered the situation before him and said, "Well, shit. Anybody for bridge?"

What made these men laugh out loud? None of them had ever played a hand of bridge; none knew how you even went about playing. Henry, Bruce, and Leroy knew a thing or two about poker, though Leroy had promised Yvonne he'd given it up. Preacher Hart knew for a fact that cards were an evil in themselves, though he might have admitted to playing a few hands of Go Fish as a child.

The preacher, dabbing the rag against his nose, spoke softly: "I think this would be a good time to offer a word of prayer."

"About what?"

As the preacher would have it, a prayer for friendship and brotherhood and letting all bygones be. Wasn't that what Jesus would do?

But Henry said, "Come on, preacher. Cut the crap. Let's have a prayer about what we really want. Me, just to get through a night without having to get up four and five times just to piss. To get up every morning and hope to take a decent dump. You know?"

As for Leroy, would his prayer be for his golden car to be restored to its perfect state, his slacks eternally creased, his wife always beautiful and adoring? Or would it be simply to live a life without always having to be constantly watching his rearview mirror?

The preacher might claim not to know, but he did. Really, truly, down deep in his heart did he not want some woman, Cindy Webb or whoever came to him in his nightly fantasies, to take him in her arms and give him what he most desired, just to get himself laid?

Didn't it all come down to finding the Getting Place, that promised place of perpetual fulfillment, that place Bruce had been seeking since he was a boy? But what if it turns out that the things we want the most can't be found there?

SELECTED EVENTS FROM ANCIENT HISTORY

When Colin told her Jeff was coming up for the weekend, Emma was not at all pleased. Denise was in the guest room and Ellie in the little guest room—really a glorified porch. Where was he going to sleep?

"I told him it was the couch. He said OK. He said he would sleep on the deck if he had to." Jeff was going through another divorce.

"You didn't see this coming?" Colin smirked and looked at the floor. Emma had seen it coming from the day of the wedding. Another one of his graduate students, another girl with stars in her eyes who'd learn soon enough.

Colin and Jeff went way back. They had been college roommates. Colin and Jeff and Emma went almost as far back. There was some history. Whenever Jeff came around, it made Emma remember things she'd rather not. Emma had gone with Jeff first, and when he lost interest—let's be blunt, he unceremoniously dumped her—she went with Colin, Colin who had obviously been waiting not so patiently for his chance. She hated fawning. And to be blunt again, she did it just to show Jeff.

"What is this, number three or four? Nobody gets divorced that many times, celebrities, tabloid fodder, but not real people. Not history professors at second-rate universities."

Colin was sensitive about the second-rate stuff. Jeff, he thought, was brilliant. Jeff should be up there with people like Simon Schama and Stephen Ambrose. He had important things to say. Just because he had a job in West Virginia was the luck of the draw. For four years, Colin had fallen asleep in their dorm room listening to Jeff rave on. Not about his studies in Greek and Roman history, which Colin really cared or knew nothing about, but about the brilliance of Jimi Hendrix, or Eric Clapton, Keith Moon, or the Everly Brothers even.

Jeff still knew how to make an entrance, Emma had to give him that. He bumped down the weedy drive in one of those things that can't make up its mind whether it wants to be a truck or a car, springs squeaking as he came. He leaped out, left his door hanging open, and took the steps in two long strides, shook hands with Colin while slapping him hard on the shoulder, giving Emma a bone crushing hug, and strode through the house, through the sliding doors and onto the deck where he threw his arms open to the late afternoon light and waves breaking against the granite ledge below. "The sea! The sea! Our mother, the sea!"

"It's still there," Emma told him.

"Still here," he corrected.

Yes. Here. That was the problem, wasn't it? Ellie had wandered out from her room where she'd been reading a *Harry Potter* book—she was old enough now. But, really, shouldn't she be playing outdoors instead of staying cooped up in her room all day? She looked at this tanned and strangely radiant man, and knew him to be some kind of magical hero, "Who are you?"

It made Emma want to jerk a knot in that child. "Ellie, this is Mr. Patterson."

"Jeff," Jeff told her and lightly took her hand.

"Jeff, Ellie is Denise's little girl."

"Man, man. Denise must be a woman fully grown, huh? I can remember when she was the size of this one."

"Yeah, well," Emma said, "if you stick around you do see them grow up."

"Emma! Sister! You know how to hurt a guy. What can I say? Mistakes were made." By Emma's count there were at least two kids out there. The oldest, a boy whose name she couldn't recall just now, would be about Denise's age. And the other? In his midtwenties by now at least.

A manly heart-to-heart was de rigueur on these occasions when Jeff crash-landed. They flattered Colin's ego, Emma supposed. What useful advice he had for Jeff was another question. She watched Jeff move gingerly across the rocks, nothing like the guy who'd bounded up the stairs, as the two of them made their way down to the tiny strip of what passed for a beach. They walked away from her, around the point and out of sight, heads bent toward each other. They could be philosophers, physicists, wise men probing the secrets of the universe instead of a four-time loser spilling his guts to the only guy who would listen. She would get whatever sad story he revealed out of Colin when they went to bed.

"Mother, don't you think you're being a little harsh?" This was Denise come fresh from the farmers' market with her cloth shopping bags of carrots, beets, green beans, and a scrawny free-range chicken. They could stretch it to five people, Emma guessed.

Denise was too much like her father, too inclined to look for the good in people and overlook the bad. But to answer her question, "No, no I don't. Actions have consequences. How can anybody claim to be a history teacher who doesn't understand that?"

"He just seems to get ahead of himself in these romances. He doesn't mean to hurt people."

"You've got an eight-year-old in the next room, so you've got maybe six more years if you're lucky to teach that child to know better." Emma caught herself menacing her daughter with her paring knife, "I should have been firmer with you."

She didn't really mean that. Denise had done her share of youthful acting out. She had a little tattoo on her bottom to prove it, not that she knew Emma knew, and she most likely had done things involving boys and marijuana not so different from what her mother had done. Of these, Emma could only guess. At the time she'd tried hard not to. But in the end, Denise turned out all right. Bob was a sweetie, maybe a little boring, but a hard worker—that's where he was now, working his butt off so Denise and Ellie could come to the beach house. Emma thought this was some silliness on his part. She and Colin had plenty of money, but Bob insisted they pay their own way. Her admiration multiplied every time she declared his foolishness.

■ ■ ■

The men returned from their walk, Jeff's faded Levi's wet to the knees, a toe in a dirty white sock showing through a hole in the top of his running shoes. He had to get wet, had to make a point of his what? His imperviousness, his wild spirit, his deep thinking that made him unaware of trivialities? His pain? Jeff went up to Denise, took her slender arms and pulled her toward him. Suddenly her shorts seemed extraordinarily short, her shoulders in her strappy top exceptionally revealing. "Denise, how long has it been? You have become a lovely woman. I'm sure you know that. I'm sure your husband tells you all the time."

Actually, Bob never said such things. He was perhaps more dull than Emma imagined. Denise blushed; Emma said, "Stop it, Jeff."

Denise stepped back toward the screen door, "There's a cat climbing into your, uh, vehicle out there with the door standing open."

"Yes, yes. My vintage El Camino. The redneck gentleman's conveyance of choice."

"It looks like it needs work."

"Past a certain age, we all need a little work. But anyway, a cat can't do any harm. Maybe it needs a home. Maybe I need a companion."

That poor cat didn't know what it was getting into, Emma thought but didn't let herself say it. She needed to lighten up. Denise had pleasant memories of spending time in this very house with Jeff and his first wife and little boy, Davie. Camping out on the screened-in porch, falling asleep to the raucous banter from the adults in the big family room with its open fireplace. Where was Davie now, she wondered. Well, maybe he was in the navy, or was it the merchant marines? Jeff couldn't say for sure. And did he hear from him? Yes, a card on his birthday, always sent from some exotic locale, Bangkok, Tokyo, Athens. Probably, Jeff suspected, Davie just sent cards to the postmasters in those cities and had them mail something out for him, just to make Jeff jealous.

"Why? Why would he do something like that?" Denise asked, setting aside the improbability of it happening at all.

"I guess you could say we're estranged. His mother and all. . . . She kind of made any sort of real relationship impossible."

That would be Naomi, a willowy blonde; Emma had judged her a pushover. But in the end, she had liked her better than any of the women Jeff had brought around, though it had taken some time to warm up to her. Later, she told herself that had more to do with her feelings about Jeff than Naomi. And that other child and that wife? If she tried really hard their names would come to her.

■ ■ ■

"So, what did he do this time?" This is Emma after they have turned out the bedroom light. Emma worn out from pulling together dinner, sitting at the table for what seemed like hours while Jeff went on and on about the grim political situation, the death of rock and roll, the new Chilean wines he was discovering—as he drank plenty of their California wine. While Colin and Denise sat rapt, she ended up getting Ellie into bed. Poor kid's head was drooping right into her plate. She left it to Denise and Jeff to clean up the kitchen. He could at least do that much.

Colin was too tired for Emma to get much out of him. "Oh, you know. The same old thing. Caught in the saddle with some other girl."

"And we're supposed to feel sorry?"

"Well, he's kind of in a corner. They did a prenuptial, and she's got a good lock on his pension—or what must be left of it after the other divorce lawyers got a piece of it."

"He wants you to lend him money? Give him money?"

To be fair, Colin was a shrewd businessman. He had graduated with his degree in accounting, gone back to his small town—Emma had gone along, too, married the weekend after graduation—and taken the place waiting for him in his parents' hardware store. But Colin quickly moved to sign on with a national franchise. Then when a hardware in a nearby town was faltering, he bought them out. By the time he was finished, Colin owned seventeen hardware stores in three different states. Then he sold them all. Emma and Colin were millionaires, millionaires several times over. Emma wasn't even sure how rich they were, but sometimes Colin would say being so rich was wrong. Boring, too. Sometimes he said they should give all the money away and find a struggling hardware store somewhere far off the interstate and start all over again.

This was the vein Emma was afraid Jeff might luck into, Colin's strange survivor's guilt: Here he was a wealthy man, while Jeff, the only genius he'd ever known, was scraping bottom. How could any reasonable person think that was fair?

"It didn't come up," he told her, and fell sound asleep like he always did.

Emma wouldn't let herself sleep. The light wind carried the voices of Jeff and Denise up from the deck below where they must have adjourned after doing the dishes. Probably enough wind to keep the bugs down too. Emma caught snatches of their talk, really Jeff's talk and Denise's enthusiastic listening. "What Dylan and Picasso have in common . . ." "Jorma Kaukonen and Jack Casady were the heart of that band . . ." ". . . drove all night to hear them live." And Denise's interjected wows and giggles finally giving over to hoots of laughter. Emma couldn't stand it any longer, she prodded Colin awake: "Go down there and tell them to go to bed."

"Let it go," he told her without lifting his head from his pillow.

"That man is trying to seduce your daughter."

"It's just Jeff being Jeff. That's all."

Exactly so, Emma thought. Jeff being Jeff. So deeply in love with himself that he cast a spell over the people around him. She remembered distinctly his coterie of friends assembled around a big table in the corner of the cafeteria tossing him softballs just to watch him knock them out of the park: Nixon? "Dick Nixon before Nixon dicks you." "Deep Throat?" "It took Nixon three times to get it down Pat." Those things seemed funny at the time. It was only over the years that she began to see how needy he was, how much he needed adulation to keep himself inflated. And his lines weren't even original.

■ ■ ■

Up early because she hadn't slept much anyway, Emma pulled on her clothes and went downstairs, took out the coffee beans from the freezer, and took down the electric grinder. She'd give Jeff a taste of his own medicine. Denise, too. She saw him out the window, sleeping in a lounge chair on the deck in his old khaki sleeping bag. She knew that bag with its printed flannel lining—red with pheasants on the wing. She knew the musty smell of it. She knew what it felt like to snuggle in without a stitch on. There it was: The kind of the thing she'd rather not think about.

In the clear light, she studied his face, still a handsome face. But he'd aged faster than Colin, his face lined deeply as any old lobsterman's. Too much living in so little time. It had to add up. And she saw, too, what she'd suspected the night before. He was dyeing his hair. Probably he'd dyed it right before he came up thinking nobody would notice. She would, she did.

Is it the animal in us all that makes a person wake up when he's being stared at? Something about knowing he may be on the verge of being prey? Because Jeff hadn't intended to wake up, and he didn't do it gracefully. He sat up and looked around at all the empties, all Colin's good Czech beer gone, "Aw shit, aw man," guessing maybe he'd screwed up with Colin, too, feeling parched and a little nauseated. Then he saw Emma watching from the window. She pressed down on the lid to start the coffee grinder.

"No, Emma," he told her, but she could only see him moving his mouth and smiled out at him. He crawled out of his sleeping bag wearing a tie-dyed T-shirt and old gray gym shorts and came into the kitchen. "Emma, sweetie," he said, "can't that wait?"

"You need some coffee. I'm making you coffee."

"Why don't you like me anymore?"

"Don't like you? I try not to dislike anybody." She gave the grinder another long pulse. "But tell me this, Jeff, why can't you . . . what is it they say these days . . . keep willie in your pocket? Why can't you see how much damage you do?"

"Just my nature, I guess." He thought she was being funny.

"Ha. Sort of like your old Greek god heroes? Zeus is it? Knocking up girls in the shape of a steer."

"It was a bull."

"A goose."

"Swan."

"A shower of gold?"

"You got that one right."

"I know I did."

"Emma, honey, you're a smart lady." She flinched. She hated those terms of endearment he threw around like a truck stop waitress. "I always liked that about you. But you've got to understand, I don't make these things happen by myself. I mean, we're all adults."

"Adults. I'll have to think about that. But what you do do, what you do all the time, what you used to do, what you've always done is create an atmosphere where what you call *things* happen." This all being said while Emma slammed the cupboard doors open and shut looking for coffee filters. She and Colin only drank tea.

"Did you know that if the earth's atmosphere were 100 percent oxygen, it'd all burn away?"

"That's a romantic thought."

"It is. It is." And then Jeff got quiet. Maybe both of them felt they'd stretched the thin skin of good behavior to the limit. How long was he staying, anyway?

When Emma's roommate met Colin, she said, "Just the kind of guy you take home to meet the folks." That kind of guy was a running joke, wasn't he? The kind of guy you wouldn't take home to your folks—that was the kind Emma and her girlfriends thought they were looking for, an edgy, leather-jacket-wearing guy. Jeff was that kind.

And to try to bring herself around to Colin, Emma had sat in the back of her child and adolescent psych class and begun to jot down Colin's good qualities in the flyleaf of the book. He was considerate and kind. He could fix anything (he had quickly diagnosed the blown fuse in Emma's VW, driven to the parts store, and had her lights back in no time). He was careful with his money without being stingy. He was neat. He studied hard for all his classes, not just for his major. He was gentle. He had good manners. He was polite. She had planned to fill the page, but she found she was already repeating herself.

Jeff had disappeared from the house, his squeaky El Camino thing going out the driveway in a faint bluish cloud. As if on cue Colin came in from his shed where he'd been since six in the morning, his usual getting up time. He'd slept fine. Now he was finishing another of the little tasks he gave himself, making a trailer out of PVC pipe for his double kayak—which he'd also made. Whether he was aware Emma had spent a sleepless night hardly mattered. It was his way to avoid conflict, even the possibility of conflict, if he could. Denise emerged from the guest room and, avoiding eye contact with Emma, made for the deck where she began to gather the empty beer bottles. "I only had one," she told them.

"That's all right," Colin told her, "it was probably good for Jeff."

"Denise." Emma waited until she came to a stop, trying to hold onto the bottles she held. "Denise, watch yourself. Think about what you're doing." What was she saying? Denise wasn't a teenager anymore.

Except suddenly and without warning she seemed to revert: the sullen stare, the huffy exhalation of breath. "Mother, I can take care of myself. I'm not a child."

"No, no you're not," Emma said retrieving her old, tired mother's voice. Denise was a mother herself, and where was that child? Ellie was not asleep in her room but holding her book in her lap in the big chair beside the fireplace. How long had she been there, big ears, big eyes, taking it all in?

■ ■ ■

Jeff reappeared late in the afternoon with a half dozen lobsters from the lobstermen's co-op, ears of corn he'd bought from a farm stand, a big tub of coleslaw from a deli, and many six-packs of Czech beer to overcompensate for what he'd drunk the night before. "Stand clear in the kitchen," he told Emma. "I'll take care of all this." And except for asking for this pot and that bowl, except for shouting out orders for Emma, Denise, and even Ellie to carry out, he did.

Colin sat at the head of the rough farm table and nursed his one beer, pleased. It always pleased him when Jeff confirmed all his admiration. Even under considerable duress, Jeff had a big heart, was a great soul. You could count on him.

Foolish man.

■ ■ ■

Emma had reached the point—maybe sooner this time than last—she reached on every one of Jeff's visits when she wished she could run out of the room, onto the deck, and throw up, vomit her buttered lobster and sweet corn and cold beer over the rail. What a goddamn fraud.

In that narrow campus world they all swam around in, Jeff's breaking up with her didn't mean she didn't have to see him again. She would be seeing him constantly. So she grabbed onto Colin, in part as a human shield against pain and humiliation.

Had she slept with Jeff? Sure she had. To his credit, Colin never asked. Maybe Jeff bragged and so he didn't have to. Maybe he didn't care. Maybe it was just the way things were then. Girls were expected to sleep with boyfriends. The ones who didn't were called uptight, or maybe they were uptight if they wouldn't do everything a guy wanted to in bed. Emma wasn't uptight either way. Avid, maybe that was the word. Though she couldn't have made it clear to her friends at the time, she felt she'd wanted to be consumed alive by Jeff, to have orgasms she could describe as out-of-body experiences. And she had.

She got in bed with Colin as soon as seemed respectable, not too long a wait in those days. He was gentle and respectful. And so damned grateful.

Now here was Jeff at the dinner table railing against the Eagles. "The Eagles signaled the end of rock 'n' roll. What wimps, what whiners. Have you ever heard Mojo Nixon's 'Don Henley Must Die'?" Of course they hadn't. "When I heard that song all I could say was, right on! And Mojo and Skid Roper doing 'Elvis Is Everywhere'?" He was off on a roll now, and Emma had gone on too many of those rolls with him in the past. Maybe somebody would stop him before he got off on one-hit wonders, session players, and complicated collaborative cross-pollinations. Bullshit, she wanted to holler, this is just bullshit. Who fucking cares? Pathetic. She used to lash out at Jeff in just those words and more when he was feeling so high and mighty and showing off how much he knew. Every time he came around, she heard all those words and more rattling around in her head. It's a wonder they all didn't spew out.

"Thank God for the Ramones," he hollered.

And Denise asked, "Aren't they dead?" Good for you, daughter, Emma thought.

"Well, yeah. 'Better to burn out than fade away,' you know?"

"Didn't they do both?" At least that brought him up short.

"Hey," Colin said, as if he'd just woken from a coma, "want to see the nifty boat trailer I made from PVC pipe? I'm thinking there must be a website devoted to uses for PVC pipe besides plumbing. I'm going to look for it and send in a picture."

"You've got a boat?"

"Well, it's a double kayak. I made it for Denise and Bob."

"And me."

"Yes, for Ellie when she gets older."

It's a small price to pay, women sometimes said to each other, meaning marriage to a man who smokes cigars or who wastes every Sunday watching ball games on television. Emma had said it herself, speaking of these parades out to Colin's shed to see his latest geegaw whether it was a coat rack made from an old wooden ski or a hobby horse made of found driftwood for Ellie when she was small, or now, this odd little cart made of PVC pipes. A small price to pay for what? In her case, for a life free of want, more than that, a life wherein any whim she had might be readily satisfied. Because after a few tough years when they were getting started, when Emma taught elementary school and helped in the hardware in the summer months, she had not had to work at all. She meant to. She had enjoyed teaching. But she quit after Denise was born and despite her good intentions had never gone back. A life of quilting, counted cross-stitch, knitting, elaborate Halloween costume making. Reading for pleasure. A wonderful life most women would kill for.

Why, why did Colin bring up this boat? Because Jeff had to see it, and now that he had, he wanted to take it for a little spin around the bay, maybe out to the lighthouse.

"Jeff, have you ever been in a kayak in your life?"

"No. But if you can do it, how hard can it be?"

"I don't. Colin and Denise have been out in the boat this summer. That's all. It's dangerous. There are ledges just under the water that you can't see. Besides, I'm not a strong swimmer."

"That's not how I remember it."

"What?" Ellie asked.

How she even got there was lost to her, in the middle of the night with a bunch of kids who were skinny-dipping in a lake near campus. She and Jeff slipped away and swam out to a little island where they had—what else?—sex, unprotected sex. Emma remembered she'd barely made it back to the lakeshore, thrashing and choking. She probably swallowed a gallon of water while Jeff lazily side-stroked beside her. She had gone around for two weeks afterward worrying she might be pregnant.

"Emma's exaggerating. It's perfectly safe out there." Leave it to Colin to say such a thing. He simply had no imagination.

"What?" Ellie asked again. "Remember what?"

"Nothing, sweetie. Jeff's just being a smart aleck."

"What's this on the front?" Jeff asked looking at the design, a wriggling snake-like thing wearing a stylized crown.

"A basilisk," Ellie told him. "A snake so mean it can kill you just by looking at you."

"That's a *Harry Potter* thing," Denise put in.

"Oh, no. There were basilisks, cockatrices long before *Harry Potter* came along. They go back to ancient times, figured in Greek mythology. There are images, dragons and such, running right up through the Middle Ages."

"See?" Colin said, "I told you Jeff would know all about this stuff. That's what he is, a professor of ancient history."

"Used to be. Now I only do my contemporary history thing. Nobody cares about Greece and Rome anymore. Kids won't take those classes. But my History of Rock class is packed."

"Contemporary history. Wouldn't that be what they call an oxymoron?"

"Funny, Emma. But really, somebody has to get in there and do the research now. It's all so ephemeral. Even as we speak, those guys are dying and taking their stories with them. Real historic artifacts are being bought up for props in bars and clubs."

" Heartbreaking. But seriously Jeff, most of that stuff we listened to was crap." Some things are ephemeral, she thought, because that's all they're meant to be.

■ ■ ■

"Crap?" Colin said that night in bed. "I don't think I've heard you say *crap* in years." No she had not. She had gradually reined herself in, that fearless, mouthy braless girl who went around singing, "Jesus was a Capricorn" now was on the official board of the Presbyterian Church in their hometown. Out by the ocean, she felt a release from all that she had let herself become. She found she liked herself better here.

Out on the deck Denise and Jeff were talking again. With no wind to help them along, their words didn't carry so well—Jeff off on some ramble about the afterlives of the guitarists in the Yardbirds—besides tonight Emma was too tired to stay up and nurse her indignity.

Jeff had been expected to stand with Colin at their wedding, but he told them he had already made plans. His graduate school studies were beginning, and he was expected to be in Greece right away for a vague sort of research project. Colin was hurt, but forgave him. Emma was relieved, and did not. He sent a telegram from Delphi instead, "Your future lies in boards," it read—Jeff's idea of a joke, a joke only he would get, and in explaining it, imply what they should know and show off what he did. This was apparently a famous pronouncement the Oracle made to the Athenians that could be taken two ways just like many of the things Jeff said. In this case, it meant that after their honeymoon, Colin and Emma would repair to a hick town and run a hardware store and lumberyard. It meant, some future. Why couldn't Colin see that?

■ ■ ■

In fact, Colin did have a pretty good imagination. Here was a guy who could pick up some stray driftwood and in a few days turn it into a rocking horse. All he did was look around him for what was possible. He dwelt in a benign universe. So when Colin saw his white boat trailer down by the path to the beach, he was not angry, not disappointed in Jeff for doing what Emma had expressly warned him not to. Instead he was mildly concerned. There was an extremely low tide. How would Jeff and Denise manage to get the boat back up over all that exposed rocky ledge? With this in mind, he began to walk up the shore toward the next cove to find a sandy spot. There was the boat bobbing maybe seventy-five or a hundred yards out, empty.

No need to panic. He walked back to the house and was calling the Coast Guard when Emma came down the stairs. She heard enough to know.

"That man. I'm going to kill him," she said and stopped short. "They could be dead. They could have drowned."

Ellie, over in the big chair, dropped her book and began crying.

"They aren't dead, they aren't drowned," Colin told her.

"Where are they, then?" The normally placid child, more like Colin than Emma, was bawling to the point of hyperventilating. Probably it had to do with reading those *Harry Potter* books.

"Well, we're just going to have to find them. People are coming to help us look for them. We can walk down the shore and look for them."

But they didn't have to. Out the screen door, Emma could see Jeff and Denise coming down the long driveway to the house. They had taken the boat out at high tide and paddled out to one of the barrier islands to explore, and the tide had turned and carried the unsecured boat away. A lobster boat had picked them up this morning and dropped them off at the co-op pier. Denise's arms and legs were covered with mosquito bites. Her hair was windblown and knotted, her eyes bedazzled, stunned. Emma knew that look. She considered whether there were bites on Denise's bottom as well.

Because she knew. She had been pulled back to Jeff after they broke up, after she was supposedly with Colin. They had done it behind his back and under his nose. And Colin, poor guy, was too trusting, too admiring, too innocent. Soon enough Jeff was off on his next conquest.

And Emma herself? What the Delphic Oracle apparently meant was the Athenians should have made a fort of wood rather than built more ships. Emma considered her own little fort of wood she'd been building since college days and wondered, was wood the best material? Was it strong enough or should it be made of rocks or steel or some space-aged material she'd yet to hear of? Because the whole trouble with the pronouncements of the Oracle was you never knew what the right meaning was until you'd done the wrong thing.

The wrong thing twice in her case.

Now, over thirty years later, Colin was still the very same. And Emma often wondered why living in a house (two houses, really) where there was never a drippy faucet, a holey screen, a loose hinge, or a sticky lock was insufficient. She told herself she wasn't being fair, there was more to Colin than that. And less to Jeff. She had recited Colin's good qualities listed in the back of her psych book like a mantra to drive Jeff out of her head. Most of the time it worked.

Once Denise had repaired to her room to rest and taken Ellie in with her to settle her down, Emma followed Colin out to his shed. "High tide. Colin, high tide was in the middle of the night." It was dark. They easily could have run on a ledge and flipped over. They hadn't taken the spray skirts or the life jackets.

"It was foolish, OK? But nobody got hurt."

He believed that? "Colin, he's got to go. If you won't go over there and tell him, I will."

"Just let things cool off a little."

Emma left Colin in the shed modifying his PVC trailer so he could go fetch the boat the lobstermen had retrieved and left off at the co-op. She'd do it herself. She would let Jeff see firsthand what the killing glance from a basilisk looked like.

Jeff was on the deck talking on his cell phone, pacing, frantic. The sturdy wire fence Colin had put around the railings to keep Ellie from falling off when she was a toddler made an enclosure, and Jeff, flinging one hand out while the other clutched the phone, dashed from side to side like a trapped animal.

Emma could only catch his end of the conversation. "I do," he said, "you know I do." "An aberration. We were just in a situation where things got a little out of hand." "She's sorry too. I'm sure she is." "No, I promise." "I swear."

"I'm on my knees out here on Colin's deck and the sun is beating down and my kneecaps are burning from hot nails." There he was trying to be funny. Wait, she wanted to tell him, look at yourself. He was like a man falling down a long flight of stairs but laughing as he went, assuring anybody watching it didn't hurt at all. Pitiful. Wait, she'd say, slow down. Go off on one of those barrier islands by yourself and sit. Stay there. Stay there until you find out who you are. But once you pass a certain age, how many chances in life are there to do that?

"You're in pain. I know that." "Me too." "Me, too, dammit."

Say it, she thought, say, "I love you." Just say it. But the longer the conversation rattled on, the surer she was he would not. Could not. It was an out; he always gave himself an out, a reliable rabbit hole cut out of words he could slip through, if only in his own mind. Yes, how many chances?

"Eight or ten hours." "Yeah, if I leave now I could be there by midnight." "Ready for me?" She heard his laugh, smug and calculating.

Emma waited long enough to be sure Jeff had ended the call and stepped out onto the deck.

Jeff said, "Hey, listen, Emma. There's been kind of a breakthrough. I think we're going to be able to work things out."

"So you won't be staying for dinner?" It was not the line she had prepared, and it tasted like disappointment when it came out.

"I'm sorry. I really am, but this could be it. New beginning. A fresh start."

"Well, good for you."

"But, Emma, you and I hardly had time to talk at all. How are you?"

She might have said, my life is tranquil and agreeable in every way; she might have said, sometimes the weight of tedium is so great I feel I must pull my hair out by the roots; she might have said, I want, I want, I want. Something she could not name but was always beyond her reach. Or she might have said nothing at all. She said, "Fine. Just fine."

"I'm glad for you," he said. A slight smile leaked onto his face.

■ ■ ■

"OK, I'm on my way," Jeff told them from the rolled down window of his El Camino, his duffle and sleeping bag thrown into the bed. "Tell Denise and her little girl bye for me."

"We will," Colin said. "They'll be sorry they didn't see you off."

Jeff pulled away.

Emma said, "Sometimes I wish he'd just go and never come back."

"You don't mean that."

At the end of the drive, the car door flung open, and a cat shot out and into the trees.

Now the hard work began. Emma went into the house to find Denise, and to find the language to forgive her, to assure her. We all make mistakes, don't we? Only how not to repeat them? That was the hard part.

LARRY'S ASHES

PREVIEW

If you happened to be driving up the Richardson Highway on this summer day, you might have seen a small procession heading into the woods along the sketchiest of trails.

In the lead were three jovial men in their late fifties or early sixties wearing knee-high rubber boots and headnets. They carried slim silver tubes containing their expensive fishing rods and wore daypacks. Their talk was punctuated with good-natured ribbing and bursts of laughter. Every so often one of the men would stop and tie a piece of hot pink flagging onto a tree limb.

A short distance behind came three others, eyes hidden behind sunglasses, but clearly not nearly so happy: a woman, also around sixty wearing comfortable jeans, a polar fleece top, and sneakers. Her name was Christine—Chris. She carried a plastic shopping bag from a local grocery store and inside it was a maroon plastic box about the size of a brick containing her husband, Larry's, ashes. Following her was a thirty-something man in heavy black boots and a leather jacket festooned with zippers and epaulets. You might have taken him for a biker, but he wouldn't know the first thing about motorcycles. And a young woman, also around thirty. She wore ballerina flats, leggings, and a knitted poncho.

Then came a man in khaki slacks and a button-down shirt and running shoes: Robert, not Rob. He couldn't decide how he felt; he was not altogether sure why he was along.

And trailing behind, not happy at all, was a slender woman also in in rubber boots and headnet and with a small backpack. Amie. She was

Larry's mistress, a word that suggested a relationship both exotic and antique. Though Robert had heard her called less flattering names the past few days.

The mosquitoes bumped against the troop like a soft, dry rain, and the four without headnets slapped and cursed under their breaths. As they went deeper into the woods, the ground under their feet gave over to muddy bogs so that by the time they had reached their destination at the river's mouth, those ill-prepared four had caked their shoes with sticky gumbo.

1.

This is what people who spend the night sleeping in the airport look like: Twisted into lumps like trash bags thrown into corners, sectioned like caterpillars stretched across three seats (seats designed not to pull apart but with awkward spaces in between), rolled up into balls under tables. They use their coats for blankets, their backpacks and bags for pillows. Some have strapped their belongings to themselves as a precaution against thieves. Some lie splayed open for all the world to see. They're alive; you can tell from their squirming and cranky groans. Robert is among them, folded nearly in half, briefcase on his lap, trying to sleep with his head on his arms.

He's put out. He didn't want to make this trip in the first place. To Alaska, to a memorial service that now he's got a pretty good chance of missing completely. Stuck in Seattle, he already knows the only plane out in the morning is a milk run, four or five stops, mostly in towns he's never heard of, on his way to Anchorage, then Fairbanks, a town he's never seen. Under other circumstances, this might have been a vacation, but to tell the truth, he never had much of an urge to go north. Not even after reading Larry's repeated invitation in every Christmas letter.

No Christmas letter for the last two years. No card sender himself, Robert figured the guy gave up on him. Now he's dead. Now Robert knows.

Larry did this thing—Robert has heard of others doing it, too, when faced with the inevitable. He made a list of those he wanted to talk to one last time and began calling them one by one. Other friends had already gotten their calls; Robert was not looking forward to his. It was worse than he'd expected.

"Robbie! Rob!" Larry's voice, always big and booming, was a hoarse whisper. Who knew, maybe he'd been on the phone all day.

"Larry, buddy, I know. I heard. I'm sorry." Then a lot of dredged up bullshit from college—water balloon fights, stoned drives to rock concerts, professors they liked, classes they hated. Robert indulged the guy. What else can you do with a dying man? Except when he tried to ring off using a manufactured need to drop off his car at the shop, Larry wouldn't turn him loose.

It was like the guy had him by the lapels of his jacket. There was a famous poem about that, Robert remembered. He'd have to Google it and see how it came out. "Listen, there's one more thing. Something I need from you."

"Sure," Robert said, but he meant, now what?

"Rob, man, you know things haven't been so good between Chris and me these last couple of years."

"No. No, I didn't."

"Well, they haven't. Not the kind of things you put in a Christmas letter."

"Right." Robert looked up at the ceiling, looked at his watch, cast a look around the room for some kind of hook to pull him out of this conversation.

"Here's the deal. I kind of got involved with this sweet lady, Amie. If this cancer thing hadn't hit, I would have divorced Chris and been out of here. But it did and I didn't and then I was in and out of the hospital. . . . Well, I'll make it short, Chris found out and made me promise to break it off with Amie."

"And did you?"

"She's got me by the balls. I've got a couple of weeks, maybe a month. I'm housebound. And if it's not Chris, it's the hospice nurse looking in."

"Hospice nurse? That bad?"

"Yeah. I'm fading, man. I know it. There's pain, and the way this works, I can ask for something for pain. Morphine. And one day a dose to ease the pain will ease me out of here instead."

"Shit."

"No, I'm ready. This is no fun. But here's the thing: Amie. I want her at my memorial."

No point in asking what that had to do with him, Robert got it. "Sure," meaning, why me?

"Really, you'd do this for me?" Then Robert heard bustling in the background, the faked cheerfulness of a nurse or Chris or somebody looking in. "I'll call you again, OK?"

Now Larry is dead. Now Robert is sitting on the plane sitting on the runway in a dinky Alaska fishing village looking at a shabby terminal that looks like something in a banana republic.

He's not allowed off the plane and finds himself standing in the galley in the tail whining to the flight attendant. "You must have been very close," she says.

Were they? Here's something he'd forgotten about, but it has shaken out of his brain, pushed out maybe by irritation alone. Larry had a nice car, very stylish notchback Plymouth Barracuda; Robert had an old beater Chevy station wagon. So when Larry wanted to go up in the mountains with Chris for a weekend, he asked to use Robert's car. Don't do it, man, all the guys told him. Let him take his own damned car. Some fire service roads would be involved. Robert can't remember if he knew this in advance, but it was pretty clear his car had been put through the wringer when it came back. And when Robert gave in, Larry promised he'd leave him the keys to his own car to use. But he didn't; he said he just forgot.

Robert has to fight down this upswell of ancient resentments, to resist his urge to simply bitch about his situation. How to say no to a dying man? There should have been a way. But he couldn't find it, and so here he is.

■ ■ ■

Robert grabs a cab at the airport and gives the guy the address. He's still in the clothes he slept in, but what can he do? He's surprised when the cab pulls up in front of a little log church. Must be Chris's choice. The cabbie says, "You're sure this is the place?" It's Robert's suitcase.

As he pushes open the door, a woman rushes out and past him. Inside, he slips into the back pew. People are making their way past the casket for one last look. All this way for not much of anything.

Chris is the only one he knows, and she does not look particularly glad to see him. Under the circumstances, why not? "You could have come sometime when he was alive; he would have enjoyed that," she tells him.

Yeah, well, Robert and Chris had never gotten along even back in college. But give her credit, she stuck with the guy. Larry could be a handful, loud, argumentative. A lawyer, a natural-born lawyer, probably a big shot of some kind based on the number of mourners. Did people call them that anymore? Mourners came to his parents' funerals. But who came to the memorials—not funerals—of friends his age? Hadn't we outgrown public displays of grief?

No graveside service, Larry will be whisked away and cremated. "Want to take a look?" The guy who asks the question looks like an old high school wrestler, wiry, knowing, combative stance even in a church.

He leads Robert up to the casket and they both peer in at Larry, much diminished, a waxen effigy of his former self. "Poor fucker," the guy says through a long sigh. "Would you be Robert, the guy from North Carolina?" Robert nods. The guy sticks out his hand, "Ted, Larry's law partner."

There's a reception sort of thing where Robert meets lots of people but can't keep their names straight. He'd just like to get in a hotel room and sleep. As he makes his way to the door, Ted catches up, "I think you know why you came."

If he needed somebody to blame, yes, Ted would be the one. Robert had looked up the cost of a short-notice ticket to Alaska. When Larry called back, he would have an excuse. But Larry never called. Ted did, and Ted had an answer, a mileage ticket. He had thousands of miles and Robert was welcome to the ticket. He was, after all, doing Larry— and Ted for that matter—a big favor.

"Look, I'm in this thing up to my neck. Legal stuff, executor of the will, all that. So all I can say is I'm grateful. You tried."

Robert waits; he feels like they are speaking in code.

"What Larry wanted to happen didn't happen, or not the way he wanted. There was some ugliness before the service and just now at the viewing. We could have used you. Be glad you missed it."

"I'm sure I am."

"But, listen, we're going down to the Gulkana in two days and scatter the ashes at this place Larry liked to fish. Come and go with us. At least it will make the trip worthwhile."

2.

The Gulkana is a river; Robert knows that now. And in this bug-infested campground are two massive "executive motor homes." This one is Ted's, and one slot over is Larry's.

Ted says the speculation is the son is gay. And the daughter is unable to hold any kind of steady job and lives with this guy who sells stereo equipment in a discount store. Neither arrived in Fairbanks until Larry was dead. That seemed to have been by mutual agreement.

Chris? "We were partners, but we didn't socialize much." And between his broad travelogue spewed out as they rolled down the twisting, nearly empty highway, Ted has told Robert his careful client-privileged version of Larry's life, a catalogue of cases won, cases lost, big fish caught, and bigger ones that broke off, a slew of animals shot and eaten, and a kind of crummy marriage to a brittle woman who hated Alaska the day she set foot in it. "Not so unusual," Ted says. "Happens all the time. What's different is she stayed. We had a Nordstrom in town then. Chris nearly bought the place out. Should have bought stock. Hell, Larry should have."

In the back, a couple of other pals have been playing a lazy game of cribbage, drinking a little, and laughing. Every now and then, one of them tunes in on the conversation going on in the massive swivel chairs, "Tell him about the moose that fell through the ice after he shot it."

"Later," Ted calls back. "So this Amie. Used to be with a *y*. The plan was for you to bring her to the service, but I'd been tracking your plane. I saw you missed your connection, so I told her she was on her own.

"Kind of a flake, what people used to call a free spirit. Teaches Pilates or yoga lessons, something like that. Lives in a dry cabin, lots of crystals hanging in the windows, cats. Great body for a woman her age, I'll give her that."

"And her age?"

"I don't know." He hollers over his shoulder, "How old? Amie? How old?"

"Forty, forty-five?"

At least, Robert thinks, she's not a kid. "Did she love him? Did he love her?"

Ted lets out a long hiss of air. "Robert, buddy, in the law game, you try not to ask questions when you don't need the answer."

■ ■ ■

It turns out Ted hasn't bothered to fill the water tank in the RV. No biggie. Robert volunteers to carry a plastic jerry can down to the campground pump.

As he passes a campsite, a woman wearing big sunglasses sitting on her table yells at him, "Hey, you," the way a person might hail a friend at a ball game.

"Hey, yourself."

"You're Rob. You were late."

"It's Robert." He sets down the jerry can and walks over. She's a slim woman, open smile, and gray roots showing in the part of her dark hair. Blue jeans and what looks to be a long underwear shirt. Braless, but maybe that's how they are up here. Behind her Robert can see a small tent and her banged up pickup truck. "Listen, Amie, I don't know," but before he can say what it is he doesn't know, she tells him.

"Those ashes? I'm going to be there. I've got as much right as she does. She's never even been down to the mouth. They can't stop me." Now the smile is gone, and her face takes on a look like a fierce little weasel.

Back at Ted's RV, the guys have adjourned outside and lit up cigars, their solution to the bug problem. It seems to be working. And in the middle of the table, a maroon plastic box about the size of a brick. "Larry. We thought he'd want to be part of this, so we went over to Chris's and got him."

Somebody starts in about Larry's famous Tabasco tie, but Robert breaks in, "Amie wants to be part of it too. She's camped about four places down."

"Shit. I'll handle this," and Ted pushes himself up. All of a sudden, he seems heavy and slow. The others are silent. "Leave it to her to fuck this up."

In the soft evening air, a sharp voice carries remarkably well. The men sit at their picnic table heads down as if they are being chewed out by a high school coach. Ted's lower voice is not as apparent. But the outcome is clear.

The problem, Ted explains, is, well, Amie is right, it is a free country—that old childhood rebellious cry. And, actually, some of the country in question isn't altogether free. To walk to the river mouth will involve trespassing on Native land. There was a sneaky element to this arrangement from the beginning, and as a result, there won't be much they can do if Amie trails along behind them. Which is her avowed intention.

What should have been a joyous meal of Ted's camp special of linguine with clam sauce turns into a collective mope. It was bad enough to have to put up with Chris and her sour kids, but now Amie on top of it. Tomorrow will be like Palestinians and Israelis, like Baptists and atheists, like whatever comparisons of hopeless situations they can come up with. No solution but to drink more whiskey.

Ted says, "Well, better get Larry back home. Don't want him to miss curfew. Coming with me?" he says to Robert. Robert understands he's going to have to start earning his mileage ticket. He picks up the plastic box and follows Ted.

Chris meets them at the door of her RV. "She's here, isn't she?" Ted drops his head. "Damn her, damn her. Why can't you tell her just to go away? Isn't there something legal you can do?"

Of course not. Chris knows as well as they do. "You're worthless, you know that? I'm getting a new lawyer when we get back to Fairbanks. "

"That would be best for all concerned," Ted says evenly.

"And Rob, why are you even here? We haven't heard a word from you in years. Why did you come here? What is it you want?"

It takes a while for Robert to get wound up; he doesn't think well on his feet, and the whiskey (he's drunk a bit, but not as much as the others) gives him an odd distance. Chris, her anger, her kids he can see through the big picture window slouched on the furniture, might as well be on television. When he begins to open his mouth, though, Ted says, "He's with us. He's my guest."

What could he have said? He is a man who finds himself in odd predicaments far too often. When a guy is inclined to withhold judgment, people tend to trust him. They take his silence for approval when it's really an increasingly rare form of bafflement. Everybody has strong opinions these days. Except for Robert.

"Well, why don't you at least meet the kids?" They are Lawrence, tall, surly, looking like he'd rather punch somebody out than offer his hand for shaking. And the daughter Nancy, so vague she seems not to be present at all. Like a couple of grade school kids, they mutter their helloes and would make their way back into the bowels of the RV, but Chris says, "Tell them, Rob, tell them something about their dad when you knew him."

The story that comes immediately to mind is one Robert would rather not remember himself, but it has imprinted itself on him over the years. They were in a room down the hall where the guys had a stereo and dynamite record collection. Robert was flipping through all their new albums, sampling tracks while Larry and three others were playing bridge around the corner of a bed. Suddenly, Larry jumped up and grabbed his partner by the shirt and hollered, "Why did you play the ten back there when you had the fucking three?" Cards flew and the other players pulled Larry and his partner apart. Robert edits his telling, "He was a serious card player, almost a photographic memory for what had been played."

"Cutthroat," Chris says. "They know that. They've seen that. He never learned to control himself. You ought to know that."

"Well, you never know. People do sometimes change."

"Generous of you to think so. Rob, I know you never liked me much, but Larry thought the world of you." Chris's eyes have narrowed to a squint, and Robert looks at her closely for the first time. She's still blonde, probably an expensive dye job, but her face has hardened and there are strong creases around her eyes. She's getting jowly around the mouth. Haggard. Blondes age that way, though. And who's to say what months with a dying man might do to a person?

Robert tries again, "He was very loyal." Not the best thing to say under the circumstances.

She talks right past him, "And I thought, I hoped, that by hanging out with you, with other guys like you, maybe something would rub off. I knew what I was getting into. I knew what Larry was, what he could do. I thought coming up here might be a fresh start. Ted and that crew . . . they're a pack of wolves, and Larry jumped in and ran with them. And you didn't do anything. You didn't even send a Christmas card."

What to say? Robert's own life has had its share of wrong turns and entanglements, not the kind of things he could wrap up in a chipper letter. For the first time Robert finds his impatience with the whole ordeal of his trip peeled away. "I'm sorry as I can be," and he means it.

Chris just sighs. "Rob, I come from good people, you know? I come from the kind of people who made their marriages work. When things got rough, you just drank a second old fashioned and soldiered on. That's what my mother did. That's what I did. But right now I don't think it was worth it."

"Well, I'm here now," meaning, he wants to think, to help.

"Oh, bullshit, Rob. Go on back to your new buddies and have another drink." Chris steps back up into her RV and the door shuts behind her with a mechanical whine.

What would he say if he knew Larry had tried a number of others before he got a yes from Robert, not exactly a *yes*, but a *sure*, a stutter step Robert had evolved as a way to buy time. Since he arrived, he has tried to piece together a version of the guy in the maroon plastic box that he can connect to the one he shared a room with for two years in college. This Larry: a woodsman, a skilled hunter. Or just a guy with a big mouth and lots of disposable income. The Alaska wild has not looked so wild from the panoramic windows of the RV. The roadside moose looked remarkably cow-like. How rough is roughing it in a vehicle that's better equipped than most people's houses?

■ ■ ■

While he's flipping pancakes on the gas stove in the RV, Ted is also looking a little frantically for an envelope containing the poem he plans to read down by the river when Larry's ashes are scattered. The others, all logy, all more than a little hungover, begin to flip through yesterday's paper, through a pile of old hunting and fishing magazines. Finally, the envelope spills out, office stationery, with the poem's title, "Ulysses," flowing across the creamy paper in Ted's secretary's flowery hand.

Ted slits the envelope and scans the poem. "Shit. This isn't it. That woman. . . ." But it is, it is "Ulysses" by Alfred, Lord Tennyson, the very poem he'd told his secretary to find on the Internet and print. He mumbles through the text as he slides the pancakes off the griddle, onto plates, and growls at the others: "Eat up, dammit. It's going to be a long day down there. Let's do this fucking right. Catch some kings, do Larry proud."

"Amen."

"Have fun."

"How about some aspirin with the coffee?"

The poem will have to do.

At eight o'clock sharp, the two RVs pull out of the campground, and as they pass a nearby site, a small blue pickup, already running at an idle, turns and follows behind.

There on the shoulder, the group makes to honor one of Larry's long-held beliefs, that their place is a closely held secret. The men and even Chris and her children race into the woods before anybody in a passing car might see them.

Robert says, "But the RVs? What do people driving by think is going on here?"

"Oh, hell, they think we all got kidnapped by space aliens, pulled up into the mother ship and examined. We'll get set back down beside the road this evening with some big fish in our packs as our thank-you."

"Hey," one of the guys says, "we're just walking here. No harm, no foul, right?" The little blue truck is nowhere to be seen.

Maybe it is the jostling walk along the trail, but something jogs Ted's brain, "Invictus," that's the poem he was thinking of. Now who the hell wrote it?

The men snigger over exchanges Robert can't hear, but he expects many of them are comments made at Chris's expense. Or the kids'. Or Amie's. Because it's at this point he realizes that she is trooping along twenty yards behind him.

Dozens of bug bites later, they arrive at the river mouth and slide down the cutbank to a narrow band of sand along the river. "Good thing it's a little low," Ted tells him.

Chris makes her way awkwardly; Lawrence is no help at all. Robert extends his arm, but she shrugs it away.

"Well," Ted says, "if nobody else has anything, I've got this little poem I'd like to read in Larry's honor—sort of gets at the heart of the guy."

"Ted, Larry couldn't care less about poetry," Chris says.

"It's the sentiment. You'll see." And he begins reading "Ulysses" in a lumbering sing-song. He should have practiced. But as he works his way to the end—it's a damned long poem—all that stuff about mariners and the setting sun and sailing out and not coming back, he develops a catch in his voice. Robert can see Larry's other buddies looking down and biting their lips while Lawrence and Nancy shoot glances at each other and roll their eyes.

At last Ted rolls up on the last line, "To strive, to seek, to find, and not to yield." Too bad it wasn't "Invictus"; it's much shorter.

Nobody utters a word until Chris says, "All right, then," and pulls the box of ashes from her shopping bag, opens them, and produces a small plastic scoop. One by one the friends and family dig into the ashes and sprinkle them onto the water.

Suddenly, there comes a high keening cry. Amie has positioned herself up on the bluff in a compact squat, arms folded over her knees, her eyes hidden behind her dark glasses.

"Damn her," Chris says. "The bitch. She looks like a harpy sitting up there." The cry goes on longer than anybody would think possible until Lawrence grabs the nearly empty box and flings it in Amie's direction. It spins off into the river and sinks.

"Hey, now," one of the friends says, "no need for that." Chris folds her bag, turns, and without saying anything more, struggles up the bank. Lawrence and Nancy smirk and follow. Ted hollers after them, "Just watch for the flagging back to the road and you'll be fine." The others are already putting their fishing rods together.

"Want to fish? We brought gear for you."

Robert snaps to; the guy is talking to him. "Me? I don't have a license."

"Won't matter down here."

"No, I don't fish." Then he sees Ted jerk his head toward the woods. Amie is slipping off her perch and heading off in the direction of Chris and family. Robert realizes what's expected of him and sets off behind her. "See you back in town," the others yell behind him. "Don't let a bear get you." Right. The men all wear side arms, he's noticed.

For a while, Amie follows the flagging through the woods, but then she abruptly breaks off and begins cutting to the right of the marked trail. Robert does all he can to keep her in sight. She strides comfortably along while he is sucking air and sweating through his shirt. Then he loses her.

There's nothing to do but walk on the approximate trajectory she seems headed. He begins to look for signs, disturbed leaves, snapped twigs, wishing he'd been a better Boy Scout. At last he hears cars on the road and makes for the sound. When he climbs up on the shoulder, he can see the RVs parked a few hundred yards to his left. Then he hears Amie's barking laugh not that far off on his right.

"Looking for something?" she asks him.

"Maybe a lift to town?"

"You don't want air-conditioned comfort?" She unlocks the passenger side door and says, "Get in before they eat you alive," and Robert thinks she probably means the bugs, but she may mean something else.

Amie flips down her tailgate, sits, and quickly slips out of her boots and into her Birkenstocks, throws her gear into the bed, and climbs into the truck. She allows her head to rest against the back window, closes her eyes, and drops her opened hands into her lap. She begins to breathe slowly, rhythmically. Robert is unsure how long she sits this way. He finds himself growing still so as not to disturb her, and wonders if she might have fallen asleep.

Her eyes snap open, she says, "OK, Rob—Robert—what can I do for you?"

"Drive, I guess."

Amie shifts her truck into four-wheel and climbs from the little hole in the woods where she's stashed it and up onto the roadway. For the first time, Robert notices the cracks running the length of the windshield. "That thing's not going to fall out is it?" Amie doesn't answer, just drops back into two-wheel and runs through the gears. Guess not. They ride along in silence, but the moose along the roadside seems bigger and more formidable, the breaks in the roadbed more jarringly pronounced, the brush more impenetrable. Lots of empty miles. At ground level, Alaska becomes more lonesome. A guy could get hurt out there.

Larry's giant RV with Lawrence at the wheel roars past, Chris in the copilot's chair, both looking stonily ahead. Amie's truck seems to rock in the backwash. "Same to you," she mutters. But they ride on in silence until Amie pulls off where some outhouses have been positioned along the same Gulkana River. "Pee break," she announces and disappears inside one of the cubicles. Robert climbs stiffly out. The walk—the hike—has been more than he was prepared for. Down below, the river opens into a rounded pool and in that pool are a dozen red salmon. He might wonder why they didn't stop here to fish. The fish don't seem intent on going anywhere, just schooling around. Still, he is transfixed and doesn't realize Amie has come up behind him. "Amazing," he says, "look at them. They don't even care if we're here."

"They're all spawned out," she tells him. "Swimming around waiting to die," but seeing the fish has opened something up in her. "Larry used to say you had to admire them. We stopped once farther downstream and had a little picnic by the river. You could see the fish working their way up. This river runs strong up here; they were working hard. 'Doing what they came here to do,' he'd say."

On that rambly phone call, Larry had told Robert he planned to wear a "Spawn Till You Die" T-shirt when laid out in his coffin. But there he was, laid out instead in a charcoal pinstriped suit.

That, Ted said, was Chris's doing. Larry had written long, detailed instructions for his memorial—songs to be sung, sung along to a karaoke machine, Grateful Dead songs, can you picture it? And testimonials. Champagne toasts, kegs of beer, and a big party. Nothing in or near a church. The air went out of that plan with Larry's last breath.

Did Amie know? "It wasn't going to happen. Anybody could have told him that." They climb back into the truck and drive, "I was a receptacle for his dreams. In a small way, you were, too, all you people he started calling there at the end."

"He said he would have married you if he hadn't gotten the cancer."

"Yeah, he needed to believe that. Chris had her claws into him pretty deep. She would have skinned him in the divorce, and he knew it. That's what he did, did to guys just like him."

The road has grown more twisty. "Did he love you?" It's a presumptuous question, but what the hell.

"Larry . . . you can ask a lot of people in Fairbanks about Larry, and they'll tell you he was a total asshole. When you got him away from those guys, those buddies, when we got out of town and came down this way just the two of us, he could be sweet. But, you know, what Larry needed to learn was how to love Larry. I thought I could help him."

"So you would have married him?"

"Me? I don't believe in marriage. Those fish back in the river, they're proof enough. That's all there is to it. You're married. Or have you been married?"

"No. Yes."

Robert sees her eyebrows shift above her sunglasses, her eyes swivel to glance into the mirror. "How many times?"

"Twice."

She allows a slight smile, "And whose idea was it to get out?"

"One each, I guess."

"So you can see, it's not that hard to do, is it? I mean you pledge your troth and all that, and then a day comes, when, what is it? The sound of her voice, out of coffee filters, the empty gas tank in the car? Just excuses. You know . . . it's just over, it's done. If you never got married, you don't have to bother with the paperwork. You just go.

"Larry and Chris. They knew. It was over a long time before I ever came on the scene. They had this sick little compact to torture each other, always a got-you-last thing. Like little kids. Lots of fights about money. Trying to outspend the other. Chris, she's probably going to be hurting for cash real soon. I kind of feel for her."

"And what about you?"

"I never took a dime from Larry. Whatever those guys told you, I'm a licensed massage therapist . . . emphasis on therapist. I probably should have been a shrink. Half the job is listening to people's problems. I should charge like a shrink."

"Is that how it happened?"

"Larry came to me to get some relief, just some relief from the misery. I would start working on him, loosening him up, and he'd just start bawling. I have this power, this power in my hands. I sense things through them. I can tell where it hurts—in your back, in your shoulders. With Larry it was all over. He just glowed with pain. I'd never felt anything like it."

"Wow," Robert says and pictures the crystals hanging in her windows.

"I told him, 'Sit up, look at me. Tell me what's going on with you.'"

"You do that?"

"No. Usually not. But I could tell this was a desperate situation. He was dying; he knew it. He was scared. . . . It was a mistake. I broke my own rules." She looks like she might break down a little, but she grips the steering wheel harder and goes on. "We had fun, small eff fun, fishing on small water, camping, cooking our fish on the grill. He was a good cook. He liked to cook. Which is good—was good—because I don't. We'd go in my truck, sleep in my tent, not in that monster thing you saw."

"And Chris? She knew?"

"I wasn't the first one. Larry told me that. But this was different. His need . . . maybe that was the difference. She was afraid she was going to lose him this time, and I used to wonder why. I mean, he was going to die anyway. And what was left to lose?"

"Yeah," Robert says. That's it, isn't it? To live this long and to have so little to show for it. So little left.

"But I've got to wonder, Robert, why you're here. I mean Larry wanted you to come because he wanted to protect me from Chris. And Ted wanted to protect Chris from me. But Larry's dead. He's dead. What happened happened. So why did you come?"

There's not a good answer. He tells Amie, "I guess I felt like I owed him something."

When they were sophomores, Robert got this girl pregnant. Larry found a doctor who'd take care of it. Across two state lines, two nights in a seedy motor court, and the deed was done. By the time they got back to campus, Robert and the girl hated the sight of each other. When she went up the steps to her dorm, he knew they'd do all they could not to cross paths again.

Larry lay on his bed reading a novel—Robert thought it might have been *Portnoy's Complaint*—when he walked in and dropped onto his bed.

"So?"

"It's done."

"You owe me one," Larry said without looking up.

"It's a little late." But he doesn't need Amie to tell him.

A better answer is, he couldn't say no. But Robert says, "I wanted to see maybe how he'd changed over forty years."

"That's simple. For thirty-nine years or whatever, I'd guess he probably didn't change a bit. The diagnosis did it. That changed everything."

3.

This place is Amie's idea, this crowded Thai place with a line out the door. They've stopped at the convenience store around the corner for beer. You can bring your own here. Robert had proposed the place in the hotel where he's staying, but Amie thinks—rightly—there'd be too many of Larry's friends—and enemies—there. This place on her side of town is better. College kids and old hippies.

After they get a table, women slip up to Amie. Some just touch her on the shoulder, some hug, and others ask, "OK?" She nods, but the hurt is plain. Now he can see it in her face.

For all that long drive, Robert has not really looked closely at her.

Sitting across from her, he sees her blue eyes. They're oceanic; a person could swim out into them and maybe never come back. Her hands with their long bony fingers splayed across the little Formica table do seem to suggest a certain power. No wonder people give her their secrets. She has been telling him about a hidden room in Larry's house—a room she has never seen of course, but one he's told her about—the room where he keeps—kept—his gun collection, valuable coins, some gold.

Robert drinks his first beer quickly; he's tired and feels weak all over. Probably dehydrated too. The ride has been harder on him than any other part of the trip. This Amie has pried the lid off. Lots of things he'd rather not think about, he'd even forgotten about, have come spilling into his thoughts.

"I think we all have such a room," Robert tells her, "metaphorically speaking."

"Probably. But hidden rooms are just that. You don't want to let just anybody in your hidden room. You don't even want most people to know there is one."

"But we all have one.

"Not everybody. Everybody hides stuff, if that's what you mean, but most people don't think much. They might go their whole lives and not know it's there, never know where they put it, never bother to look inside. At least that's my experience."

"And Larry?"

"Yeah, maybe he was like that. When he stumbled into his room, everything in there came puking out. Not a nice way to put it, but that's how it was."

Robert has felt a growing urge to confess to her, to lay bare memories he's carried around for decades. That abortion, for example. Though the girl, and up to this minute, Robert himself seemed to have felt little remorse. He says, "Maybe I'm that way."

"You're not." She's scowling. "There's too much space between what you say and what you're thinking."

Would this be an insult, a challenge, or what? But he catches himself up short; that's just what she means. Can he find an answer that's not an evasion? He says, "I'd like to see where you live."

"Why? So you can see how many cats I have and whether I really have tie-dyed curtains?"

"No. That's not it. No. It's nothing. Forget I asked." He's aware he's already had three beers. "But can I ask this: Did you love Larry?"

"I did. I thought I knew what I was getting into. I thought it wouldn't cost me much since he was dying anyway. It did. It cost a lot. And that's why it hurt so much when Chris shut me out." Now she is crying, tears running out of her eyes squeezed shut. She doesn't sob, doesn't hyperventilate, doesn't do anything that would cause anybody to look their way. She dabs her tears away with her napkin, "I could have helped him at the end. I could have soothed away his fear."

Amie has hardly eaten anything at all. She says, "I've got to get out of here," and asks the waitress for a go box. "Come on, I'll take you back to your hotel." She smiles a slight smile, "But first let me show you my place."

∎ ∎ ∎

The cabin is spare and neat. There is one cat, a slinking black presence named Elvis Peacock. And no tie-dye to be seen. Prints, maybe those are the very mountains they drove through today, hang on the walls, ceramic vases and bowls carefully placed on the counters and tables, a small couch under the window with a throw made of some Indian fabric—the only hippie element, Robert thinks. Well, maybe the candles in the windowsill. Many books and a compact stereo—all orderly arranged on shelves. A rocking chair, clearly handmade, but behind it a high-intensity reading lamp. Her bed must be up the narrow stair to the loft. The place is daunting, self-contained.

In one corner are two silver fishing rod tubes of the type Robert has seen Ted and his buddies carry to the river ages ago this morning.

"Yeah," Amie says, "Larry gave me those. I took them; they were the one thing I thought would hold him close."

When he gave them to her, the last little time they had together, Larry told her the two rods and the reels were worth more than her truck. Even then, could he not see the measure of their value was not in what they cost, but in how much they might mean? Amie had hoped she showed him how to look at the world differently, how to see himself in it differently.

"And did you?"

"Who can know."

She has not invited him to sit. She has not offered to open the two beers they carried away from the Thai place.

"So where's your massage table?"

"In my office, of course. House—office: two different things. It's in a building near the university I share with a dentist and an acupuncturist. This is my home, my sanctuary." She pauses, but only briefly, "OK. You've seen it; you got your treat. Let's go."

There's a kid-who-got-no-Christmas look on his face.

"You were coming on to me back at the restaurant."

"No."

"Yeah, you were. Not like some redneck guy backing a girl up against the side of his pickup. A wimpy kind of come on, a 'save me, save me' little squeak oozing out around your words. . . . You thought we would come up here and fall into each other's arms and go to bed and fuck through our shared sorrow and come out the other side all better. And who knows? Maybe I would even want to follow you down to Carolina or Virginia or wherever you're from. . . . You don't have a clue. I would drown you in my sorrow."

"No," he says again, but he doesn't say anything else. There is more than a little truth to what she says. But there is more to it than that. He has been made—provoked—to feel this terrible need. Not as great as Larry's might have been. An opened hole in the world and he can't see the bottom.

Again she says, "Let's go." And they go. Down the hill from her cabin to the town lying in the dusky not-night.

"Thank you, Amie," he says when they pull up at the hotel door.

"You'll be all right," she tells him, reaches over, and pulls the passenger side door closed behind him.

In his room, Robert looks out his window at a misshapen town of mismatched buildings, still a little stunned. Amie's words stung sharp as a slap. If he could, he'd say to Larry, thanks for nothing. Except it wasn't by accident that Robert had bumped up against Amie's love for the guy. Maybe he had it coming.

He considers that Ted had loved Larry, too, in his ol' boy towel-flipping way. So had Chris, at least for a time. There must have been something to the guy. But Larry, well, Robert sees he never really knew him even when they were roommates.

He takes his suit he never had an opportunity to wear off its hanger and folds it into his suitcase, slips his still-muddy running shoes into the hotel's plastic laundry bag and packs them too. He takes a shower and changes.

Robert finds himself considering a Chris version, a Ted version, an Amie version—all Larrys competing with each other to be the actual Larry that Robert might carry home on the plane. And the actual Robert? That's another matter.

He goes downstairs to the desk clerk and tells her he'll be leaving early in the morning and he'd like to settle his bill now. She checks his room number in the computer and says, "Everything is taken care of. You're set." Ted's doing. "Did you enjoy your visit to Alaska?"

He might as well be polite. "Yes, I did. Mostly. I was hoping to see the northern lights, but I guess they're not out in the summer."

"Oh, they're always up there. You just can't see them."

THE DISCOVERY PROCESS

When I came to this town, I wondered if people would know me. When I walked down the street, I wanted to think they remembered, that they knew me as one of their own, or almost one of them. It turned out some of them had. It had gotten to be a dumpy place. The Western Auto was gone and the little ladies' wear store. One bigger place, a department store, had been cut up into small antique booths. Another sold used clothing, all piled up on tables for customers to fork through.

We called our place an office, but really it was an old storefront too. Once it had been a dime store, then a place that sold well-used appliances and other household odds and ends. There were three of us and a hand-painted sign in the window, Legal Aid of Southwest Virginia.

My desk was a great steel hulk, olive drab, army surplus maybe, with the Formica starting to peel away from the metal underneath it. I had no computer but an electric typewriter instead with coal dirt worn into the once-white keys. Coal dirt was everywhere here, though coal had not been mined nearby for almost twenty years. I loved our office. Its rough-and-ready appearance said we meant business; we were here to do justice.

A person who knows me now might wonder where I got such a notion. There is this: my brother and I getting home from basketball practice, and before our parents came home from closing our grocery store, flopping onto the couch and watching bad television, *Roller Derby* featuring the Bay Area Bombers, reruns of *Superman* and *Perry Mason*. Perry was two kinds of good lawyer, wasn't he? He was good, and he was good. Square-jawed, stern, he was always fighting for truth and justice and the American way, no different from the other guy. We made fun of them all.

And this: two women from my law school class—Pam and Marcia, do-gooders, people would have called them when I was a kid, people who came back into the hills to save us from the mine operators, from environmental degradation, and mostly from ourselves—it was their idea.

Pam, funny, always ironic. We joked around, me doing my best George Reeves as Superman, "Are you all right, Miss Lane?" Pam as Lois, "Thanks to you, Superman." What did we think we were after? Was it truth, justice, or the American way? It made Marcia furious. Goodness was nothing to laugh at. It was something to work at. Yeah, I would agree, just to keep the peace. Still, there was something genuine in Pam, I believed. Why else had she come here? She just needed to keep it hidden.

People probably called the three of us do-gooders, just not where I could hear them. I had not grown up in this town, but two ridges over. Close enough. The women thought I would be their ticket.

I wonder if I could have explained why it wouldn't work that way before I sat at my desk and waited for the phone to ring, for the little bell over the door to jingle. It seemed like I had forgotten what hillbillies were like: stubborn, suspicious of strangers, inclined to hold grudges. I was a hillbilly myself.

I thought if I was a legal aid lawyer, I should dress the part: khaki pants, work pants really—I was proud of my Dickies—button-down shirt, sleeves rolled up, tie loosened at my neck. On the back of the door I hung a couple of worn sports coats and a blue blazer to throw on when I strode across the street and into the county courthouse.

This guy Henry would come in once or twice a week. He had been our first serious client. We had tried to get him a claim against Island Creek Coal for an old back injury and failed, of course. But he forgave us. And I guess we forgave him too. It turns out his version was filled with invention and embellishment. I was a sucker; I fell for it. Now he brought in things for sale: A cheap pistol, whiskey bottles in the shape of Elvis, or old cars, or locomotives. "They're worth more with the liquor still in them," he told us, "but they're still worth something." Maybe Pam bought something from him once.

Henry only matters because when we took his case, we got a visit from Wiley Crawford, the commonwealth's attorney. Or I got a visit, since Henry was my case. When I came out here on a scouting mission for our practice, I found this building and did most of the work cutting it up into offices myself, making dividers out of two-by-fours and cheap sheets of fake pecan paneling. Flimsy hollow-core doors, hung crooked, gave us the illusion of privacy since the walls were just eight feet high and the ceiling another twelve above us. That way when the phone rang, a person could just yell over the wall, "Can somebody get that? I'm busy."

When we set up shop, we had made a reception area in the front by the big plate glass windows, outfitted it with an old schoolteacher's desk painted gray, a vase full of artificial flowers, some framed photographs of rows of full coal cars lined up under tipples, miners coming from work—a way of saying we knew what our clients had come from. We'd briefly hired a receptionist but had to let her go.

Wiley Crawford just walked right in, let himself in the front door, looked into the open door of my office and when he saw it was me, threw the door shut and dropped himself into the empty chair. The wall swayed behind him. I knew who he was; he obviously knew who we were, but we'd not met. Probably this was a wrong thing, bad manners at least. We were the new folks, I thought, so he should make us welcome. We had different but necessary roles to play before the law.

He probably thought we'd entered his domain, and we ought to pay him court. "I'm not going to fart around," he told me. "Why are you taking Henry Blankenship's case?"

I started laying out what I saw as the facts of the matter: Henry's long-running fight to get Island Creek to pay up for what amounted to a lifelong disability.

"Bad back he told you?"

"Yeah," I said.

"Son, if Henry Blankenship ever got a back injury, he got it falling off a bar stool. Listen, I'm here to do you a favor. Don't mess with that guy. Don't take that case. You're just going to look silly if you do."

Wiley Crawford had been the commonwealth's attorney over here since before I was in high school. I looked at Wiley Crawford, his florid face, messy yellow-gray hair, tie with stains I could see from four feet away, and a belly that would never let that coat be buttoned. People claimed he was in the coal operators' pocket. I was inclined to believe them; right then it was necessary for me to believe them. If we were good guys, there had to be bad guys. Wiley looked the part. ("Truth, justice, and the American way!" Pam would sometimes shout at me over the wall as a client exited the office.)

Then he surprised me. "You don't think I know you, but I do. I re-member you; I remember that ball team you played on. Damned good team. You boys got hoodooed out of the district championship right over in that gym," he said meaning the local high school.

We had been hoodooed. My dad had used the very same word the next morning. I had not forgotten; I'm ashamed to say I thought about it more than often passing by the school building. We might have been state champions. Maybe this is the time to own up to my former self, the kid who could get through law school still thinking the world could be neatly divided between good guys and bad guys, who believed that when left to their own devices ordinary people would do right most of the time. The law was there to protect them from getting run over. Just like Perry Mason, our other rerun TV hero. In the nick of time, Paul Drake would drive back from Bakersfield with the exculpatory evidence.

In truth, winning a basketball game would have changed nothing about how my life spooled out from there, how I came to this place. Sometimes it's not what you think you know, though, is it?

It was a civil case; Wiley Crawford had nothing to do with it. The day of the trial, Henry came to court with whiskey on his breath. His chiropractor, my star witness, didn't show. The lawyers from Island

Creek tore me to pieces. They came in with file folders an inch thick, filled with their very substantial and factually supported version of Henry. They even had x-rays to pass around to the jurors with affidavits from doctors to back them up. On my way out of the courthouse, Wiley poked his head out of his office and declared I was a dumbass. I just looked at him.

"Aw, hell, forget about it. Let me buy you a beer." I told him no.

That was then.

Maybe Pam still has whatever it was she bought—a whiskey bottle, an old movie poster, a baseball with a blurred autograph Henry claimed was Lefty Grove's. I get a Christmas card from her every year, always the same: Her family, the two boys getting bigger every year, standing out in front of a colonial-style house. She's with a powerhouse firm in Richmond these days; one of their clients is a tobacco company. That's enough information for me to be able to picture her furniture, the cars in her garage, the CDs scattered on top of her entertainment center. Over the years she has written, "Love you," "Keep in touch," "Hope you're well." I've not written back.

Business was slow. It wasn't what we had in mind. It wasn't what Marcia had in mind. Marcia was an only child in a well-off family. She was from Northern Virginia, and her first trip out to the coalfields was with me. "Oh my God," she told me again and again looking at the slate dumps, abandoned tipples, disused appliances and cars pushed over creek banks—creek banks with sewage pipes coming straight out from them and dumping into the coal black creeks below. "Oh my God."

Here was a woman looking for a cause where she could unburden her weird sense of guilt at having been born lucky, and here was the cause.

Marcia: I do know more about her, a glowing little hot stove. I feel the heat from her righteous anger wherever she might be.

Probably Wiley Crawford was right. Representing Henry had been a mistake; letting him come around the office was another one. Was it that people didn't trust us, or had we become a joke? Because people in this town will do you that way, make fun of you behind your back, smile at your face. So you might be in the town but not of it.

One day the bell on the outside door jingled, but before I could get up to pull receptionist duty, here was this hillbilly standing in my doorway—wiry and taut, full of a ferocity trying to find its way out. I supposed he was looking to sue somebody. He wore a snap-button shirt and blue jeans, a pair of discount store running shoes. I estimated he was my age or not much younger. With this type, you never can tell.

He looked at me carefully, silently.

"Do I know you?" I'm a tall guy; people complain that I loom over them. I caught myself leaning forward, anticipating some movement as if he might run at me.

"You know me," he said.

"I know you?" I said acting like I was processing this information, acting like somewhere in my head I was looking for a memory of him. I was glad for our eight-foot-tall walls. Back beyond us, Marcia and Pam were tuned in to this exchange.

"Tom Tabor. Tommy Tabor. They called me Sputnik."

"Yes," I said, "I do know you."

"Yeah," he said, and he turned around and left.

"What was that about?" Pam asked over the partition.

Up the old wagon road that ran up the valley, right on the uphill side of a steep curve, a house sat on stilts with a rough garage underneath. Polly Tabor lived in it then, rented it from Shorty Johnson. She was what my folks called a good customer, which meant she made big orders and paid her ticket in cash on delivery. Somewhere in the world she had a husband, I guess, but in the black ledger where my mom kept accounts, Polly Tabor was Polly Tabor.

Saturday mornings, she would have an order big enough to fill the bed of our pickup by itself. My dad and I would run it up to her house. "Polly-wolly-doodle," he would sing out when we went through the door. He had jokes and nicknames for all his favorite customers. Then, while I carried the boxes of groceries in and unloaded them onto her kitchen table, my dad and Polly Tabor would talk. Getting our boxes back was important; there would be other orders to fill throughout the day, throughout the rest of the coming week until the wholesalers delivered again. Big boxes like what soap powders—detergent—came in were especially valuable. Polly Tabor's order would fill several of those.

Meanwhile, her kids milled around the table picking at the bags of candy and cereal like Cocoa Puffs that my mom would not let my brother and me have. There were maybe four or five of them, Sputnik among them, the oldest. He must have been born in the Sputnik year; by then he must have been nine, maybe ten, a tow-headed kid, who like all of Polly Tabor's kids, never spoke a word.

Her house was neat as a pin, the kitchen table all emptied off to receive her groceries, her sink shiny white and her dish drain empty. Little rag rugs sat in front of the door, in front of the sink. This was different from other houses where dirty kids were running around half naked, where their moms' scabby legs stuck out from under baggy housedresses. I did my best not to track in any dirt on the scrubbed linoleum.

As soon as I put them on the table, Polly Tabor took a pack of Salems out of the carton she'd ordered, packed them against the kitchen counter like a man would, took a cigarette out, and lit it. While she smoked, she kept on talking a blue streak to my dad. People were always talking to my dad like that. My father was a much-loved man in our town. In his day, he had not been a sports star at the high school. He was not a civic leader or active in our church. He was a patient man, patient with his children, his customers, his help. The only times he lost his temper with me were when I dropped a good customer's watermelon on the third of July and he had none left to replace it, and when he tried to teach me how to drive. It was the clutch. We owned a car and a pickup truck for deliveries, and both had stiff clutches. I just could not get the hang of the clutch.

What my father did was listen. People simply allowed themselves to go around the meat case and into the butcher shop where they boasted about their kids' accomplishments, whined about their aches and pains, aired their grudges against their families or the members of their church. My father never gave any advice as far as I know. He just listened, and he knew to keep things to himself.

Polly wore a man's flannel shirt with a couple of buttons undone, neat blue jeans, and Keds with worn spots where her big toes were trying to poke through. And glasses, glasses that made it feel like when she was looking at me she was really seeing me. The skin on her chest was still a little tanned from summer sun, and it made me think of bread just out of the oven, warm and comforting.

After a while, clients began to present themselves. A man wanted to sue his neighbor for shooting his dog. The next day the neighbor wanted to sue the same man for letting his dog maul one of his sheep. Women came seeking help getting child support or alimony out of men who'd left for parts unknown or else were living right down the road, laid off and out of work indefinitely. A man wanted to sue for falling off a porch rail at somebody's house when it turned out he was drunk off his ass at the time.

We became a kind of counseling service. People would come in, we would listen, and the best we could often do was to try to get both parties together and patch things up out of court. I believe there are daytime TV shows that handle that kind of thing today.

If we had come here with a sense of purpose in mind, this wasn't it. And maybe I'd gone along just to be agreeable. My dad had shown me the value of being agreeable. In Marcia's eyes, though, I was a project. Or maybe a cause. I'd been a scholarship basketball player at a second-, maybe third-tier liberal arts college where I'd sat the bench and studied little. I didn't have to. Suddenly at law school I did, and I didn't know how. Law school, for a boy whose mother had expected him to be a preacher, was a fallback. The least I might do would be to try to go out into the world and right some wrongs. My parents' store had never been a big money-maker, but that was all right. Our family had money enough, and I grew up understanding there had to be more to life than that.

Pam and Marcia, roommates, took me in. I had a room in a house in town full of undergraduates, guys who drank, smoked dope, and threw open their windows when things got too much for them and hollered, "Fuck this shit," out into the world whether it had to do with midterms, or no girls, or running out of beer. The women and I were all in the same first-year curriculum, struggling with constitutional law and legal writing, so we pooled our efforts and studied together. When the hour grew late, I crashed on their couch.

We law students would not run out of beer; we could go to Graduate Happy Hour every Friday afternoon, sponsored by the ROTC department in hopes of luring us into the army. Fat chance. Pam went home for a weekend; Marcia and I got a little buzzed. You can guess the rest.

When she came back, Pam knew in the way women know things. Or maybe she and Marcia had planned it out beforehand. Marcia was a sturdy, determined woman, captain of her all-women's college field hockey team. She told me once she'd pulled an earring out of an opponent's ear in a particularly intense game. When she told this story, I found it hard to judge whether she'd meant to or not. Regardless, she wasn't exactly sorry. I liked her; I admired her spunk. I admired her sense of purpose. Pam was the pretty one, the funny one.

When I slipped down the street for some lunch I saw Wiley Crawford sitting at the counter with two chili dogs and a mess of French fries on his plate. I would rather he'd not seen me, but too late. "Hey, you arrive at a just and peaceable resolution of the crime of the century? That dog-shooting, sheep-killing massacre?" I knew now. He was sending us those hopeless cases. "You're wanting some clients. I'm trying to help."

I told him no thanks.

"Come on. I been listening to that kind of bullshit more years than I can count. People don't know the difference between criminal and civil law, think I'm like Matt Dillon or some such, going to set things right, want me to string somebody up just to get even. You mess with them awhile." I didn't mean to laugh. "Haw! That's right, might as well see the humor in it." I carried our sandwiches back in a bag and told the women.

"So what," Marcia said. "We're doing something good here. It may not be exactly what we imagined, but we're disrupting the status quo. We're helping people think differently."

Pam wasn't so sure, and besides she was getting tired of eating grilled cheese sandwiches for lunch. Truth and justice took on a sharper ironic edge by the day.

This much was sure, we were disrupting the status quo. To begin with Marcia and I had rented an old farmhouse in the country, Pam took a little apartment in town. But since we were so short of income, we agreed she should let the apartment go and move into one of our extra rooms.

Henry Blankenship sidled into my office and invited me outside to take a peek at a very special item he had in the trunk of his car. And it was, an old brass lantern from the N&W railroad. I could only think about how it would look if I were found to be receiving stolen goods, so I declined. "Listen, then, tell me this: You putting it to both them ladies like they're talking around?"

"No. Absolutely not. I'm married to one of them."

"Which one?"

"Marcia."

"Oh, well," he said, and laughed a little, "too bad."

Marcia and I got married the week after we graduated from law school. Of all the things to explain, this is the hardest. Here are some reasons: My mother. This place. That time. Respectable people got married. Trashy people shacked up in trailer courts. Yes, Marcia and I had been sleeping together, living together for the better part of law school. A university town and this place might as well have been on two different planets.

At some point after I had gone away to college, my parents' marriage stiffened. There was no joy in their household. Maybe the pleasure they took in my brother and me and our ball playing and good grades was all there had been to it. My father seemed smaller, more turned inward. He had always been one to hug the pretty women, to slap the men on the back. He was a kidder, but gentle in his kidding.

One day he disappeared. That is to say, my mother looked back to the butcher shop where he had been cutting some pork chops and he was gone. Gone, dead on the floor, dead of a heart attack and still in his fifties. My mom quickly closed the store and withdrew from the town, coming out only for church and the bookmobile. She must have read a murder mystery a day, and I have to wonder what that could do to a person's mind, that protracted study of the various methods of snuffing out a life. But in that world the guilty were always guilty.

I'm not sure Marcia, being Marcia, believed in marriage. After I studied law in the Commonwealth of Virginia, I understood her position. Virginia wasn't very forward looking in lots of ways. Still isn't. Beyond seeing the necessity of it, I'm not sure I believed in marriage either. If we were to practice law in this town, if we were to do some good, our marriage had to happen.

Pam said she wasn't sure, were we doing something good, or nothing at all? I had forgotten how hard hillbillies could be on strangers. Pam and Marcia were young and well-dressed. Sometimes they wore dresses and skirts, but they wore pantsuits, too, even to court, though it was clear certain judges didn't like that. They complained that people looked at them funny, looked into their carts at the grocery store to see what they were buying, watched to see if they went in the liquor store. Marcia wore her hair in one long thick braid down her back and Pam let her long curly hair fall free. Hippies, people probably thought, just scrubbed up a little.

Wiley Crawford was as bad as Henry Blankenship in thinking he could just walk into my office and take a chair. He would lean back and look around at the pictures on the walls of the tipples and coal cars. "Not a one of those buildings is standing today, you know that?" I told him I did. "Kind of makes you think," he paused a little, "kind of makes *me* think, why in the hell did you come back in here? This whole country's emptied out. Anybody with any sense is long gone." Those days, I had no good answer.

He studied my framed diploma. "You got that high tone degree and brought it back here. I just don't see it." I sat there quietly thinking he would go away. "Hey," he said, "ever try that barbeque place out on the highway?"

Riding in his car, a fifteen-year-old Chrysler New Yorker, ashtray full of butts spilling out into the floorboards, he started in as we drove past the high school, "Oh, yeah, I remember that ball game you all lost like it was yesterday. You didn't foul that boy, you know the one I mean, right there at the end, did you?"

I told him most ball players didn't believe they'd committed half the fouls they'd been called for.

"But that one. That one they called blocking on you when everybody could see it was a charge."

"No," I said, "I didn't make that one."

"I lost a pretty piece of money on that game."

"Sorry."

"No need to apologize to me. That's the trouble with you, with all you kids in that office, you want to be sorry for something you never even done." I didn't answer that. We rode along a little farther, and Wiley said, "Aw shit, you'll learn." Then he said, "That game was rigged, you know. That wasn't a standard-issue bad call; that was a bought and paid for bad call."

I watched Wiley Crawford polish off a plate of pulled pork, hush puppies, and fries plus a piece of pecan pie. I didn't have much appetite myself. It had never occurred to me the game had been fixed.

That evening I could not tell Marcia and Pam. That bubble was popped, and I didn't need a smart-mouthed comment from Pam for confirmation. I didn't remember much about that ball game except the last call, the call that went against me, the call that lead to the free throws that lost the game for us. What I did remember was that we had a hard time finding our rhythm that night, that every time we seemed to get rolling, somebody would be called for traveling or for being in the lane. We stuttered along; but we were the better team by far. I didn't doubt that. We just couldn't shake them. When it came down to the end, it was my foul, my fault.

As for the refs, I always thought the refs were our friends. Playing hillbilly basketball could be a rough way to go. Gyms were crowded and hot. Sometimes you couldn't hear a teammate ten feet from you yelling for the ball. People jeered, hollered out threats, threw rocks at our bus after we won, chased us in their cars as we tried to drive away. Through all that, I always thought the refs were there to keep things fair, to protect us if it came to that.

If Wiley Crawford could have read my mind, he would have said something he'd said a dozen times to me already, "How could a bunch like you all go to a highfalutin law school, must be some kind of smart, but be so damned dumb?"

In my case maybe it was hereditary. My father saw the good in everybody. Sometimes a guy would lurk around the sidewalk until he was sure my mom was out of the store and slip in. He'd pick up a few groceries, stack them on the counter, and then as my dad was toting up his bill, ask for credit. There was always a hard luck story to follow, laid off, broke-down car, sick kid. My dad would give him the yellow copy of the ticket and spike the other on the nail beside the register.

That night when my mom did the books she would find it, have a fit. Probably there was still an unpaid balance from last time. "Cash and carry," she told us. "One day I'm going to put up a sign."

After his death, after the funeral when everybody had gone home and Marcia, my mom, my brother, and I were left to nibble off the ham and macaroni salad and all the cakes and pies that'd been left us—for in the hills food remains the surest way to express your love—my mom said sourly, "Your father was a terrible businessman."

I remember a Christmas Eve when a good customer's order spilled off the counter, took several detergent boxes to fill, and I was moving as fast as I could to fill them and carry them to the trunk of her waiting car. My dad came by, reached up to the top of the produce rack, and brought down a huge box of candy and stuck it in her order. When she protested, my dad said, "No, no that's for you, that's yours. Merry Christmas."

Later my mom said, "There went your profit on that order."

And he said, "We weren't going to sell it anyway. What did it hurt?"

Really, what had it hurt?

■ ■ ■

Before a case goes to court, you do a little dance with the other side, the discovery process. It's kind of like playing Go Fish. The defendant asks the plaintiff if he has any information on this or that aspect of the case. And if he does, the plaintiff is supposed to say so and show what he has. And if he doesn't, he kind of says, "Go fish," go out there and see what you can find out yourself. When the lawyers from Island Creek didn't come around asking, I thought they knew they had no case. What I couldn't figure out was why they didn't offer to settle. A little like that ball game. I thought I knew what I knew, but I had no clue.

I had seen Sputnik from time to time, maybe coming out of what used to be the Western Auto or the pool room, or standing on the street jawing with his buddies, other out-of-work miners, I guessed. When he saw me, he made a point of shooting a stream of tobacco juice onto the sidewalk. Then one day, he turned to face me as I walked toward him, as if standing in to take a charge. "Momma says she wants you to come see her."

I was not shocked that Polly Tabor was alive. Probably she was not much more than fifteen or twenty years older than I was. But I had not thought of her as present in this place and time. I had kept her under a kind of house arrest in her place on stilts up the old wagon road when in fact I knew she had disappeared from there years ago. One weekend we'd delivered the usual big order, the next the house stood empty as we passed it on our way to the row of company houses farther along.

I didn't see how I could tell Sputnik no.

I followed him in his ragged old Camaro out the highway until we turned onto a slick clay farm road. A guy could high center if he didn't watch himself. I tried to stay in Sputnik's tracks as his car jounced from side to side, riding the high spots and avoiding the ruts. We passed into a grove of trees, and there sat two other vintage Camaros stripped of parts, a doghouse made from scrap plywood, rusty barrels, and other assorted junk. Across a yard pounded to dirt, a turquoise and white house trailer poked out of the scrub pines.

I parked so my car pointed back toward the hardtop and followed Sputnik into the house. It was dark and smelled of dirty clothes and cigarettes. Polly Tabor sat in a recliner with an oxygen tank beside her, the clear plastic tube running up behind her head and splitting off to come round and stick in her nostrils.

"Come on in, honey," she said just as she had said when I appeared at her door with the first box of groceries. I stood in the doorway there, feeling my hair just brushing the door frame. "Good lord, you're tall. Are you the big one or the little one?"

I knew what she meant. Though my brother is a powerfully built man, in the world of our parents' old customers I will always be the big one, he the little one.

"Sit down." She told me. "Tommy, clear your junk off that couch so the man can sit." His junk looked to be the many pieces of a tape deck that might fit in a car's dashboard. He pushed it all to one side, and I sat.

Polly Tabor looked at me, her glasses thicker than I remembered, looked at me like she was searching for something that might pain her if she found it. "You look just like your daddy." I had been told that before. I always took it as a compliment. I told her my father was dead, that the store had closed sometime back. She knew that, she said, "I seen it in the paper." But she had not been among the many people at his funeral service.

"I don't get out much," she told me, guessing what I was thinking. I told her there was no need to apologize. We sat. A game show ran on the TV with the sound down. A dog came from somewhere back in the trailer and wanted out. Sputnik got up and led the dog to the door, went out with it, and sat on the stoop smoking.

She was waiting for this. "I loved your daddy," she told me.

"Everybody loved my dad."

"No, I mean he loved me too. He loved me back."

I'm not sure what I could have said besides, "Oh." Maybe, that's not true. Maybe, I don't believe you. Because I didn't.

"You just don't know." But before she could say anything more she began to cry and then broke into a ragged cough. "Get him," she said. Sputnik was already coming back inside. He gave her something, maybe some kind of medicine, maybe a sip of whiskey. "Help me up." Sputnik turned off the oxygen bottle and undid her plastic tubing. We led her to the door where she lit a cigarette and smoked as much of it as she could manage. "I got to sit back down."

This was the kind of information Paul Drake never delivered. Information that changed everything, but instead of it sliding into place like the last puzzle piece, it seemed to undo everything.

Sputnik told me I'd better leave. I was happy to go.

■ ■ ■

Finally, we three—Marcia, Pam, and I—had a ferocious fight in the office. Pam dropped her ironic mask and said she was sick of it, sick of grilled cheese sandwiches, our drafty farmhouse, no clients, and what clients we did get having no case to take to court regardless. The money we imagined would come from big class-action lawsuits tapped from an underground vein of anger and rage didn't happen, did it? It had been a good experiment. She admired Marcia for talking us into it. This was the wrong strategy. The more Pam argued against our enterprise, the more Marcia dug in. Ours was a higher calling. We were the ones who stood for justice, for everything our country stood for. ("Truth, justice, and the American way!" I could feel that sentence hanging in the air waiting for Pam to roll it out.) And in an honest moment, Marcia might admit she was blowing smoke. She might admit that in most respects, Virginia was as reactionary as a state could be. Now wasn't the time to remind her.

I watched Marcia and Pam go at it like a couple of the women wrestlers we watched on TV when I was a kid, terrified that women could generate such spit and venom, forgetting for a while that it was all fake. What went on between Marcia and Pam was not fake. I said as little as possible as each one tried to pull me into the argument on her side.

"You're my husband," Marcia said.

"I know," I said. I might have said more.

Shortly after that, things went to hell in a handbasket as Wiley Crawford liked to say. Marcia declared she needed a week of R&R and took off to see her parents in Northern Virginia.

"You're coming with me?" Though she offered me a question, all I heard was a command.

"No." I told her I had work to do in the office. And I did.

Pam and I sat on our little concrete back deck drinking beers and grilling hamburgers on the hibachi. I sat on the slab and she sat behind me in a folding chair. I let myself lean back against her and she began to knead my shoulders. It had been a hard week, no real clients, the fight. Underneath it all, the recognition that we had no money.

Pam knew. "Tell me the truth. Aren't you sick of this?"

"No," I said, "absolutely not. I want to spend the rest of my life buying Henry Blankenship's rusty guns, busted television sets, and commemorative whiskey bottles."

"Empty bottles."

"Empty."

I drooped my head over backward until it fell into Pam's lap. She bent down, awkward as hell, barely possible, and kissed me on the mouth. I kissed her back.

Our sex that week bordered on the violent. We popped buttons, tore shirts and blouses, hollered out loud when we came. And we could not get enough of each other. All day at the office, I could feel her wanting coming over the partition between our offices. Whenever we could, we cut out early. Did we know what we were doing? Did we know we were breaking things past fixing?

■ ■ ■

When I left Polly Tabor's trailer without Sputnik to follow, I let my little car slip into the ruts a time or two, killing the engine, having to start it, and back the car up a bit to take another run at getting away.

It was then, when I engaged the clutch that I felt the sharp prick of a memory. My dad and I were headed up the old road, me at the wheel. He liked me to drive, liked watching me do almost anything as if wonderstruck at his boy, at the star ball player I had become. A big black car came flying right at us and I had to swerve hard toward the creek that ran along the road keep from being sideswiped. "Fool," my father called him.

Polly Tabor looked dazed, frazzled, not like herself. "We got to talk," she said to my dad when we brought in our first load.

He stopped, thought a minute. "All right. OK. Son, you bring those boxes in and then run back to the store for the next load and come get me."

So I went, but when I came to a steep uphill curve, I missed my downshift and killed the engine. The truck had an accelerator pedal and a starter on the floor beside it the way old trucks did then, and I tried to start it the way my dad did, one foot on the clutch, the other with heel on the brake and toe reaching toward the starter. It started fine, but I killed the engine a couple of times trying to let the clutch out on that gravelly uphill. Pretty soon, the engine flooded.

I'd done it before, so I knew what to do, got out, popped open the hood, and took the wingnut off the air cleaner, lifted it off the carburetor, and let it breathe. Usually it didn't take long for the gas to evaporate. Here came a little Black boy running and bawling down the road. "The house," he hollered, "the house." I looked up the hollow and saw the heavy black smoke rolling out of one of the company houses there.

The truck wouldn't start; I couldn't help him. Soon enough I heard the fire whistle and soon after that, the fire engine came roaring at me still blocking the road. Normally, my dad would have been among the volunteers on the truck, and I was relieved he wasn't. Two of the firemen helped me push the truck out of the way and the fire engine went on.

The house was lost. Probably it would have been anyway. The minutes lost to getting the truck out of the way were negligible. Those company houses were tinderboxes just waiting to go. In my head I knew that even then, but I couldn't stop blaming myself. The burned out family had been good customers. Though I didn't tell him about stalling the truck, my dad gave them their groceries that day and for weeks after. A lot of time had passed in what seemed like minutes. I'd always remembered it that way, time gone missing while a house burned down.

Now I wondered, how had my dad passed that time at Polly Tabor's house? What did she need to talk about? Did they just stand around her kitchen table while she smoked half a pack of Salems? The car that ran us off the road was an old Hudson Hornet, ugly, but a heavy, powerful car preferred by moonshiners and other types who might be in a hurry to get somewhere. Or to leave.

Leave, that most American of options. I thought we would shut things down in the office, and Pam and I would go off together. Marcia would go off to the shelter of her parents' house. Which wasn't what she did at all. After days of storming and fighting, days when our office did not open, when I went by myself into town and made a recording for the answering machine, Marcia left with her loaded car and drove over the mountain roads she hated to my mother's house. She told my mother everything, and my mother called me and told me she was ashamed of me and that I was just like my father.

I tried to imagine Polly Tabor's kids having been safely shooed out the door so she and my father could be alone to say whatever needed to be said. I tried to imagine my father putting his arms around Polly

Tabor, kissing her, helping her out of her clothes as she helped him out of his, stepping with her the few feet into her bedroom. I tried to imagine what promises had been made and which would be broken. I could not, any more than I could imagine the act of my father making love to my mother.

Pam and I did not go off together. "Listen," she said, "just because we love each other doesn't mean we should have a relationship." What was that supposed to mean? Pam loaded her car up a few days after Marcia was gone and dropped me off at the office on her way out.

■ ■ ■

Our office was empty and cold. I would go back into the women's offices and look at the debris they'd left behind: paper clips, cheap ballpoint pens, legal pads with a few sheets left on them. Nothing personal; they each made sure of that. I admit I missed Pam more. I admired Marcia, admired her stubbornness, her commitment to an ideal even if it turned out to be far-fetched. But Pam. Maybe I didn't get enough of her in that one week. Maybe I thought we could burn through all that great sex and come out the other end, pure and cleansed, and still horny as hell.

For the next week, I had to hitchhike home or try to bum a ride from Wiley Crawford.

One day when he gave me a lift, he said, "You might ask your buddy Henry what he's got in the way of automobiles. I'm sure he can fix you right up. Just make sure the serial numbers match."

"Ha ha," I told him, but before another week was out, I was driving a twelve-year-old Chevy three-quarter-ton pickup with 150,000 miles on it. I learned the off-brand gas station sold recycled motor oil and bought myself a case to keep in the bed.

"Couldn't help yourself, could you?" Henry said.

"Meaning what?"

"Oh, I don't know nothing for a fact, but, you know, just like everybody else, I can put two and two together."

Sometimes a lawyer might have to say to a not so clever client, "Don't tell me anything you don't want me to know." That way you don't have to lie. As for the clients themselves, after a while you come to understand that everybody lies, plaintiffs and defendants, you just need to decide what to believe.

I didn't need Henry Blankenship to tell me what I already knew. Between the bitchy one and the pretty one, I had picked the one when I should have picked the other, so no wonder it turned out the way it did. Proof enough that I wasn't a man to be trusted. I could sit in my office until the cows came home. The phone wouldn't ring; the bell over the door was not going to jingle.

What might make a lawyer a good lawyer, at least one kind of good lawyer, is that he learns from his mistakes and doesn't repeat them. I suppose I wanted to be both kinds of good lawyer, had wanted to win for my clients, had wanted to seek truth, do justice. And I had not managed very well. One of my law professors had told us that some people see a flaw in our justice system, a flaw in the discovery process. That a clever prosecutor always has an information advantage. He knows more than a defendant and so he always will win. There was much I had not known.

When I went out to see Polly Tabor, what had I expected? A woman grown to a late middle age, a woman at ease with herself and the world? I actually knew such women, the mothers of guys I'd gone to college with, women whose beauty continued to bloom. Would we take tea? What was I thinking?

I guess I could have joined Henry and taken up drinking, but instead I drove by the schoolhouse one night and saw the lights on in the gym. It was late summer, and inside were a bunch of men about my age playing basketball. They invited me to join them, and I went home and got my shoes. I had nothing else to do.

■ ■ ■

Wiley Crawford came into my office and took a seat. It was getting on toward Thanksgiving time. "Busy time of year," he said, "what with all the drunk driving and assaults and whatnot, we get kind of backed up across the street. Won't settle down until sometime in the New Year."

I sat there thinking, knowing what was coming next.

"I don't suppose you could see your way clear to giving us a hand?"

Sputnik. It is the fall of 1957. My folks, my brother, all the people who live on our hill are standing out in the road on this dark, starry night. There, just as they promised on TV, goes the thing, coursing across the sky, winking its little green light, making us know it's smarter than we are, that it has our number, that we'd better look out. Of the vast information in the world, who can know the all of it? Who can know the why of his own life, the why of what he does? Sometimes a person has no choice.

THE LIFE OF CHARLIE WINTERS
AS FIVE DISAPPOINTMENTS

This small creek with native brook trout wasn't far from Charlie Winters's cabin on the ridgetop. He knew it well. So when he came on the hole with the great gray rock, he planned to fish it like he always did, by climbing up on the backside of the rock and casting from his knees into the long deep pool on the other side.

But something went wrong. He felt himself sliding down the rock face, first on his knees, then on his belly. Maybe if he got enough of himself against the rock, he'd stop. He didn't. Instead he went into the water, folding up like a jackknife and going all the way under. At some point, his Leonard cane rod and Hardy reel went clattering out of his hand and off the rock.

Over on the bank, Barnes Henderson was standing there looking into his fly box for a lucky choice. He'd been fishing the whole damned day and had not caught a thing. He looked up when he heard the splash. He smirked when he saw Charlie in the water, maybe he snickered a little too. Served the old bastard right—no doubt what he was thinking.

By the time Barnes crossed the tail of the pool—Charlie had left him the thin water along the shallow bank—Charlie Winters had crawled up on the water's edge, flipped over on his back, and thrown his legs in the air to drain his waders. His ball cap hung in the water about six inches under the surface. Barnes retrieved it and handed it to Charlie.

"What do you expect me to do with this?" Instead he took Barnes's rod, a not-inexpensive graphite rod and began to probe the hole for his own rod, swishing it this way and that and prodding it under the big rock where he was sure his rod had come to rest.

He poked around hunting for his rod long enough for his wet clothes to start him shivering. Barnes had to help him up the steep bank to the road above, then to his car. "You drive," Charlie told him. This was something different. Charlie Winters had never been known to ask for help from anybody as far as Barnes knew, definitely not Barnes. Barnes Henderson was Charlie Winters's son-in-law.

"Not so far from this creek, on the North Fork of the Rivana, William Lewis was swept off his horse when he was trying to cross in high water. The horse drowned, and William Lewis took a chill on the walk home. It turned into pneumonia and he died."

"Tough break," Barnes said.

"You know who William Lewis was?" Charlie waited a minute. It was obvious Barnes had no idea. "Meriwether Lewis's father. That day the boy had to start becoming a man."

"No kidding," Barnes said.

When he said something like that, so utterly dumb-assed, Charlie could never tell whether the boy was stupid or just didn't want to get it. "Fortunately, these days there are antibiotics."

Charlie Winters had grown up loving history, particularly the history of grand exploits and adventures, whether it was Lewis and Clark or John Wesley Powell or Xenophon, or even Odysseus or Aeneas. Those, too, were histories, no matter how sketchy the facts, true histories of the heart and soul.

Once he imagined the possibility of himself a part of some grand event. As a fourth grader he had sat in the back of his classroom reading his Virginia history book cover to cover and over and over while the rest of the class diagrammed sentences. After reading of brave boys marching three days to the Battle of New Market, he made up his mind he would somehow attend Virginia Military Institute. And he had. Crawling on his belly up a sandy beach on a Pacific island had shaken that heroic notion of history out of his system. And now? He read his history every night before switching off his bedside light, mostly history of warfare, history of what had been called the War Between the States when he was coming up, not reading anymore for exploits and adventures but to confirm his sense of the continuing march of human folly.

Still, a part of him never let go of the idea that some greater purpose could still be in store for him. Everything that was to happen hadn't happened yet. He had tried. Too small for football, too slow for track, he had found his sport in wrestling, was captain of his college team. There, in the nearly empty gym, he dominated other boys, intimidated them, hurt them, sometimes hurt them permanently. Quick like a weasel, he pinned his opponents fast and got his matches over. The referee raised his hand above his head and his teammates gave a little cheer. That was that and never enough.

At the cabin, Mary Frances ran a tub and made a hot toddy for Charlie while he got out of his wet clothes. When she came from the bathroom, she said, "Barnes!" as if discovering his presence in the small sitting room of the cabin was the most wonderful surprise a woman could wish for.

This is the way Mary Frances talked to everybody, her voice as radiant as her smile, a blessing descending on whomever she cast her glance. Goddesses probably operated just this way. Barnes was no different than any other man in her life regardless of age or background. He was smitten the minute he met her. He would do anything for her. Mary Frances Winters was Barnes's mother-in-law.

"Barnes," she said, "Charlie cannot stop talking about that fishing pole. You know he has had it for I don't know how long. Longer than he has had me, I believe." Barnes had no idea of the value of the rod, only that he had never been invited to cast it, or even touch it for that matter. The thought of the empty aluminum tube and rod sock in the trunk of Charlie's car gave him a smug pleasure. "I know it's getting late and going to be dark soon, but would you please go down to that creek and see if you can find it?" Barnes went out to his own car. He would go hunt for the rod; he didn't even feel resentful.

Barnes parked on the road right above the hole with the great gray rock. When he started down the bank, he thought maybe he saw a glint, maybe the reel or a ferrule. When he got down to the water, he was sure. The rod lay out in front of the rock in deep water, probably six or eight feet right there. Barnes stripped to his skivvies, waded out as far as he could on the rocky bottom, and then took the plunge. So simple. He brandished the rod high in his hand when he surfaced.

Now darkness was coming on fast. Barnes stood on the bank feeling like the only man on earth left alive. He checked Charlie's line to see what fly he had on. Blue wing olive. Probably he'd been using it all day and never told Barnes his secret. Wearing nothing but his white underwear, now seeming to glow in the dying light, the creek water steaming off him, Barnes fed out some line and began to false cast, feeling the easy rhythm of the bamboo rod, drying the soggy fly. He waded a few steps up beside the big rock and threw a cast into the pool. Nothing happened. He picked up the fly and false cast a couple more times and laid the fly just on the edge of the rocky wall that marked the deep side of the pool, a lucky cast. He heard the fish take the fly more than saw it, a tough little fish, maybe more fish than he thought. Barnes worked it slowly, slowly to him as he backed toward the water's edge.

There it was. It was a big fish, and he had caught it. The fish was ten, maybe eleven inches long, a brook trout, sharp white rays outlining its amber under fins, belly a soft yellow gold, olive sides covered with hundreds of haloes of red and orange. Barnes brought it into his hand for only seconds, then set it back in the water, took the shank and let the fish back itself off Charlie Winters's barbless hook. Gone so quickly, it was hard to believe it had been there at all.

Though he would never again catch a brook trout as big or beautiful in any of these creeks, Barnes would tell no one about this fish. A small miracle had been visited on him. Some things are to be kept and pondered. Besides, a fish story without the fish to go with it is just that.

Barnes dried himself off with his shirt and pants as well as he could, went up the bank, broke Charlie Winters's rod down and threw it in the trunk of his car. When he drove up to the cabin, warm light spilled out the windows into the spring night. Inside, he could see Charlie Winters in his robe and pajamas nursing another toddy. Mary Frances met him at the door, "Did you find it?"

He just looked down and shook his head. Why, a person might wonder, would he do a thing like that?

"Oh, honey, I'm so sorry," she said, and she meant it for Barnes and Charlie both. "Look at you. You went swimming after it, didn't you?" This much was true at least.

In Mary Frances's view, if a stiff drink couldn't fix things, a good dinner could. "Come on, Lizzy, help me with the table." Over in the corner under a stooping lamp, Liz had been there all along. Neither tall nor short, pretty or ugly, having at some point adapted the protective coloration of a sculpin, she could sit right in plain view and still be unseen. All day, she had read a book wherein a woman accidentally causes the death of her best friend's child. Though she had no children herself, Liz believed she knew every pang this character felt. Sometimes she liked to call herself a long-suffering woman, and often believed she really was one. Liz was Barnes Henderson's wife and Mary Frances and Charlie Winters's only child.

As Mary Frances lit the candles and called everybody to the table, she said, "Tomorrow you and Barnes can go down to the creek and look again. I'm sure you'll find it."

"I can go by myself. It doesn't take two men to look for a fishing rod."

"All right then: Barnes, you carve the ham. I'm not sure Charlie is at his best tonight."

But before Barnes could come to the table and take up the carving knife and fork, Charlie raised himself out of his armchair and made for the ham. "I'll carve." And he did cut clumsy slabs of ham for all four plates, which was not like Charlie Winters who took some pride in being precise in all things. Maybe it was the drinks.

"You can always get a new one," Liz told him.

"I can't. They don't make them like that anymore."

"Not that kind exactly, but I bet there are other kinds."

What Charlie Winters wanted to holler out loud was that the world had gone to shit. Nothing was good anymore. Everything had grown half-assed and sloppy. Everybody too. Maybe it was the drinks. He caught himself looking across the table at Mary Frances, at her brown eyes grown wide. He knew what she wanted, tranquility: the air made warm by the woodstove, the softened light of the candles, the table elegantly laid. More than he would care to admit, she had made this world of his, and she had the gift to lift him up out of himself and into a still place of calm. The candles fluttered; the plates were piled with plenty. All Mary Frances's doing; he was a fool for her still. "Yes," he said, "there are other kinds."

Neither Charlie Winters nor Barnes Henderson went looking for the rod in the morning. Instead, Mary Frances woke Barnes and Liz at 5:00 a.m. Charlie had a cough that would not let go of him and a touch of fever too. Maybe they ought to pack up early and head down the mountain and find a doctor. Thank goodness there were antibiotics.

HIS SON-IN-LAW

In those days, colleges held mixers. In those days, the South was full of small colleges for men and similar colleges for women. Some good ones and some average ones. At all of them, the romantic lives of their students was a problem that had to be dealt with somehow. Men's and women's colleges partnered up and bused their students off to one another's campuses in hopes that their students would meet somebody right for them. Actually, the wise men and women who planned such events were thinking, the right kind of person, a person with good taste and good manners and, most importantly, of equal social standing. That's how Barnes and Liz met. They were the leftovers when the more socially adept students had buddied up, had begun to dance, and with any luck had moved on to other things in darker corners of campus.

Liz was a funny-looking girl in a way Barnes couldn't put his finger on. Her clothes and hairdo didn't seem to match her body. She wore more makeup than most of the other girls. And she didn't have much to say. Neither did he. They walked to a coffee shop near the women's

college campus where breakfast was served twenty-four hours a day. All
Barnes could tell you he remembered was eating grits for the first time
in his life. Just the same, a month later he invited her to be his homecoming date. Who else could he ask? And she accepted. What else was
there to do?

Do? Barnes's hall counselor was a senior who regaled his charges with
his tales of sex with older married women, coed conquests, his adventures with whores and b-girls. His last year's homecoming date excused
herself to the ladies' room and when she came back, stuffed something
in the pocket of his sport coat. Turned out it was her panties. They left
the game soon thereafter. Inspired by these stories, a guy who lived next
door to Barnes and had a terrific record collection and stereo made a
chart with all the guys' names on it and categories they might check off
after the weekend: Feel her up. Finger her. Hand job. Blow job. Fuck.
The whole thing embarrassed Barnes, not the ambitions expressed by
the chart so much, but how unlikely anything like that might come his
way. Check off? How about jack off? That was the most likely category
for him.

The ball game was boring; the home team was terrible. Barnes
caught himself wishing he could do like the characters on *Star Trek* and
beam himself the hell out of there. He could see other couples nearby
laughing and talking and not watching the game at all. And he thought
maybe there must be something he and Liz could talk about, but what?
They were freshmen, they'd already established they had no idea what
they were majoring in or why they were at college. If they had read any
books or seen any movies in common, they couldn't think of them. Af-
terwards, they walked the campus waiting to eat dinner in the cafeteria where the least connected of students wound up. At least, Barnes
thought, the dance would be loud, the room would be dark. And then
he could stuff Liz in the car with the two other girls she'd ridden up to
his campus with.

"Dance?" he asked

He already knew she wasn't a very good dancer, just sort of hopped around and not exactly in time with the band. They sat the slow ones out. "Good band," he told her.

"Let's go outside," she told him. "It's too hot in here."

He swallowed down a yawn. Outside, inside, it didn't much matter.

Seated on a little concrete bench, Liz seemed to heave a deep sigh. She turned to him and kissed him hard on the mouth. She kept at it until Barnes felt his mouth getting numb. Then she guided his hand under the hem of her dress. After a while, she said, "Can't we go to your room or something?"

Girls were forbidden in the dorm, but even Barnes knew enough to see that circumstances demanded he let that rule go by. He pictured his hall counselor hovering somewhere up above them grinning and nodding. He barely got Liz to her rendezvous in time; her pantyhose crammed in her purse. Hot shit, he thought, I am hot shit.

Where was that chart? Barnes Henderson would put a big gold star right on "Fuck." Yes. Except the big weekend was over. Another thing about college Barnes had yet to grasp was classes. Maybe for a weekend guys drank too much, partied too hard, but now they got back down to work. The silly chart was last seen in the big trashcan at the end of the hall. That was then, this was now; now was lab reports, papers, midterms. Even the hall counselor hung a Do Not Disturb sign on his door. He was a pre-med, after all.

Barnes had to wait until the middle of the week when a bunch on his hall were playing lazy hands of hearts waiting for the cafeteria to open. So who got laid last weekend? That. Guys laughed sad laughs. "I did," Barnes said.

"Bullshit."

"I did."

That strange girl? That girl with the blue eye makeup all over the place and that Cleopatra hair? Well, damn. Good deal. Shows you just never could tell. Among the pre-meds and pre-laws, the jocks who swaggered up and down the hall, Barnes suddenly had some standing. He felt himself swelling before their eyes.

"But, you know, I think I'm going to dump her," Barnes said, never knowing he had such a thought until it came out of his mouth. Guys nodded their heads. Nailed her, now on to the next one. So before going over to the cafeteria, Barnes went into his neighbor's room and put on the Byrds, turned the stereo up loud, went back to his own room and took out a creamy sheet of stationery with the college seal, and began to write a kiss-off letter with his cartridge pen.

Before coming to college, Barnes had scarcely listened to music at all. Now it was everywhere. Mostly on this record, it was Roger McGuinn's jangling guitar. He'd never heard anything like that. But now he heard, "I'll feel a whole lot better when you're gone." That was it, that was what he was getting at. Music explained everything. Except the rest of the song might have made more sense to Liz than him. He danced around his room until the record was over then caught up with his hall mates at dinner.

OK, he felt a little guilty, though he never admitted it to anybody. And he expected to hear something back from Liz, something hurt, something mean. For a while, he heard nothing at all. Then he got a very short note. It said she had missed her period. He went to see his hall counselor who was poring over a comparative anatomy book thick as a dictionary. "Girls miss periods all the time," he told him. "Don't worry about it." Barnes got a few more notes. Sometimes the pay phone at the end of the hall rang and rang and nobody answered it. Just as well, he thought. Then he got a letter saying Liz missed her second period.

His hall counselor shut the door this time. In his vast experience, the hall counselor had been in this spot too. "Listen, there are ways of handling this. She has to be willing, too, though." He knew who to call. Barnes went down to his room and took out another sheet of his stationery with the college seal. He laid it all out for Liz, then he mailed it. He wasn't sure how he could get the money. He didn't hear from her. Maybe that was her solution.

One day he was sitting in his room with a calculus book open on his desk trying to study. Every problem had to do with the rate at which events happened over time. He'd gone next door and listened to *Surrealistic Pillow* real loud until a jock from down the hall came in and told him to turn it off or he'd break his arm. It was late in the semester, school was hard, exams, final papers, and projects were starting to stack up on everybody, but not as heavily as they were on Barnes.

This work-study student from the admissions office knocked on Barnes's door. "Henderson?" He'd been the one who'd given Barnes and his parents their campus tour, but he didn't remember that. Barnes just nodded. "The dean wants to see you in his office."

When he said, "About what?" Barnes knew it was a stupid question.

Until this day the dean of students didn't even know who he was. But Barnes knew who the dean was, a little man who reminded him of a mole. He'd seen him skittering up the hall in bedroom shoes and a cardigan sweater. Barnes imagined him a harmless man. Now he had on his suit jacket, his face was red, and he was waiting in the hall outside his office for "Mr. Henderson."

Inside the dean's office Liz sat on a big leather couch. Her hair was cropped short and was a dirty brown color, not the shiny black he remembered. Her face was flushed red, but plain, and she wore glasses. The lady to her left looked wild-eyed as if she was still getting over a shock; maybe somebody close to her had just died or maybe she had been robbed. Barnes couldn't say; he had no real experience with either. On Liz's left sat a man dry and hard as a hickory axe handle. That man stood. Though he was shorter than Barnes, Barnes took a step back. He did not offer his hand to shake. Barnes thought that in other circumstances, the man would have hit him, and he was sure he would have run. This was the first time Barnes met Mary Frances and Charlie Winters.

HIS DAUGHTER

She was not accomplished. That's what Jane Austen called it, and Beth Winters, who'd always been a reader, knew what became of girls who weren't accomplished. That was one thing. The other was the inescapable feeling she must be a disappointment to her mother. Her mother

206 ■ THE GETTING PLACE

sang beautifully, could have sung professionally had she wanted. Her mother cooked lavish meals. As a girl, she had made most of her own clothes and as a mother had made clothes and costumes for Beth when she was growing up. Mary Frances was a great beauty with brown eyes, dark hair that formed a perfect widow's peak, with slim legs that would turn a man's head even as she aged. Nobody ever said Beth was not like her mother; they didn't have to. She had a habit of sucking on a strand of stray hair when she read or studied. Her handwriting was clumsy and without character. She spilled food on her lovely clothes and ran her shoes over. Her legs were thick, her breasts heavy. Sometimes she thought it must take all her parents' mustered goodwill to love her. They did love her.

And they sent her to a very good college for women, the very college Mary Frances had attended, the college where she sang a solo at a Christmas concert that Charlie Winters happened to be in the audience to hear. Older professors still spoke fondly of Mary Frances.

Beth's roommate was a sly, funny girl, a wispy, mischievous girl. Her suitemates were two upperclasswomen who majored in drama and art. They wore short skirts and no bras and made daring gestures with their hair. It's only hair, they told her, it grows back, this after each had shorn herself almost to her skull. They smoked cigarettes and marijuana too. Beth's roommate fell right in with them, and the three agreed to make Beth their project.

That's how Beth became Liz. Mary Frances had named her Elizabeth because it offered so many choices: Would she be a Betsy, a Betty, a Lizzy? No, she became a Beth early on and stayed that way. Liz, though, was a glamorous girl, wasn't she? A girl who crossed her legs as she looked men in the eye, a girl who laughed a knowing laugh through a cloud of cigarette smoke. Her suitemates called her Liz, would call her nothing else. They cut her hair, dyed it, puffed it up with some mousse. They insisted she try contact lenses and made up her eyes to look bolder. They lent her clothes.

And they talked incessantly about the men in their lives. Sex was a game they played with these men, a weapon they used at their discretion. Even Beth's roommate had some sexual experience, the backseat of cars kind. The older girls were firm in their dislike of cars: never in cars. If a guy couldn't find you a room and a bed, he wasn't worth the trouble. Beth didn't have to say anything; they knew she was a virgin.

When the freshman girls set off for the mixer, Beth—no, she was Liz, the older girls had so insistently called her Liz that all the other girls in her dorm and her professors had, after some initial confusion, begun to call her Liz too. She was Liz and couldn't go back. Liz was on a mission, a mission about as inviting as parachuting out of an airplane.

Maybe if Barnes Henderson had been better looking. At eighteen, he was already getting pudgy. His tummy slouched a little over his belt. His pants sagged. His hair was tousled, not in a charming, offhandedly sexy way, but in a messy way. Liz had heard stories of girls who fled from these affairs, slipped away at some opportune time back to the dorm, and hid until the chartered buses pulled away. Given her prospects, she considered it. But her suitemates would be waiting and would only push her back into the mix.

Barnes Henderson approached her. Though they both wore nametags, he said, "Are you Beth?"

"It's Liz."

"I thought they said Beth." She could only blame whatever they was out there, the they who planned this massacre, brutal sadists they must be. Beth had been painfully shy, and Liz was no better. Back in the dorm, her suitemates had made her up and led her to the mirror—there with her bold mascara and eye shadow she was a stranger to herself. "Sexy, sexy," they chanted. And Liz could almost see it. If she could jut her jaw a little and wipe that look of panicked befuddlement off her face, she would almost be sexy. It was a lesson she understood in principle but could not apply.

They balanced their picnic dinners on their knees. They tried not to spill their food, but Barnes did anyway, baked beans down his shirt. He tried to dab it off with a napkin, which only made it worse. "The band is supposed to be good," he told her.

"I hope so."

"Do you like to dance?"

"Not so much."

"Me either. Not really. Do you like music, though, I mean to listen?"

"Yes," she said. Yes, she did. The sound of her mother's voice had filled up their house when she was a girl. No person could sing as wonderfully as her mother.

"Who do you like?" Barnes asked and began to name names from the collection of the guy with the stereo next door. Cream, he said, Jefferson Airplane, Iron Butterfly.

Liz had never heard any of these bands. In truth, she liked musicals. Her mother sang songs from *My Fair Lady*, *The King and I*, *South Pacific*. She said she liked Julie Andrews.

"From *Mary Poppins*," he said, and she was embarrassed, though she shouldn't have been. Barnes was as happy as any *Jeopardy* contestant at asking the right question.

When the boys finally boarded the buses for their own college, Liz felt a relief akin to having made it to a bathroom just in time to take a long pee. "Well?" the suitemates said.

"He was nice." Which seemed like the truth. Really, there was nothing wrong with him, just a guy who if you passed him on the street you wouldn't give a second look.

"Nice? What's that?"

Liz was tired; she would not be badgered by these girls. "He was just a nice regular guy. He'd never eaten grits. Maybe he's a Yankee. I mean from up North or something."

"Oh God, a stranger in a strange land! A mysterious stranger."

"No," she said, not wanting to admit to the truth she felt instantly. Barnes Henderson didn't have a mysterious bone in his body. Liz just wanted to crawl into bed, which she did. And she fell asleep without washing her face until her roommate came in three hours later. Her

date, she announced, was a dip; she ditched him by going to the pow-
der room and climbing out a window. She'd hooked up with some cool
townies and gone drinking with them. Climb out the window, why
couldn't Liz have thought of that?

When Barnes Henderson called to ask her to homecoming, she
told him she'd have to think it over. "Go! Go!" the suitemates cheered,
"you've got to go." They could find her a ride with friends of theirs who
were going. They reminded her she'd said Barnes was nice, which they
all knew meant boring. She could always treat the date as a scouting
mission—meet cool upperclassmen, get the hell off campus. When he
called again, she accepted.

Away from the older girls back in their own room, her roommate
said, "You know, you ought to seduce this guy. Trust me, it won't be
hard to do."

Liz looked at the girl. Some things girls didn't do. Not just having
sex with boys. In the past weeks, she'd gotten beyond that. It seemed
like all the girls on her floor had or at least were better at acting like they
had. But to be the one who started it?

"It's not too fun the first time, but once you get past that it's a blast."

"I can't do that," she said.

Her roommate laughed.

■ ■ ■

Charlie Winters had declared he would strangle the boy with his own
hands, but he knew he would not even before Mary Frances told him
he'd do no such thing, reminding him it took two just as it had in their
own history. That Charlie Winters had already considered, but things
were different then. There was a war on; lovers parted thinking—thinking with good reason—they might never see each other again. Besides,
"We were smarter."

"Lucky," she corrected. And, though she didn't say it aloud, in love.

How could her daughter go to bed with a boy she scarcely knew? They both wondered.

What about sending Beth off to take care of a sick aunt? Mary Frances and Beth had already talked it through. She wanted to keep the baby. To his surprise, so did Charlie. If there was going to be a grandchild coming into this world, he was going to claim it. Still, the boy was a pitiful specimen, a soft baby face set on top of a slack body. One look told Charlie the toughest thing he'd ever done was make a trip to the dentist's office. Why did Beth have to pick him?

They had left the boy and the dean back in the office to talk over his options when truly there were none. Charlie, Mary Frances, and Liz-not-Beth walked across the campus to inspect the chapel in the company of the campus minister, a gutless Friar Lawrence. How many times had this man tied the knot for heartsick kids who had no idea what they'd gotten themselves into? How many times had he stood by and let the shit hit the fan? This man was Charlie's coconspirator, and Charlie hated him for the part he must play.

Charlie would never know the primitive coupling Liz and Barnes had managed on his dorm room bed. Though he never told her so, his daughter was already a disappointment to him. She was no beauty; she couldn't sing. Now he was wondering if she wasn't very smart, either, or simply incapable of making good judgment. Maybe they amounted to the same thing. Look at the boy.

The following night, Charlie and Mary Frances lay in their bed at the Oaks Motor Lodge and looked at the dark ceiling. Their Beth was now Liz Henderson. She and her husband would move into a grimy bungalow on the edge of campus, housing the college maintained, it seemed, for just this kind of emergency. Barnes Henderson would continue his studies while Beth would be a stay-at-home mom. Next semester, she might sit in on a class or two until the baby came. Barnes Henderson would take a job, second shift at a textile mill. Charlie Winters snorted out loud: the idea of that boy as a family man.

"Don't," Mary Frances told him. Her grief was deeper than he could know. She—they—had lost their only child, cast her out into the wilderness.

There was no point in asking whether they had done the right thing. As Charlie saw it, there was only one thing to do. Actions had consequences, and grown men owned up to them. Grown women too. He had not been able to look his daughter in the face since the day she had told them her news. He could picture well enough Liz-not-Beth and Barnes Henderson lying in a bed not so different from this one, looking at a dark and infinitely receding ceiling of their own, having nothing to say, not even, "I'm sorry."

"They're young," he told Mary Frances. "They'll figure it out. They've got no choice."

There was no helping them now; Charlie and Mary Frances drove home the next day. Mary Frances would send care packages, but boxes of cookies and chocolates did not seem appropriate to send a new wife. She wrote her daughter, slipping in checks from her mad money account; Charlie didn't need to know. And her daughter wrote back; Liz was lonely, scared, sick every morning, sick in a way she had no recollection of when she thought of her own pregnancy. There was a pay phone at the gas station down the street where Liz could call collect. Could Mary Frances send them a radio? Finally, Mary Frances talked Charlie into paying to put in a phone. What, she wondered, if there was an emergency?

Shortly, there was one, an emergency. Barnes Henderson called at two in the morning. He was at a hospital. Liz was in surgery right then. At first they thought she had appendicitis, but it turned out to be a tubal pregnancy.

Driving through the night, driving on unfamiliar roads, through a maze of unfamiliar streets, Charlie and Mary Frances reached the hospital at first light. Nobody met them; they found Barnes dozing on a couch with a cup of coffee and a half-eaten doughnut beside him. Liz was still in recovery, and the doctor was off making his rounds. Charlie Winters took Mary Frances's hand and pulled her through pairs of

No Admittance doors until he found his daughter. "We're here, honey," Mary Frances told her.

Charlie Winters felt himself balking, angry, thinking his daughter deserved this, the worst thing. But when he looked at her still groggy in her bed, not yet aware of what had happened, that one kind of pain had just been substituted for another, he gave way. "We can fix this, all this," he told her.

What did he mean by that? What he might have wished was that he could bundle his daughter up in her blanket and carry her out to the car as he had when she was a child, carry her away from that silly goose in the waiting room, carry her back home, and set her upright and let her start college life all over again. Make it right.

Mary Frances felt his shift. On their ride back home, she said, "Why don't we have Thanksgiving at the cabin? It would be good for Barnes and Liz to get away from that little house. You could get to know him."

"Huh." Which was as close as Charlie Winters would come to saying he agreed. Despite the loss of the baby, he was probably stuck with the son-in-law. Get used to it.

Unlikely he forgot how it had been between Mary Frances's father and him. That man looked at Charlie Winters and saw a slight hillbilly boy with bad teeth and bad grammar. And he was right. People had been underestimating Charlie his whole life, and he had learned to use it to his advantage. Charlie would learn to play by the old man's rules so when he came back from the war—came back with his bronze star and purple heart—he got himself into the same law school Mary Frances's father had attended, the one that shared its campus grounds with VMI. What could he do then but welcome Charlie into his practice when he graduated?

As the time grew near, Charlie Winters found the prospect of bringing that boy to his cabin less appealing. Some years it would grow unexpectedly warm at Thanksgiving and a man could get out of the house and run some nymphs through the deeper pools on the creeks he knew. It snowed wet and heavy instead.

He asked Barnes, "What is your course of study?" Asked him again, actually, because he had not cared to remember the answer the first time.

"Sociology," Barnes told him. In truth, he had chosen no major. Somebody told him sociology was pretty easy, though.

"What would you do with that?"

"I think I would like to be a public defender." It was Barnes's former roommate who was bent on becoming a public defender. He was a boy who wore a peace sign every day (Barnes had had to ask him what it meant), who was a genuine conscientious objector, who was gentle as a child except when he began yelling about social injustice. This injustice he proposed to take on one case at a time. Barnes had thought he was a little bit kooky. He sounded like one of the songs from *Hair*. Liz had led Barnes to believe, though, that saying he was interested in law might be a way of getting Charlie Winters's respect.

Charlie screwed his face up sideways as if he were going to bore right into Barnes's sternum. "You think those fellows in jail are all innocent, do you?"

"I don't know. Some of them, maybe."

"Let me tell you something, there's not a single guy in the joint who doesn't think he's innocent. Not a one. But let me tell you something else: They all believe in the law. Somebody done them wrong, some scallywag or another who snuck away scot-free, but the law is the law. The truth. They believe." Both Mary Frances and Liz had heard this speech before, both saw it coming. Charlie Winters, too, believed in the law, believed the law was as real and as solid as the table they sat around eating their turkey dinner. Virginia Military Institute, the United States Marine Corps, and the law . . . sacred institutions. Charlie Winters believed too.

Barnes muttered something about social injustice.

"What?" Charlie Winters was almost hollering. "Have you taken a look the Constitution lately? Social justice is built into it. It's what we do; it's who we are." Words from the heart.

Barnes looked at his plate. He had never read the Constitution ever.

He and Liz started back for the college Sunday night; he had to be in classes in the morning and then off to work at the mill. As they worked their way down the winding mountain, she suddenly said, "Pull over." And he got the car off the road and stopped just in time for her to open the door and puke. Probably she had too much to drink on top of too much of her mother's rich food. Liz climbed out of the car and worked her way around the fender to the front. She threw up again, illuminated by the headlights. It could have been the sight of the last of it running down her chin or the sour smell, but Barnes felt his own gorge rising. He jumped out of the car and joined Liz at the bumper, heaving into the gravel on the shoulder. They took turns for a while, retching back and forth until they were both exhausted and emptied out. And then they started laughing. Just then they felt closer to each other. This could almost be love.

But mostly their life together at the men's college was a gray time. It rained. It rained all the time, muggy rain in the spring and summer, chilling rain in the fall and winter. Barnes took his classes in the morning, ran home and studied for a few hours, then was off to his job until he came home sometime after midnight. With no baby to prepare for, no baby to raise, Liz began to sit in on classes. The college would tolerate her attendance, allow her to earn her grades, but would not let her take a diploma. The men students seemed to scorn her—did they all know her story, did they blame her? She took a job at the college library, shelving books, then working at the reserve desk. She felt like a fixture.

Maybe Barnes could have made it as a public defender, or a teacher, or even a professor. But the odd crucible of bull sessions and dorm room debates that shaped his fellow students as much as their time in the classrooms was missing. While they struggled to know who they were and what they believed, Barnes worked, slept, and ate. He had little to say to Liz; he had little to say to anybody. Sometimes he would think he saw a guy from his former hall cutting across campus, but everybody had grown long hair and beards so he couldn't say for sure. Probably his old roommate enjoyed his spacious room; probably his neighbor was happy not to have Barnes coming in and playing his stereo all the time. His hall counselor was deciding where he would go to med school.

What held them together? Their fights, lots of fights, were over leaving shoes out in the middle of the floor, not putting gas in the car, getting the wrong kind of cereal, dirty dishes, dirty laundry. Nothing, really. Maybe they should fight about things that mattered, but they didn't know enough to know what they were. Sex. They had sex. Liz's old suitemates had known all about how to get birth control pills and were going to tell her soon enough. Now it was easy. Sex turned into a kind of fighting too.

Left alone in their bungalow, they had nothing else to do but grow closer, tangled, wrapped around the same turning axle. Four years of college and the textile mill was enough for Barnes to dig into a deep resentment of Charlie Winters. The man had money, plenty of money. To make Barnes and Liz live the way they did was cruel. They had to practically beg for everything they got from him: Charlie's worn out car Barnes drove to work. Their TV, the stereo when Charlie Winters knew how much Liz loved music. Liz was angry too. How long would it take for her father to forgive her this one big mistake? Their resentment pulled them together, too, that and their mutual admiration for Mary Frances. She, they agreed, was a saint.

For Christmas they had given her the soundtrack from *Hair*, a different kind of musical. Some of the songs were real songs, but others were sort of musical doodles. That next summer, they heard her singing in her beautiful alto, singing to herself in the kitchen: "How can people be so heartless? How can people be so cruel?" And they thought to themselves: "Especially people who care about strangers and social injustice?" That was Charlie, they agreed, who cared more about his clients and his laws than his own daughter and son-in-law.

HIS WIFE

How could a woman as lovely and gifted and charming as Mary Frances possibly be a disappointment to Charlie Winters? She died. She died, according to those who had been out of touch and had not been privy to the details, suddenly and unexpectedly. From Charlie's perspective, she died slowly, painfully, and too fast. What began as a fainting spell became a yearlong slide into death.

That same night after Charlie Winters's Leonard rod and Hardy reel tumbled to the creek bottom, he followed Mary Frances to bed where he found her crying. "Why," she said to him, "can't you let that boy do anything?" Barnes Henderson was far from boyhood, now thirty-five years old. He had finished that degree in sociology and had used it to bounce from job to job: manager of a mall record store, insurance salesman, car—used car—salesman, unsuccessful realtor (but at least he had passed the examination). Just now he worked in a big local hardware store in the paint department. With the help of a clever computer, a brand-new gadget, he could mix paint to any shade a customer might want. He never stopped talking about the wonders of that machine. What else did he have to talk about? He didn't even follow baseball.

Charlie and Mary Frances had been here many times before; she being of the opinion that if Charlie could relent and say a few encouraging things to boost the boy's confidence, he might still amount to something. But it had never come to tears. Mary Frances never used tears as a weapon as Charlie had heard other women did. Probably she was just tired. And in the morning, it was Charlie's cough and fever that had caused them all to quit the cabin sooner than planned. Only after he was in an examination room and being seen to, did Mary Frances slide down into a chair in the waiting room and fall into a faint.

It turned out she was anemic. It turned out she was anemic because she had uterine cancer and it was pretty far along. How could Charlie have missed this? Yes, she had been tired lately. She had begun falling asleep over her novel or in front of the television set. Maybe she had looked peaked. He should have paid more attention. Surely she had been bleeding. Surely she had been in considerable pain. But she had been a constant in his life so long, he looked at her no more closely than the clock on the kitchen wall.

For the first time in his life, Charlie Winters felt scared, scared because he was helpless before this disease. More helpless than on the beach at Iwo Jima. There, danger had been real and tangible; there a man with his wits about him could at least pretend it was in his power to save himself. Now he could not save his wife. The threat lay in Mary Frances's own body gone haywire, her body turning on her. A doctor, a man of their longtime acquaintance, cut her open and found too much cancer there to try to remove. He sewed her back up and went out to where Charlie Winters sat waiting.

It was all Charlie Winters could do to keep from hitting that man. It was all Charlie Winters could do to keep from hollering out loud like a kid who'd slammed his hand in a car door. Charlie could not save himself either.

The chemotherapy made her sick; she couldn't keep anything down. Always slender, Mary Frances became bone thin. They stayed home, stayed to themselves. Always gracious, she grew sharp and angry. They weren't good company to anybody but themselves now. Sometimes he wondered if she couldn't try harder against this disease; other times he wondered how it was she didn't give up entirely. But this disease cared nothing for what Mary Frances did or didn't do, or what he thought or wished for. Mary Frances' lovely brown hair grown silvery gray now fell out in handfuls. She could not bear to be seen this way. He didn't argue with her.

Every chemo treatment landed Mary Frances back in the hospital for days. Charlie cornered the oncologist in the corridor. As he saw it, the medicine was killing her as much as the cancer. She couldn't eat; her hair had all gone, her gums bled, her teeth were falling out too. "What's the good of any of this?"

The man, a young man still, said, "I'm not sure there is."

"What would you do?"

He looked carefully at Charlie Winters before he said, "I would stop it. I would take your wife home or wherever and pray for her ease and peace."

"Pray!" Otherwise the doctor had judged the man standing before him correctly. Charlie Winters took his wife home to her own bed, propped her up with many pillows, and read to her from the books she had held onto from the time she was a child, the same ones she had read to Liz when she was a girl, a shelf of them he assembled by the bed: *Peter Rabbit*, *The Wind in the Willows*, *Anne of Green Gables*. At the end of that line, *Middlemarch*, *To the Lighthouse*. They would not get that far. Charlie would not know Lilly Briscoe's plaint for Mrs. Ramsay. He would not guess art might be a person's salvation. He would not have believed it anyway.

Toward the end, the drugs kept the pain back so she slept most of the day and most of the night too. He stayed by her, bringing her water, bringing her soup, which she could not keep down though she kept trying. He made himself coffee. As he stood waiting for Mr. Coffee to dribble into the pot, he heard her cry, "Charlie, come quick."

She was gone; whatever she had meant to tell him was lost. He sat by the bed until the sun came up. Maybe she weighed eighty pounds, probably less, with no hair or eyebrows or eyelashes, Mary Frances had turned into a little girl, the little girl she must have been before he ever met her. Cold all the time, she wore a knit ski hat and a pair of Charlie's wool fishing socks on her feet. She wore a slight smile. All done.

He turned on the stereo where he had cued up a recording of *Fauré's Requiem*. He had planned to play it for Mary Frances when she felt her time was near. As he listened to the soprano singing in a language he did not understand, he thought of the medieval cathedrals Mary Frances and he had visited in France. That soprano voice was a kind of soul (though he did not believe in souls, that was another thing war had done to him), a spirit maybe, like a bird that had gotten in by accident and was flitting around that high ceiling trying to get out. As the voice trailed off, he saw that spirit loose in the open sky, flying up until he couldn't see it anymore.

He got up and walked through the house, her house filled with plush pastels, a sitting room designed for languorous cups of tea or gin and tonics. A room that often held three card tables and lady bridge players sitting around them. Chairs and settees with bowed little legs, shelves with china plates and porcelain figurines on display. Antique tables and chiming clocks. All just so, all as she would have it. Without her, without Mary Frances, he had no place in this house, among these things. She had graciously made him feel he belonged in her world. Now that she was gone, it was clear he did not.

Subsequently, Charlie Winters became a man fearful to Liz and Barnes Henderson. He resigned and sold his interest in the law firm that bore his name and that of his dead father-in-law. He sold the house he and Mary Frances had lived in for the past forty years, gave Liz her pick of the household goods, and sold the rest at auction. He sold his Buick and bought an inexpensive pickup truck. And he moved himself to his mountain cabin.

There, he stripped it bare of all the homey flourishes Mary Frances had brought from town. The place grew spare as his old barrack room at Virginia Military Institute. He had his fly rods, his tying bench, his shotguns for the occasional bird he took, a twenty-two for varmints. He had his library of favorite history books. After a year or so, he came down from the mountain and set up a small law office in the nearest county seat. There he wrote wills and contracts, settled divorces. If a man believed in the law, he must practice it.

In that same year Mary Frances passed, Barnes and Liz Henderson divorced. Barnes Henderson had loved Mary Frances achingly, longingly. Foolishly, too. He could not explain the power she had over him, but once she was taken sick, he stayed away. At the visitation, he would not look in the casket. He could hardly speak her name then or for weeks afterward. The last thing he needed was to climb that twisty road to Charlie Winters's cabin. Nothing much had changed between Barnes and that man since the day they met. He drew all his courage from Mary Frances, and now that she was gone, who could imagine what Charlie would do to him?

Death had muted Charlie's urges to punch doctors, chew out nurses.

Still angry, he was too tired to do much of anything. He cooked his spare bachelor meals. He tied more flies than he might ever manage to fish if he lived to one hundred. Sometimes he did fish, though he often would stop and sit down on a river rock for long stretches, and he often would just climb up the bank and make the slow walk back to his truck.

HIS COUNTRY

Anybody who was in the Krispy Kreme place saw a man in his eighties, ramrod straight, khakis sharply creased, his white VMI ball cap set smartly on his head. Charlie Winters had come in for his black coffee and single cake doughnut. As he waited, he glanced at the television hung from the ceiling above the counter. There the city of New Orleans was drowning under twenty feet of water; people clung to their few possessions and waved for help at passing helicopters. "By rights that ought to be the end of that bunch, but we're stuck with them for three more years," he told the little girl who took his order, pretty if she would get rid of those piercings. She knew what he meant; it had been going on for days. But did he feel anger or shame? He could not say, and he could not say how his country had come to this sorry pass.

On VJ day, he had been among other marines on a Hawaiian beach practicing landings for what they all knew would be the invasion of the Japanese mainland. They had heard the news of the first bomb, and then the second, and they had begun to hope in a fatalistic soldierly way.

His buddies and he found an old car and some aviation gas and tried to run into Honolulu where they guessed big doings were on. They blew the engine instead and had to walk. It took a long time, but the party was still there. Just then everything seemed possible. All it took was a little gumption.

When Barnes Henderson and Liz came to the cabin in the summer of 1970, his hair had grown down past his collar and he wore scraggly sideburns that ran off the end of his jaw. She wore a long skirt that came to her ankles and flip-flops. Both of them wore matching shirts, his a T-shirt with wads of orange and brown dye shot through it, hers a man's undershirt. "So you all are hippies now," Charlie Winters told them. At least Liz was still wearing a brassiere. He knew: All of them, college kids, looked this way now. And mad, as if they had reason to be mad.

"Let them be" is what Mary Frances told him that night. Of course Liz was still wearing a bra; she was too big up there to go without.

"Would you? Go without?"

"Maybe," she told him with a sly smile. Something had gotten into her too. She played that record from that *Hair* musical just to see what kids were listening to. Now she sang some of those songs when she went around the house. One was just a string of dirty words, well not exactly dirty words. She had to look three of them up to see what they meant. And she wondered: Did people really do those things? A pleasant thrill ran through her at the thought. Not her and Charlie. Who they were, what they did in private was long established. But the idea that people did. The world was wider than she had thought.

Nothing people might do surprised Charlie Winters. He had been in the service; he was a lawyer. Surprise was one thing; disappointment was something else. He read the papers and looked at the TV news and he felt the world drifting away from him. Many a Thanksgiving Day, Mary Frances and he had gone into Roanoke and watched VMI play the Tech boys, the two corps marching in the parade and on into the stadium. The bands. A good marching band on parade still gave him chills. But this past year some of the Tech students, for they now had many students not enrolled in the Corps of Cadets, stood along the roadside and jeered, jeered at their own classmates. It occurred to Charlie Winters that he was mad too. But maybe he had good reason.

Some years later, he sat with one of his old classmates at a football game, a cold November football game, but not against Virginia Tech. That school had moved along. And his own? He preferred to think it had made the more honorable choice, which seemed to mean losing to one pitiful outfit after another. "You know," the man said, leaning into Charlie confidentially, "we could have won in Vietnam if we'd stuck it out."

Yes, it had enraged him to see Jane Fonda straddling that artillery piece like a man's big dick. When those exercise tapes of hers came around, he would not let Mary Frances bring them in the house. And then she turned up in the box seats at Braves games. Enough to put a man off baseball. But now Vietnam was just another country. A dictatorship, but no kind of communists Karl Marx would recognize. We got along with them better than some, and he had to wonder if we would have gotten along with them sooner if we had just stayed away from there. "What," Charlie asked him, "would we have won?"

Just the same he had asked his mailman up on the mountain with his "POWs/MIAs never have a nice day" bumper sticker. "Do you think boys are still out there?"

"We can't rest," the guy said in a preacherly voice, "until we account for every man." Here he was in his fifties and wearing a ponytail and tie-dyed shirt as if he had to live the rest of his life being a hippie because he was in 'Nam and missed out the first time around.

Yes, the Greeks had rallied around the corpse of Patroclus to save it from desecration at the hands of the Trojans. A study in comradely loyalty. But what you learned in real war was that men stepped off landing craft into riptides and got washed down before the enemy even took a shot at them, or got blown to bits so thoroughly there was literally nothing left. Still, he understood the mailman's impulse to take corrective action, to try to right things as best he could.

Some years ago, he had been invited back to Virginia Military Institute for graduation—the fiftieth anniversary of his own. As the ceremony progressed, the traditional roll call for the boys fallen at the Battle of New Market was made, and the traditional answer came from boys in those same companies on this day, "Died on the Field of Honor, Sir." As in his own days as a cadet, he felt the tears squirt from his eyes.

He looked at those boys, and he saw among the ranks colored boys, Black men, African Americans as they now wanted to be called. And he wondered what this ceremony, over 125 years old, meant to them. Charlie Winters had gone to an all-white high school, an all-white college, an all-white law school. And this was far from the first time he had marveled at the fact that he had grown up in a town among Black people but had never known any of them by name. His adult life had been filled with Black people, also strangers to him, who had done his wash, cleaned his house, done his yard work. They had picked up his trash and fired the furnace at his office.

Though he had never said much more than a hello to the women his wife hired, he had come to know the man who cleaned his offices. Because Charlie was an early riser and in the office by six in the morning, he often encountered the man finishing up his night's work. They talked, talked about nothing much, ball games, goings-on around their town, the weather. Gradually this evolved to friendly bets, a soda on a big game; gradually this man, Pierce, was entered into office betting pools where he did well. He studied the sports page as carefully as any man. And the rest of the paper too.

In a half-hearted way, Charlie had wondered whether the law firm ought not hire some Black person as a secretary or even a legal secretary and see how that worked out and maybe then they might look into hiring a Black lawyer. But they never had. And when he read that Pierce's daughter, a child not so different in age from Liz, had been killed in an auto accident, he sent flowers on behalf of the firm. He expressed his sympathy privately to the man but did not go to the funeral. Why not? Maybe it was class, maybe it was race itself, maybe it was their time and place. But mostly he understood it was history, history itself pressing down on him, a weight too heavy to lift off himself or Pierce.

History could be a crooked thing. Once he had fished an unfamiliar creek and at some point, he realized the hole he had just fished was just over to his left. Without sensing it, he had fished around a tight oxbow. He thought about what he had told Barnes Henderson those years ago. It wasn't until the Thirteenth Amendment that the Constitution itself started to own up to the claims the Declaration of Independence made. That was history. And the law? Could it still be said to be solid as a table?

HIMSELF

Charlie Winters found the nest of an animal behind his woodpile. Probably a varmint of some kind. He loaded a couple of rounds into his twenty-two and set it by the door. But what he saw was a cat, gray from head to tail, an old jowly tom with pieces missing from his ears. Charlie had dogs as a boy; as a young man he had bird dogs he took pains to train properly. He'd never had much to do with cats. So his first thought was just to shoot the thing. He didn't. Instead, he put a little turkey meat out by the woodpile, and after a few days, the cat made up with him. It wasn't in good shape; somebody dumped it up here on the road. When the cat would let him pick it up, Charlie took hold of it, slapped it yowling into a cardboard box, and hauled it down the mountain to a veterinarian, a lady vet to his surprise.

"Worth saving?"

"Oh, yes. He's got some pustules under his skin, probably from fighting. Those need to be lanced, some antibiotics. He should be wormed. But he's healthy; he's not been on his own too long."

"How old?"

The vet peeled his lips back and looked at his teeth. "I don't know, six, eight years. A cat can sometimes live for twenty years or more." While she held the cat on her examination table and began to work her hands in his fur, the cat actually began to relax, and then luxuriate as she scratched around his ears and head. "He's a sweetie," she told him.

"My God," Charlie Winters told her, "he'll outlive me."

"And what's so wrong with you? You look like you've got a little life left in you."

Charlie Winters felt his ears go red.

"Want his nuts nipped while he's in here? It might not change much at his age. He may still be a rover, but it might keep him out of a little trouble."

Though he knew nothing of this veterinarian, this Martha Grimes, DVM, he felt she was flirting with him, toying with the cat and with him.

He let her keep the cat for a couple of days, picked it up in a new cat carrier, and left with an encouraging smile and a big bill from Dr. Grimes. "Enjoy your new pet," she told him. As soon as he got back to the cabin and let the thing out of the carrier, it tore off into the woods. Probably never see it again.

But the next day it was back. He called it Odysseus, thinking not so much of the crafty schemer slipping inside the walls of Troy but the man come home disguised as a beggar. The cat claimed for himself the other reading chair, preferred, it turned out, to have a lamp shining down to warm him. The two got on companionably enough, and Charlie began to carry on a running monologue: "I'm not talking to myself," he said at the cat. "I'm talking to you." After a while, Odysseus morphed into Oddball, "just between us." To rare visitors he remained Odysseus.

Because if he were honest, Charlie Winters was a lonely son of a bitch. He made himself this way. Sometimes Liz would drive up the mountain to see how he was, to make sure he had enough food in the refrigerator, to make sure he was eating right. Now she was a middle-aged woman. Now she was the head librarian at a rural county library where she was the only person with a proper degree. Really, Charlie wondered, how much of a degree did a person need for such a job? Liz, so full of promise as a girl, had wasted her life, wasted years of it on Barnes Henderson. Whose fault was that? Charlie wouldn't let himself go there. Instead he went around in a constant state of cranky irritation.

So it happened he was driving along the twisty part of the road near his cabin when he came upon a truck nose down in the ditch. It was the first snow of the year, and the road had grown icy. Charlie pulled to a stop and saw Dr. Martha Grimes climb out of the cab. She had come up on the mountain to put a horse down.

"Hardly a good day for it," Charlie told her.

"There's never a good day for it," she said.

"Seems like they could have just shot it like people used to do."

"People get attached to their animals," Martha Grimes told him.

"They do. These folks should have put this horse down months ago; it was time, but they couldn't let go. It's hard."

"I wouldn't know about that," he told her.

"How about that cat?" she asked him. "How's it doing?"

She had him dead to rights. After he yanked her truck out of the ditch, he asked her to his place for coffee. As he drove along, being careful to keep her in his rearview mirror, he felt excitement and some dread. By his estimation, she was not much older than Liz.

When he offered a slug of whiskey in her coffee, she took it. This was not a workday, just a house call for old friends. She took her mug and drifted around the walls of his cabin, nosing at things as the cat had weeks earlier. "You a professor?"

"I practice law." It's what he always said; it's what he always meant too.

"And a fly fisherman." She leaned over to examine the nymph he'd finished but was still clamped in his vise, a hare's ear. Early winter was the time for making nymphs, then on to blue wing olives, light and dark Hendricksons, yellow sallies, each in their turn anticipating the season of their best use. And she held her cup out to him for a refill. "More high octane would be all right too." She looked closely at his rod and reel set in the windowsill to air. "Though I would have thought you'd be a bamboo man."

"That's a long story I won't bore you with."

"You know, the bead head nymphs work pretty well on these creeks."

"I don't hold with anything new-fangled like that. I'm a mean old man, set in his ways."

"Not so much."

"Not what?"

"Not so old; not so mean."

After she pulled on her boots left by the door and tied them snug with double bows, she stood straight up and kissed Charlie Winters on the mouth. "Next time, I'll bring you some of my bead head nymphs." Then she was out the door, into her truck, and gone.

"What the hell was that supposed to mean?" The cat in its chair fixed its yellow gaze on him and didn't make a sound. A man as parched as Charlie Winters should have been grateful, joyful even, to receive such an unexpected gift. "What the hell does she need with me?" He thought of Mary Frances, gone now ten years and more. He had quit missing her particulars, was ashamed at all he had forgotten, if that was the word for it, the familiar pattern of their lives worn away by his thoughtless acts, the acts of a man just getting by. Even so, Mary Frances persisted, a blurry presence, an ache. "Next time? Don't get sick," he told the cat.

Martha Grimes was a big-boned gal; she told him she had grown up on a farm bucking hay with the boys. He could see it in her shoulders, in the sure way she held herself, standing with legs apart, arms crossed across her chest as she talked, laughing out loud, more like a man than any lady. She was no lady; she could have told him that.

The next time happened when he looked at the weather forecast and saw a warm front rolling in. He called her up at her veterinarian's office and asked her did she know a certain creek? She did. He said she might want to meet him there if she could shake herself free for the day. When she said she'd have to see, he told her he'd be fishing there regardless. Was she just fooling with him?

Charlie Winters preferred fishing alone; most serious fishermen did, he thought. Going out with his ex-son-in-law had been more of a babysitting operation than a fishing trip, watching him tangle his back cast in the bushes, splash over rocks, and spook the pool before he even made a cast. What casts he did land on the water showed he had no sense at all of how fish live in a river. It still pissed him off thinking about that boy. And his lost Leonard rod.

So why had he invited Martha Grimes? When she rode up in her big truck with the magnetic sign advertising her office tucked behind the seat, he felt a surge of relief and surprising fatigue. The night before he hadn't gotten much sleep.

Quickly, she jumped into her waders and strung up her rod. He'd caught a glimpse of the shape of her behind and legs in her long underwear—either by accident or design. But they came here to fish, and she eased down the bank and stepped into the back of a short pool. Charlie Winters watched her cast into the gap in the mountain laurel on the far bank and drift the nymph down under the overhanging foliage. On the third or fourth cast, she had a fish. Charlie found he spent more time watching than fishing as the day went on. She handled a fly rod well.

Early that morning, he had decided, what he might be up to, to ask her back to his cabin to eat some pork chops. Pork chops were among the few things he could cook. He was afraid she would decline and equally afraid she would accept. He bought good dark beer to go with them. Charlie Winters allowed himself a glass of beer or wine with his dinner but never drank anything else alone. He was afraid of himself, too, afraid of what he might become if he didn't watch himself.

She let him cook without butting in; he appreciated that. And she told him funny stories about bringing cows, reaching inside and getting the calf straightened out so it could come out easily. She told him stories about people and their pets, not showing off what she knew and what she did but showing what she believed, that you could judge people by how they took care of their animals. Charlie Winters told her his mother's old saying, any man who'd kick a dog would beat his wife. Back in the mountains where he'd grown up, it was probably true. He wound up telling her more about himself than he meant to.

Martha Grimes had surmised as much; she knew what she'd gotten into. After they had eaten, when they had pushed back from Charlie's little table, she took her coffee and went around to him. Rather than sit crosswise on his lap as Mary Frances had done, she straddled his legs, put her arms around him, and looked hard into his face.

He felt himself retreating; he felt he'd let another wrestler get him in an unexpected hold. He felt himself aroused. "I'm not sure," he said, something he was not in the habit of saying. And he would have said more, but she didn't let him.

Charlie Winters had never made love to a woman who was not his wife. As Martha slept beside him, he considered what he had done. Something satisfying, pleasurable, necessary even. Something wrong.

For years to come, he and Martha Grimes got together this way, several times a month. Sometimes they took trips out west to famous trout streams they had both wanted to fish. Carrying on, as Charlie put it. He thought of how he and Mary Frances used that phrase in talking about his former neighbors, clients, people from the country club who were carrying on—lives elicit, licentious, and sneaking along without interruption or shame. Now he found his was a surprisingly pleasurable life in its sub-rosa way, though Martha kept insisting neither had anything to hide.

"Pleasure is not immoral," she told him. "Fun is not wrong."

"Fun."

They gave each other small gifts, exchanging flies, his carefully tied traditional patterns, hers more updated with the new synthetics. They mocked each other's taste and style. One day she presented him with a collapsible wading staff; it fit in a little holster that could go on his belt. "This proves it. I'm too old to be going around with you."

"People in their twenties and thirties use these things. It's a tool, something to give you a little more stability in deep water."

"Maybe I should keep to the shallows."

She had no patience when he talked that way. "Bullshit," she told him. He didn't really believe it either.

It was his knee, getting more and more unreliable, an old wrestling injury and the marines hadn't helped it any. Martha came around a bend in the river and caught him sitting on a rock in midstream rubbing it. "If I were an old horse, it'd be time to put me down."

"If you want to keep fishing, you're going to have to get a new knee. The choice is yours."

He got the artificial knee, waiting until late in the fall when the best fishing had passed. When Martha Grimes drove him back to his cabin from the hospital, he saw she had ordered a small TV satellite dish installed. There it sat right out in the clearing on a four-by-four post, ugly as any jar in the woods in Tennessee. "This way you can watch your World Series while you do your rehab." For the first time in a while, the

Red Sox were in the Series. The thought of watching the games softened him considerably, but he tried not to let it show. At least the cable to the house was buried.

When that odd-looking bunch, those hippies and rastas and whatever they imagined themselves to be, won the Series, Charlie wondered how had it meant so little to him when it was all over? How was it that as Martha Grimes slept soundly, lovely and buck naked beside him in the bed, he lay awake?

He was careful with words around her. That she would outlive him was a certainty so best not to pull them both in too deep. She had her money, her practice. Probably there had been other arrangements in her life. She'd have no trouble finding another. But no matter what she claimed, this had become more than fun.

Liz had withdrawn from him even more since Martha had come into his life. She, too, was comfortably off and would be more so when he died. Every time he saw her, she was heavier than the time before. Letting herself go. He wondered if there could ever be another man in her life, or a woman even, somebody to come home to. Though he knew, too, that he had been as responsible for her marriage to Barnes Henderson as anybody. There was that. If there were a way to forgive himself and to ask forgiveness, to fix things, he could not manage to say it.

Mostly, though, he wanted there to be something better, something more to show for the life he had lived. He had come home from the war with a sense that having lived through that, he could manage anything. He had done OK; his work, his marriage, even this unexpected bonus with Martha Grimes. Shouldn't there be something more, something more to show? A sense of accomplishment, of completeness, a feeling of a job well done? Whatever was missing, he could not name, but he knew it was never enough.

■ ■ ■

When the family had quit the cabin suddenly those twenty years ago,